WERE THE HANDS THAT CARESSED HER STAINED WITH HER HUSBAND'S BLOOD?

Anna could not deny the feelings that Paul Kuragin stirred in her—but she could not shut her ears to the rumors surrounding this strong and ruthless man.

Had he in truth killed her husband in a duel over the ravishing woman whom both men wanted as mistress?

Was her husband indeed dead—or was he a prisoner of the rebelling tribes that had turned the wild and beautiful Caucasus into a bloody labyrinth of ambush, abduction, and slaughter?

The answers lay at the end of the most daring and desperate journey a woman ever took through a nightmare of danger to the ultimate limits of love. . . .

Heir to Kuragin

"THRILLING . . . KEEPS YOU EN-TRANCED TO THE END!"
—*South Bend Tribune*

Big Bestsellers from SIGNET

Heir to Kuragin

Constance Heaven

A SIGNET BOOK
NEW AMERICAN LIBRARY
TIMES MIRROR

Copyright © 1978 by Constance Heaven

This is an authorized reprint of a hardcover edition
published by Coward, McCann & Geoghegan, Inc.

SIGNET, SIGNET CLASSICS, MENTOR, PLUME AND MERIDIAN BOOKS
are published by The New American Library, Inc.,
1633 Broadway, New York, New York 10019

First Signet Printing, January, 1980

1 2 3 4 5 6 7 8 9

PRINTED IN THE UNITED STATES OF AMERICA

Part One

The Caucasus

A world of wonder, whose soaring peaks
Are hit by veils of mist and men live free
As eagles . . .

Mikhail Lermontov

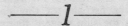

1

Why had she come to the Causasus? Why had she ever dreamed that it would solve anything? It was a question Anna had asked herself a hundred times during the thousand-mile journey over appalling roads. Of course there was the house at Kumari, there was the appeal from Gregory's grandmother, there was his last letter, but she did not need to go there immediately, the lawyer had told her that, the legalities could proceed without her, and now when she was less than half a day from Pyatigorsk, the first step on her long difficult road to Tiflis, the purpose that had driven her so powerfully for the last few months seemed suddenly futile.

She pushed open the wooden shutter and stared across the rolling plain to where the snow-capped peaks rose steeply, so delicately etched in silver against the evening sky that they might have been an illusion . . . the mountains of the fabled Caucasus, Elbruz between whose twin peaks the Ark had rested on its way to Ararat, Kazbek where Prometheus had been chained for his presumption in stealing fire from the Gods and bringing it to man, the legendary land of Colchis, where Medea had woven her magic spells and Jason had come with his Argonauts seeking the Golden Fleece . . . they were the myths with which Gregory had enchanted her in the early days, not the grim reality that had brought tragedy to the man she had once loved. Yet as she drank in the pure cold air, she was ravished by wonder in spite of herself, the oppression beginning to lift for the first time since they had brought her the shattering news.

Perhaps soon, when she knew everything, the misery and guilt would fade and she could begin to live again. After all, as Papa had said, meaning to comfort, life does not end at twenty-three because your husband has disappeared, vanished inexplicably one morning as if he had never existed. But then Papa didn't know, had never once guessed, so clever she had been in concealing it, that the marriage which had begun in

3

such a blaze of glory had become only a source of bitterness and reproach between two who had loved too violently. He had not heard the taunting words Gregory had flung at her before he had gone out of the apartment, slamming the door; he had not seen how she ran to the window, clawing at the bolts, hammering her fist against the glass, watching with tears of baffled rage the slim elegant figure climbing into the waiting troika, never realizing that it was the last time she would see him.

A sleepy voice from the bed behind her murmured complainingly, 'Do you really have to keep the window open? There is a fearful draught. I'm slowly freezing to death.'

'I'm sorry.' She pulled the shutter towards her and fastened it. 'I'm a pig. I keep forgetting.'

Cousin Marya, exhausted after the long day over roads that were little more than tracks, opened one eye and said humorously, 'Not quite a pig, Anna my love, just a mite thoughtless. Wake me up when Yakov brings our supper.'

'I will.'

She picked up one of the fur travelling rugs and crossed to the bed, tucking it around the older woman and dropping a light kiss on her cheek. It was not yet dark and she had a longing to breathe the fresh cold air of the April evening, to feel the wind on her cheeks, free from the stifling dingy room which was the best the posting house could provide.

She went down the rickety staircase past the main room of the inn. From the babble of voices it was crowded. She had a quick glimpse of the motley group of peasants, camel drivers, packmen, carters, tribesmen and soldiers clustered round the yellow wooden table with the steaming tureen of cabbage soup and the huge mounds of buckwheat *blini* stuffed with spicy meat. The waiter in his greasy apron was hurrying to serve a couple of officers, sitting apart from the others, aloof and disdainful. A hot gust of air thick with the mingled smells of food, wine and sweat nearly choked her, then she was outside on the dirt track.

Here, so far south, the snow and ice had already disappeared and there was a scent of spring, a faint breath of the exotic land beyond the mountains. Deep impenetrable forest came down on one side of the road and on the other lay the vivid green of a field of young maize. She stood still for a moment breathing deeply the sharp freshness of pine and larch, feeling the breeze lift her hair from her hot forehead. She walked a little way into the blue dusk aware that she should not go too far. She had been warned constantly that the roads could be dangerous and no one was safe from brigands or even from enemy horsemen swooping down from the hills like a pack of hungry wolves.

Her mother had burst into tears when she had first spoken of her intention. 'You can't go to the Caucasus alone,' she had wailed. 'Stepan, you must forbid it. Anything could happen to her amongst those savages, anything . . . she could be murdered like poor Gregory.'

'Now, now, my dear Nadia,' her father had said placatingly. 'It's not so bad as that. If what we hear is true, then the war is at a standstill. And it is not at all sure that Gregory is dead. I have certainly not given up hope. He could well have been taken prisoner. Stranger things have happened.' He had drawn Anna to him putting his arm around her shoulders. She had always been sure of his sympathy and understanding.

'There is another thing,' he went on gently. 'It is right that Anna should go to her husband's country, meet his grandmother, see the house where he grew up. The Caucasus is beautiful in the spring, and if it will bring her peace of mind, then I think we should do all we can to help. Gregory would have wished it.'

Would he? She was not so sure but if it had not been for Papa and Cousin Marya she doubted if it would have been possible to make the trip at all.

The war in the Caucasus had gone on ever since Anna could remember. For more than fifty years Russia had been fighting the rebellious tribes of Daghestan. The Caucasus was the gateway to Asia; once bring the whole region under the sway of the Tsar and the road was open to Persia and the riches of India. Anna had heard her father talk of it a hundred times with a certain admiration for the heroic peoples who fought so hard to preserve their independence. In the last ten years the daring and ruthless strategy of a new leader, the Imam Shamyl, had united the tribes into the savage fanaticism of a Holy War, Moslem against Christian.

But despite the terror he inspired and though Russian soldiers died in agony from wounds, from fevers, from frostbite in the high peaks, it had never prevented the wealthy from travelling to Pyatigorsk to swelter in the hot mud for their rheumatism or drink the sulphur water for their overworked digestions, and even the occasional kidnapping or murder did not stop them from journeying on to Tiflis and the Black Sea to revel in the pleasures of the viceregal court and perhaps pick up a husband or a lover in less formal surroundings than Petersburg or Moscow. When her friends heard that Anna was going to the Caucasus, they were immediately fascinated; how romantic, they exclaimed, how thrilling! They had said the same when she had married Gregory, Prince of Kumaria, so dashingly handsome. All the other girls had been green with envy. How little they had known! How little she had!

She walked on down the empty road enjoying the exercise after the weeks of travel cramped into the bone-shaking carriage. Then suddenly she stood still. A man had come lurching out of the forest, a tribesman by his dress, a Tartar or a Circassian perhaps, but whether enemy or friend she could not be sure. The long close-fitting coat was ragged and filthy, the boots thick with mud, the dark hair hung in wet streaks over his face. Somewhere he must have fallen into a bog or swum a river. She could not decide whether to turn and run or simply ignore him and while she hesitated, he took a few staggering steps towards her and keeled over, falling on his face, his arms outstretched, his hands scrabbling in the dirt of the road as he tried helplessly to raise himself.

Drunk, she thought, drawing back her skirts in disgust, but then something caught her eye. She stared down at the muscular hand at her feet, stained and encrusted with dirt, yet not quite the horny hand of the peasant, and on one finger a ring, large and square with two tiny hands that held an onyx seal, a ring she had last seen on Gregory's hand . . . or was it?

Momentarily her heart seemed to stop beating and her vision blurred. It couldn't be true. She must be imagining it. It was one of those insane chances that just don't happen in real life. She closed her eyes and then opened them again, staring in disbelief. Swayed by a sudden dizzy hope she fell on her knees beside him, but the brown high-cheekboned face half turned away from her was not Gregory's and a sickening wave of disappointment surged through her. She put a hand on the beggar's shoulder, shaking him.

'Where did you get that ring? Where? You must tell me.'

She spoke in Russian. The head turned, but the eyes looked up at her vacantly through the matted hair. He mumbled something and then groaned. She saw with horror that there was blood on her hands and that it streaked the ragged coat in long dark patches. She knelt there for a moment, puzzled and disturbed, then she got to her feet and ran back down the road. At the door of the posting house, she looked for Yakov and saw him at last talking to the waiter. She beckoned urgently and he elbowed his way across to her. Yakov was a serf from the family estate, a man who had grown up with her mother, and whom she had known all her life. Despite her marriage he was still inclined to treat her as the child he had taught to ride her first pony, who had climbed onto his broad shoulders and tugged at his thick grey beard.

He said indulgently, 'What is it, Barina? Are you anxious for your supper? It is almost ready. I have ordered these idle wretches to prepare something better for you and Marya Petrovna than this hog wash,' and he waved a disparaging hand towards the cabbage soup.

'It's not that, Yakov. There's a man up there on the road. I think he has been badly hurt.'

'A man, eh?' he smiled at her foolishness. 'And what if there is? There are beggars everywhere, little mistress, robbers too, most of them. They know all the tricks, then quick as a snake, steal your purse. You don't want to concern yourself with rogues of that sort.'

'He is bleeding, Yakov,' she insisted. 'He cannot be left there to die. You must fetch him in. Let the people here take care of him. I will pay.'

Some of the men in the room behind Yakov were staring at her, their eyes alive with curiosity. He pushed her gently through the door and pulled it shut.

'No need for them to hear. Ears long as a donkey's,' he muttered disgustedly. 'Now tell me again. Did this son of Satan harm you?'

'No, no, it's not that at all.' She was impelled by a feverish urgency. If she was not wrong, if that really was Gregory's ring, then the man might know something, but it took time to persuade Yakov and he went off at last still grumbling. She watched him disappear into the darkening night. In a very few minutes he was back.

'Not a sign of anyone, my lady. Are you sure you didn't dream it? Maybe he wasn't there at all. In this light it is easy to deceive oneself.'

'Of course he was there,' she answered angrily. 'I spoke to him. Are you sure you looked everywhere? He could have crawled into the ditch or into the field.'

'Not a chance, I swear it.' He grinned infuriatingly. 'He's gone back to where he belongs and left this behind him,' and he held up a long strip of stained blue wool. 'It must have caught in a branch as the rascal pushed his way into the forest.'

'But he can't have vanished like that. It's not possible,' she exclaimed in sharp disappointment and then saw Yakov looking at her curiously. She really was behaving very stupidly. She pulled herself together. 'It doesn't matter,' she went on more quietly, 'it is not at all important. If our supper is ready, you may serve it now.'

'Yes, my lady, at once.'

She went slowly up the stairs while Yakov shouted to the waiter to hurry and bring the food.

'Oh there you are,' said Marya as she came through the door. 'I was beginning to wonder what had happpened to you. I'm starving.'

'I went for a little walk. I needed the air.'

Marya glanced at her young companion shrewdly but said nothing more as the table was spread with a white cloth. Anna went to wash the blood off her hands while Yakov bustled around, harassing the waiter, examining the plates to make sure they were clean and bringing out their own cutlery from the travelling basket.

'That will do,' said Marya, 'we will serve ourselves.'

Yakov bowed and went out, pushing the waiter in front of him and leaving them alone.

The food was surprisingly good, a dish of eggs with pieces of chicken, well roasted and tender for once, followed by a local speciality, hot cheese pies served with *smetana,* a kind of rich sour cream that was quite delicious. Marya attacked it vigorously and Anna looked at her with affection. She was her mother's cousin but so much part of their household that as she grew up, Anna had always thought of her as an elder sister, and sometimes felt closer to her than she did to her own mother.

Anna's father was English. Stephen Crispin had come to Russia as tutor to the daughter of Count Kuzinsky and had fallen in love with her. Dismissed with ignominy as soon as it was discovered, he had refused to be beaten. Stubbornly he had fought his way to recognition, writing articles on all kinds of subjects, pursuing his study of literature, starving in a garret until at long last he had won a teaching post at Moscow University and Nadia had run away from home to marry him to the fury and disgust of her aristocratic parents. Later, Marya, her orphaned cousin who had lived with them all her life, came to join them in their unfashionable apartment, eking out their income by giving music lessons and outraging convention by taking her own lively part in the intellectual circle Stephen Crispin had created around himself.

In the midst of the arguments as to whether or not Anna should go to the Caucasus, it was Marya who clinched it in her quiet way.

'You know, Stepan, I've been suffering from severe attacks of rheumatism all this winter,' she said serenely, 'and my doctor swears there is nothing as beneficial as the mud baths at Pyatigorsk so I think I shall take a course of treatment as soon as the roads are open in the spring. Perhaps Anna would care to accompany me.'

So miraculously her path had been smoothed and here they were, the worst part of the journey already behind them.

They did not talk much while they were eating and it was only when Marya got up to light the samovar and prepare the tea that she said, 'You've eaten scarcely anything, Anyushka. Has something happened? I thought you looked upset when you came in.'

'I don't know.' Anna played with the handle of her spoon before she looked up to meet the kind short-sighted eyes behind the thick spectacles. 'Promise you won't think me crazy if I tell you.'

'Why should I think any such thing? I've never believed that you lacked common sense, my dear.'

So Anna told her everything just as it had happened and Marya was silent for a moment before she said quietly, 'There are several possible explanations. First and most likely Yakov is probably right and you imagined the whole incident.'

'I couldn't have done,' she said obstinately. 'He was there and I saw the ring. I couldn't help but recognize it. Gregory wore it so often.'

Once, in one of his wild rages, he had hit her across the face and the sharp edge of the ring had cut her lip. She could taste the salt blood now.

'All the same, it was evening and growing dark. You believe you saw it because your thoughts were already full of him and maybe the beggar was wearing some object that momentarily appeared to be the one you recognized.'

It was so plausible an explanation that Anna's certainty began to waver and yet something inside her refused to be convinced.

Marya cut the lemon into thin slices and began to pour the tea into the tall glasses. 'Secondly,' she went on slowly, 'let us suppose for an instant that you were right. Isn't it just possible that Gregory has been captured by enemy tribesmen or brigands who would of course rob him of everything of value . . . his watch or any jewellery he might be wearing . . . and these objects could pass from hand to hand as they do among thieves and by pure chance have ended up on the finger of the man you saw?'

'It seems so incredible and yet . . .'

'There is still a third theory,' said Marya, spooning in the sugar and sipping the boiling tea with relish, 'even more improbable but just within the bounds of possibility. Suppose there is someone who knows what has happened to Gregory and for some reason is trying to convey a message to you, using that ring as a passport, something you would immediately recognize . . .'

'Message? What kind of message?'

Marya shrugged her shoulders. 'Ah there you have me. Impossible to guess at it without delving into the realms of fiction.'

'But why should he be so injured? And why vanish when Yakov went to look for him?'

'Who can tell? Perhaps there are others who want to prevent whatever it is from reaching you.'

'Do you really believe that?'

'No, I don't,' said Marya sturdily. 'I think it is not only vastly improbable but quite ridiculous.'

Anna was silent for a moment, thinking of Gregory's letter, so unexpected, so unlike him, imploring her to come to the Caucasus and then before she could reply or decide what to do, he had vanished with no explanation, no further word.

'Tell me, Anna,' said Marya refilling the glasses with tea, 'I have never asked. Why did Gregory go off to the Caucasus so suddenly?'

'There was some family business to settle after his father's death . . . his grandmother wrote to him. It was more than twelve years since he had been to Kumari. He was brought to Petersburg as a child, a ward of the Tsar.'

'Why didn't he take you with him?'

'He said he did not think it safe.'

But that was not the real reason, she knew that. He had wanted to escape from her, he was bored with Petersburg,

bored with the wife he had never really wanted . . . the wife
it had amused him to humiliate so cruelly.

'Well,' said Marya, getting up and stretching. 'Do you
know what I think? We are letting our imaginations run away
with us and there is no explanation at all. I think we should
forget the whole incident. We have to be up very early and it
is time for bed. Let's put all thought of it out of our minds.'

But that was easier said than done. Anna could tell herself
that what she thought she had seen was nothing but the result
of nervous tension arising out of the brooding hours spent in
the carriage while Marya dozed and yet all the same it added
another facet to the mystery she had come so far to try and
solve.

'I'm not one to keep on asking questions,' Marya had said
soon after they set out, 'but what is the real reason behind
this trip to the Caucasus?'

That was one of the blessed things about her. Shrewd and
worldly wise as she was, she did not keep on badgering for
explanations and so Anna had been able to tell her and know
she would understand.

'You see if someone dies of a sickness or even is killed,
then terrible as it is, it is also final. No questions unanswered,
no doubts. But if he disappears, if he simply goes out one day
and never comes back, then how can you accept? You must
know before you can go on living.'

'And what do you hope to discover in Tiflis?'

'How can I tell? I shall talk to the people he knew, I shall
meet his friends, his relatives, the people he spoke with every
day. Somewhere there must be someone who can tell me
what I want to know, what I must know.'

'Did you love him that much?' she asked quietly. 'I did
sometimes wonder.'

But that was a question Anna was not prepared to answer.
It was too painful. She could not talk about it to anyone.
Marya had not liked Gregory, nor had her father for that
matter. She had evaded the question and her cousin had not
pressed her.

The bed was hard and the mattress lumpy, but mercifully
free from the unpleasant inhabitants that had tormented them
at so many of the posting stations. Marya fell asleep almost at
once as easily and peacefully as a child, but Anna was not so
fortunate. She lay wakeful, staring into the thick darkness,
hardly daring to move lest she disturb her cousin, the
memories that can resolutely be banished during the day

crowding in on her remorselessly, brought vividly to life by
that queer encounter on the track. Had there ever been anyone so guileless and trusting as she had been? It sickened her
to think of it. The first time she had met Gregory, she was
barely eighteen and in her last year at the Smolny. It was her
grandmother, the Countess Kuzinsky, who had insisted that
she should be sent to the aristocratic school founded by the
Tsarina Elizabeth for the daughters of the nobility and still
under imperial patronage.

She had descended on them in their humble apartment in
Moscow one afternoon in a wave of perfume, trailing her
rich furs. 'If you have seen fit to cast aside your heritage,' she
said icily to Anna's mother, 'then don't deny it to this innocent child. My granddaughter should be trained to take her
place among her equals.'

'Anna has been very well educated,' said her father calmly.
'I have seen to that myself.'

'I've no doubt you have, Stepan,' said her grandmother, her
eyes sweeping around the book-lined walls contemptuously,
'taught her all the things that don't matter. That won't help
her to make a good marriage.'

'The child is only fourteen,' protested her mother, but she
shrank visibly under the eagle stare of her formidable
mother. No one dreamed of asking me, Anna thought resentfully. She had never had any wish to be sent to the fashionable boarding school. She did not want to be presented to the
Tsar. She loved the warm informal life in Moscow where the
students came and went, where her father encouraged her to
study and hold her own in debate and argument. But her
grandmother insisted and so off she went on the verge of
tears that she stubbornly refused to shed.

From the first she had hated it. Among the young Coun-
tesses and Princesses who were now her companions, she was
like a fish out of water. They had only two ideas in their
pretty curled heads, the fit of a new gown and the man they
hoped one day to marry. She despised them as much as they
disliked her. She had never become one of them and their
spite turned to a sharp malicious envy after the ball at the
Winter Palace.

During their last year the girls were escorted to a number
of social events to prepare them for their future position in
society and it was there in the mirrored hall with its marble
colonnade, its pillars of jasper and malachite, among the py-
ramids of fresh roses under the glittering chandeliers with the

thousands of wax candles, that she saw Gregory Gadiani, Prince of Kumaria, raven-haired and ravishingly handsome in the white and gold uniform of the Imperial Guard. He was twenty-one and it was his first appearance at Court as it was hers. He was the sensation of the evening and it was not only the girls who couldn't take their eyes from him. But it was at Anna he looked, with Anna he waltzed . . . Anna Stepanovna Crispin in her white lace ball gown, cream roses in the red-gold hair, as innocent and ignorant of life as a kitten.

She stirred in the hard bed, her eyes hot and sleepless, while outside a dog howled its miseries to the moon. It was so easy to look back now with bittter experience and condemn her folly, but then, deliriously in love for the first time, she had been enormously flattered that it was she and not her companions despite their wealth and aristocratic birth, who had captured the charming newcomer with the fascination of his wildly exotic background in the far distant Caucasus that made him so different from all others.

They were strictly guarded at the Smolny, but when has there ever been a time when young love couldn't find means of evading watchful eyes? All that spring and summer at the concerts, the opera, the garden parties and the soirées, Gregory would contrive to be unobtrusively present. In crowded rooms there were smiles, exchanges of looks, a touch of the hand. They found enchanted moments to be alone together; there were stolen kisses made even more enthralling by the fear of discovery.

One evening she spoke to him in the English she had learned from her father and he laughed softly, touching her hair with one long slim hand . . .

'She walks in beauty like the night
Of cloudless climes and starry skies . . .'

That he could quote Byron to her, that exciting and dangerous poet, forbidden reading at the Smolny, but whose verses she had devoured avidly in her father's study, seemed to her a dream of perfection. What a romantic idiot she had been to believe that kisses and poetry had anything to do with marriage! She shuddered to remember the fool she was then, so unfit to cope with what lay before her.

All that year she lived in a blissful dream until an evening in early autumn. It was Nina who put the crazy notion into her head. The Kuragins were one of the wealthiest families in

Petersburg and their masked ball held on one of the islands of the Neva was the most talked of event of the season.

Nina Astrov was fifteen, lively and frivolous as a butterfly, but the nearest to a friend Anna had at the Smolny. 'It's the most marvellous affair,' she sighed. 'Papa has told me about it often. There are the Tzigane, the gypsy singers and the actors from the theatre and the ballet, the trees are all hung with coloured lamps and they dance until five in the morning. Mama is Countess Kuragina's sister but she won't let me go. She says I am too young. Gregory is sure to be invited. Oh Anna, wouldn't it be wonderful if you could go with him? There are dozens of guests. No one would notice you among so many.'

At first it had seemed too daring an escapade even for Anna who had always been something of a rebel against the strict rules of the Convent. Then, walking in the Nevsky Prospect with three of her companions and their dragon of an escort, they ran into Gregory and under cover of polite conversation, she had been foolish enough to mention it and he was on fire with the notion at once.

'If they find out, it will be dreadful,' she whispered, half afraid, but she had never felt herself bound by convention like the other girls and he was very persuasive. Nina, trembling with excitement, made the excuse that Anna had been taken by a violent migraine and must remain in her darkened room. Giggling she poured the prescribed medicine out of the window and helped Anna to dress. The porter on the garden gate, well bribed, had always been a friend. He let her out and promised to be there when she returned. Gregory was waiting with the carriage.

It was an evening to dream about for a lifetime, a magical Petersburg night when the light faded to a pearly glow and the river was a sheet of silver under the stars. They danced and danced and under the shade of the acacias where the late roses spilled out of the great stone jars, Gregory kissed her with a passion that made her tremble with mingled delight and terror. All might have been well if Gregory, driving more wildly than usual, had not collided with a cart bringing vegetables to the market and smashed the carriage on their way back. They were thrown amongst the turnips and the potatoes, little hurt except for a few bruises, but it was nine in the morning by the time they reached the school and disaster fell on them.

Anna's absence had been discovered and poor Nina con-

fronted with their stern guardians broke into a passion of
tears and confessed.

The storm that followed was out of all proportion to what
had actually happened. What after all was so sinful about
spending an evening dancing with an honourable young man?
'Accidents can happen to anyone,' she had said defiantly and
was locked up in a shocked silence while the scandal grew.
Malicious tongues gleefully related damning details of the
summmer's stolen meetings. Her father was sent for from Moscow, her grandmother complained angrily to the Tsar who
deeply resented any slur being cast on the honour of the
school he favoured.

'I've done nothing wrong. Why should he make such a terrible fuss about it?' she said rebelliously. 'Everyone knows
that Barbara Nelidova is his mistress.'

'You shouldn't speak of such things,' said her grandmother
in icy reproof, 'and if you cannot understand the difference
between what is done in public and what is permitted in a
discreet privacy, then you had better return to your bourgeois
father and the vulgar life you appear to like so much.'

She quailed under the lash of her contempt, distressed beyond measure at what she knew Gregory must be going
through. They were called before the Tsar. She had seen him
more than once and was still terrified. Tall and handsome, he
possessed a manner that could charm and at the same time
freeze you to your marrow. He fixed them with his cold grey
eyes, hard and inflexible as pewter, furiously angry at behaviour that seemed to reflect on his Court. If Gregory had been
Russian, he might have been exiled to some unspeakable
provincial town or even to Siberia, but he belonged to one of
the oldest families in Georgia and they must be kept sweet or
they might damage Russia's influence in the Caucasus. As it
was, there was nearly a diplomatic incident. Authority bore
down heavily on the young Prince, the English Embassy was
moved to protest, the Kuzinskys brought pressure to bear, a
featherlight romance had suddenly turned into stern reality.
They were marrried in December with the extremely reluctant
consent of her father. Frost dusted the snow with diamonds
and her wedding bouquet of white hothouse roses was frozen
hard as porcelain when they came out of the Cathedral and
Gregory handed her into the sleigh.

She stole a glance at the sullen young face beside her. He
was staring in front of him.

'Well. that's that,' he said, 'and devil take it! We shall have to make the best of a bad job, won't we, my dear?'

The chill in his voice was more withering than the wind that blew off the Steppes and she shivered despite the fur mantle. Then he began to laugh in the reckless way he had and drew her against him, pushing back the veil and kissing her violently. But the icy breath that had touched her then, never quite vanished, not even in that first year . . .

Anna moved restlessly and Marya mumbled something, turning over and taking the blankets with her. She tugged them back firmly but gently.

Where was Gregory now? Where was her young savage of a husband with his beauty, passion and furious rages when things did not go his way? Was he lying somewhere in the mountains, imprisoned, tortured, dead? She did not know whether she loved or hated him, but she had to find out if only to still the nagging doubt that it was she who was responsible, that it was she who had driven him to ride out alone into the wilderness that day and never return.

—— 2 ——

It was astonishing how gloriously hot the sun was though it was not yet May and Anna, sitting on the bench outside the bath house and waiting for Marya to finish her treatment, felt it warm her through and through, bringing her back to life. She opened her book but after a second or two her attention wandered and she leaned back. The air was filled with the scent of the lime flowers and there was a faint sweet music from the wind blowing through the Aeolian harp in the little belvedere two or three hundred yards higher up the mountain. Through half-closed eyes she could see the group gathered around the well, laughing and grimacing over their glasses of sulphur water. She felt peaceful and relaxed for the first time in many months and it was then that she was aware of the curious sensation of being watched.

She shifted her position a little as if to avoid the brilliant light from falling on her book and stole a swift glance from under the brim of her bonnet. Yes, there he was again. In the same position as he had been the day before, leaning against one of the pillars of the covered terrace. He wore the plain uniform of an officer in the regiment of the Line, but the excellent cut and the scarlet lined cloak slung around his shoulders gave him an air of distinction very different from the soldiers of the garrison or the other young men idling away their leave or convalescing from their wounds in the little spa town.

There were couples strolling in the lime-shaded alleys and several people were climbing up the steep narrow path to the Elizabeth Spring, but in some way he seemed isolated from them and she felt suddenly uneasy. So far as she knew, she had never seen him before in her life so why should he look at her so intently? She got up hurriedly and the book on her lap fell to the ground, skidding along the gravel almost to his feet. He looked down at it, flicking it shut with the stick in his hand, but he made no move and with a tiny exclamation she went quickly to pick it up. As she rose, she had a swift impression of a lean high-cheekboned face, slanting eyebrows, dark hair under the peaked cap.

He said quietly, 'Forgive me, Mademoiselle, if I appear discourteous. It is either that or falling flat on my face at your feet. Do you enjoy reading poetry?'

'Sometimes. You are wounded?'

He gave an almost imperceptible shrug. 'You might call it that.'

'Are you in pain?'

'Nothing to speak of.'

There was a hint of a smile about the full mobile mouth. She met the dark eyes surveying her ironically and felt confused as if she had been trapped into showing sympathy towards a complete stranger. She said hurriedly, 'Excuse me, my friend will be waiting for me.'

He inclined his head and she walked quickly towards the well, taking a glass of the medicinal water and sipping it before moving to the bath house. Marya must be coming out soon. She was angry with herself. She was no schoolgirl to be disturbed by the frankly appraising look in a man's eyes. Someone spoke to her and she answered absently. Out of the corner of her eye she saw that the young man was slowly limping away from her towards the town. How stupidly she was behaving. Because of Gregory she seemed to read significance in the most innocent of looks. Probably she had imagined his interest.

They had been in Pyatigorsk for three weeks already and unexpectedly she had found herself enjoying it. The little town cradled in the mountains had a great deal of charm. The air was fresh and invigorating and their rented cottage with its thatched roof was clean and pleasantly furnished. Flowers bloomed in the garden and outside her bedroom window the boughs of the cherry trees were hung with clusters of snow-white blossom, the petals sometimes blowing across her dressing table.

She had discovered almost immediately that it was not going to be easy to continue their journey to Tiflis. The Commander of the garrison to whom she was advised to make application was extremely discouraging. Captain Maxim Gorsky was a small grey man, grey hair, grey whiskers and tightly buttoned into a grey military frockcoat. He was a hard-bitten soldier aged by long years of service in the Cau-

casian army and not at all disposed to listen kindly to young
ladies disturbing his daily routine with frivolous requests.

All Russian officials have a passion for documents, she
thought impatiently, watching him examine their passports
and letters of recommendation at least twice before looking
up at her curiously.

'Your husband is Prince Gregory Gadiani, Madame, he is
therefore Georgian.'

'Yes. I am on my way to visit his estates at Kumari.'

'Which lie some miles outside Tiflis?'

'Yes. What is the reason for these questions?'

He re-examined the papers in front of him before he said,
'May I ask, Princess Gadiani, why you are travelling under
your own name and not that of your husband?'

She had no ready answer because she was not certain herself. It had been almost as if she wished to be free of
him, to be herself, a person in her own right, something
which he had never allowed her to be. 'I think that is my affair,' she said at last curtly.

'Maybe you're wise,' said the Commander dryly. 'There are
some among the Georgians whose allegiance to Russia has
been a cause of grave suspicion.'

'Not my husband. Prince Gadiani is an honourable man.'
Strange how nearly she had said 'was.' Did she believe him to
be dead already?

'And the other lady?' pursued the Commander.

'Marya Petrovna Kuzinsky is my mother's cousin and is
travelling with me.'

'I see.' He leaned back in his chair, joining his hands together and looking at her gravely over his eyeglasses. 'Well,
Madame, it is quite obvious that you cannot possibly under-
take the long and dangerous journey to Tiflis without a military escort and that, I am afraid, it is not in my power to
supply.'

'But why . . . ?' she began to protest and he raised a hand
politely to silence her.

'Perhaps you are not aware that we are in the midst of a
war, Madame,' he said ironically. 'The Gregorian Military
Highway and particularly the pass of Krestovaya are under
constant attack from the Tartars. Only a month ago, a cara-
van was brutally assaulted in the Daryal Gorge and the
travellers were fortunate to escape with their lives.'

He was trying to frighten her, thought Anna, and her resolution hardened. 'We understood that after the last great victory the war was virtually over,' she said boldly.

The soldier smiled grimly. 'That was two years ago and whatever they like to tell you in Petersburg and Moscow,' he said sarcastically, 'here in the Caucasus conditions are very different.' He looked down at their papers again, turning them over and studying the signatures.

'They are perfectly in order,' she said angrily.

'I don't doubt it, Madame, but they will not help you to cross the mountains.'

'Well then, what are we to do? There must be some means of travelling south. I was given to understand that parties of travellers journeyed to Tiflis at regular intervals during the spring and summer, or are you trying to tell me that my cousin and I must make our own way?'

That roused him. 'I would most certainly not advise you to attempt anything of that kind, Madame. If you were attacked, it might be quite impossible for us to protect you and do not, I beg of you, do not cherish any romantic notions about the chivalry of these mountain people. They are in many instances no more than savages who follow the tenets of Islam and they have little or no regard for women except as slaves or bargaining counters for the exchange of prisoners. To be kidnapped by them . . .'

'Would be a fate worse than death,' said Anna dryly. 'I understand perfectly, Commander, you need not elaborate on it. But in the meantime I am waiting to hear what we must do.'

'It is just possible that there may be a company of soldiers who are marching south. It does happen from time to time,' he said reluctantly, 'and with the permission of the Captain, it might be in order for you to travel with them, but I warn you that he may not wish to be burdened with the responsibility of ladies in these difficult conditions and the journey will be rough.'

'We are not afraid of that and if necessary we are prepared to ride. We do not need the luxury of a carriage, only mules to carry our baggage.'

'You are intrepid travellers I see,' he said with a frosty smile, 'and indeed there is no other way of crossing these heights. I will bear it in mind but I must tell you that you may have a long wait.'

'How long?'

He shrugged his shoulders. 'Who can tell? Circumstances change from day to day. In the meantime I suggest you enjoy the amenities of Pyatigorsk. The town provides a number of diversions to help young ladies like yourself to pass the time very pleasantly.'

'It seems I have no choice,' she put out her hand to take her papers and he stopped her.

'I will keep these until such time as you need them.'

'I intend to go, Commander, with or without an escort.'

'But not without your papers, Madame, I will make sure of that,' and he swept them into a drawer of his desk and turned the key.

'You cannot do that,' she said indignantly.

'I am afraid I can,' he said calmly. 'It is my duty to make certain that you take no unnecessary risks. I have the lives of my men to consider as well as your safety. They will be returned of course at the appropriate time. And now, Madame, may I wish you good day?'

He rose, bowing courteously, and there was nothing she could say. After a moment she swept out of the office. The soldiers of the garrison sprang to attention as she went through the outer room and she felt their eyes follow her as she walked down the path.

It was maddening and she raged to Marya about it, but there was little they could do and after a day or two of frustration and rather against her will, she began to enjoy the peaceful routine of the little town. There was a pleasant informality about life in Pyatigorsk. They had not been settled in their cottage for more than a few days when they had their first visitor. Fellow patients eagerly discussed their symptoms with Marya greatly to her amusement. Bored young men welcomed an attractive newcomer among the young ladies and anxious Mamas hoping to marry off their plain daughters were thankful for the rumour that the elegant young woman who had suddenly appeared in their midst was already married but for some mysterious reason was travelling incognito. Their conversation might be a little dull and concerned only with trivialities, thought Anna, at the concerts and soirées to which they had been invited, but it was harmless enough and it was a relief to be among strangers who knew nothing of her and Gregory, free of the innuendoes, the jealousies and intrigues of Petersburg society.

'You're looking exceedingly pretty this morning, Anna,' remarked Marya, coming out of the bath house and taking her cousin's arm. 'Who has been paying you compliments?'

'No one,' said Anna quickly, a little annoyed to find herself blushing for no reason at all. 'I have been sitting in the sun and reading. Hadn't we better walk? You mustn't take a chill after the heat of the bath.'

'Being immersed in hot mud to the chin is a most peculiar experience but it is certainly doing wonders for my rheumatism,' said Marya cheerfully as they walked briskly down the steep path.

'I don't believe you have rheumatism at all. I think you invented it as an excuse to come with me,' said Anna, giving the arm tucked in hers a grateful little squeeze.

Marya grinned. 'Perhaps I needed a holiday as much as you did.' She stole a glance at the slender young woman beside her. 'You look a different person already, my dear. I always knew it was a mistake shutting yourself up in that apartment after Gregory went away.'

'It was our home,' she said defensively. 'Besides I had plenty of friends.'

But had she? Acquaintances perhaps but no one who really cared and they very soon ceased to call when Gregory was no longer there to excite and intrigue them. In the time they had been together she had never really fitted into the frivolous society life into which she was plunged. It was more than a year since he had left her and in all those months there had only been that one letter. After a while she had almost stopped going out, finding it difficult to answer the questions, hating the pitying looks, resenting the edged remarks meant to hurt. She had felt deserted, gnawed by a sense of failure. What had gone wrong? Was it her fault or his? Was she foolish to mind so much? If only the baby had lived. To have a child to care for would have made all the difference.

'My dear girl, what do you expect?' he had said when she raged at him, accusing him of amusing himself with other women. 'You hardly let me come near you.'

He should have understood how difficult it had been for her in those first months after her confinement, the grief, the disappointment, the depression . . . had he been unfaithful? She didn't want to believe it and yet there had been someone. She was almost sure of it.

'I think I shall take a nap after we have eaten,' said Marya taking off her mantle in the tiny hall. 'All that hot mud makes me sleepy.'

'Very well. I shall write to Papa. I owe him a letter.'

When Marya had gone upstairs to lie down, she sat down at the table and took up her pen.

'Dearest Papa,' she began, 'I've begun to keep a journal as you suggested although very little of importance has happened to us yet. The country around here is beautiful beyond belief and I am eager to see as much as I can since we are forced to stay until a suitable escort is supplied to take us on to Tiflis . . .'

She paused, nibbling the end of her quill. She had written little as yet in the red-covered diary at her elbow. That had been another cause of friction between her and Gregory. Encouraged by her father she had always kept a journal, filling it with her impressions, her thoughts, her inmost feelings. When Gregory came across it one evening in her desk, he had opened it, holding it high when she tried to take it back, reading snatches of it aloud, making them sound ridiculous in front of some of their closest friends while she writhed in shame and resentment.

He had never wanted her to have any kind of independent life apart from him. Perhaps it was the oriental streak in him inherited from one or other of those Persian ancestors; his wife had to be his slave, sitting meekly in his harem, mother of his sons. She had screamed that at him one day in exasperation and he had laughed at her, but it was true all the same, and yet there had been moments. She shivered, remembering his arms round her, his mouth on hers, the wild abandon of his love-making which had first shocked her and then become almost like a drug when she forgot everything else. Sometimes at night she ached intolerably for his kisses. She shook herself free of unwelcome memories and turned back to her letter. She was halfway through the second page when she was interrupted by the maidservant. Darya was a Circassian, round and plump, with eyes black as sloes and cheeks like cherries.

'A gentleman to see you,' she announced and threw up her hands in wonder, 'and such a gentleman, as fine as a prince.'

'Don't be ridiculous, Darya. I don't know any princes and certainly not here. Did he give you his name?'

'No, Madame. He said you might not remember it but you'd know him when you saw him.'

'Oh very well. Show him in and you had better tell Marya Petrovna that we have a visitor.'

The young man who came through the door stooping under the low lintel was wearing the handsome uniform of the

Hussars, the cap set at a rakish angle on the blond hair, and she stared at him uncomprehendingly for a moment.

'Don't say you've forgotten me, Anna Stepanovna. I should find that very discouraging,' he said gaily. 'It is two years since we met but you were very well acquainted with my sister Nina.'

'Of course.' She stretched out her hand. 'I remember now, Prince Nicolai Astrov. How extraordinary that we should meet here. What on earth are you doing in the Caucasus?'

'I've been appointed to the staff of the Commander-in-Chief. I'm on my way to join him in Tiflis.' He kissed her hand and then perched himself on a corner of the table. 'I couldn't believe my ears when someone mentioned the name of Anna Crispin and I couldn't resist finding out if it could possibly be you.'

'I am travelling under my own name. It seemed easier somehow,' she said a little awkwardly. 'I'd be grateful if you would remember it.'

'Certainly if you wish.' He hesitated. 'Nina told me something of your husband's disappearance. Have you news of him?'

'Not yet. That is partly why I made up my mind to come to the Caucasus. Gregory's grandmother has invited me to Kumari.'

'In that case perhaps we can travel together . . . that is if you would be kind enough to accept my escort. I have been in touch with the Commmander of the garrison and he informs me that I must wait until I can attach myself to a military party going south.'

'He told me that too,' she said ruefully. 'I thought it was just that he had a prejudice against young women travelling on their own.'

'I think Captain Gorsky has a grudge against anyone coming from Petersburg, but maybe he has reason on his side,' said Nicolai lightly. 'We are in pretty wild country after all. Perhaps we can see something of one another while we wait. This is all new to me. I thought I might explore the mountains a little. Would you care to ride with me one day?'

'I'd like that,' she confessed, 'but it's not at all easy to hire horses. When I made enquiries, I was informed that the Cossacks of the garrison had commandeered all the best available.'

'Leave it to me,' he said confidently. 'I may be able to pull a few strings.'

Then Marya came down and there were further introductions. Darya brought tea with slices of lemon and little almond cakes and Nicolai chatted gaily giving them all the latest Petersburg gossip before he took his leave.

'What an attractive youngster,' remarked Marya watching him take the reins of his horse from his servant and swing himself into the saddle. 'How well do you know him, Anna? Was he one of Gregory's friends?'

'Not really. His sister and I were quite close when we were at the Smolny and so we used to meet occasionally.' The first time had been at the Kuragin ball, that fatal night that had been the beginning of everything. She remembered him now as a boy of sixteen with the ash-blond hair of his mother, only then she had had eyes for no one but Gregory.

'He admires you, my dear, that is quite obvious.'

'Oh don't be absurd. He is so young. He can't be more than nineteen or twenty.'

'I should cultivate him if I were you. If he is on Prince Vorontsov's staff he may be able to do quite a lot for you if we are ever permitted to get as far as Tiflis. It always helps to have a friend at Court.'

'Perhaps,' said Anna doubtfully.

But it was not entirely for that reason that she took pleasure in Nicolai's company during the next few days. His attentions and the admiration which he took no pains to conceal acted like a tonic. The fact that he was Nina's brother seemed to put them on familiar terms almost at once. Marya, watching her with affection, was glad to see the old sparkle back in her eyes, to hear her laughter at some absurd joke and note the bloom returning to her cheeks. It was time, she thought, that Anna took a fresh interest in life and learned to love again, less disastrously this time, and she found herself quite unrepentantly wishing that Gregory Gadiani had vanished out of his wife's life once and for all.

The ball at the Assembly Rooms usually took place on a Friday and by the time Paul Kuragin strolled up the Boulevard after his solitary supper, the orchestra and the dancing were in full swing. It was a quiet night, the warm air fragrant with the scent of the acacias, the only sounds the occasional cry of the sentry from the outposts of the garrison, the creak of a cart bringing vegetables to the market or the clop-clop of a solitary horseman. He walked slowly savouring the return of health. Thank God, the pain had gone at last and this damnable hold-up to his plans had come to an end. Another week and he would be free of this wretched little town. He had not attended any of the concerts or evening parties, partly because he had not felt well enough, partly because of the unutterable boredom of having to make himself agreeable in this stuffy provincial society. He had had no intention of attending the ball but as he heard the wail of the violins and saw the lights streaming through the pillared portico, he abruptly changed his mind and went up the steps and through the restaurant into the hall.

He ran his eye over the crowded room. There were the usual frumpish dowagers sitting straight-backed on the gilded chairs ranged along the walls, their heads adorned with feathers, their eagle eyes watching their charges whirling around the ballroom. Hardly a girl there worth a second glance, he thought critically, except for one, the young woman who twice before had attracted his attention. She was waltzing with Nicolai Astrov, the red-gold hair, satin smooth, swept up and away from the small ears, revealing the pure lines of her cheek and neck. Her pale yellow gown with the fine lace foaming around the slender shoulders had a classic severity that pleased him, but it was her eyes that he found fascinating. 'Velvet eyes', he had read that somewhere and thought it absurd, but it described exactly the dark lashes, long and curling against the creamy pallor of her skin that bestowed on them a mystery and a depth that intrigued him.

Then he pulled himself up short. God, what an almighty fool he was even to be thinking of such a thing! It must be the effect of the fever that had bedevilled his recovery and hung about him still. Hadn't Natalie caused him enough pain during the past two years? Never again he had sworn to himself, never again would he give any part of himself to a woman, never again allow himself to be enchanted by a deceiving beauty or endure the bitter humiliation of knowing himself betrayed. He would take what pleasures he wanted and to hell with the consequences! He ground his teeth, envying Nicolai's youth and gaiety, envying the radiance on the lovely face raised to his. He regretted the impulse that had brought him there and was on the point of leaving when the dance came to an end and Nicolai saw him. The young man waved his hand and then began to elbow his way towards him across the crowded floor.

'Paul,' he exclaimed breathlessly as he came up. 'I've only just seen you. I thought you'd decided not to come.'

'I looked in for a minute or two, that's all. I'm not staying.' He smiled. 'I see you've captured the pick of the bunch as usual. Who is she?'

'Anna Crispin. She is by way of being an old acquaintance. She was at school with Nina.'

'Crispin? I should know that name.'

'You probably do. Her father is professor of literature at Moscow.'

'An English intellectual who holds liberal views, I remember him now. Very unpopular with some of the die-hards at the university. Is his daughter like him, a revolutionary, a blue stocking? Not with those looks surely?'

'Judge for yourself. Come and be presented to her.'

'I think not. I'm not up to dancing yet.'

'Well, if you're sure . . . by the way I've been meaning to ask you. Do you happen to know where I can hire horses? Anna has promised to ride with me.'

'Has she indeed? You're not wasting any time.' He shrugged his shoulders. 'You can borrow one of mine if you wish. I've four of them eating their heads off in the stable.'

'May I? It's dashed obliging of you.'

'Can she ride? They are Kabardans, the best I could buy, spirited as the devil, but very sure-footed in these mountains.'

'Acccording to Nina, she is a veritable Diana.'

'There seems no end to her acccomplishments,' said Paul dryly. 'You had better take care, Nikki. Paragons can have feet of clay.'

'Don't be such a cynic.'

'You forget. I speak from experience.' Then he laughed and clapped the young man on the shoulder. 'Enjoy yourself, boy. I'm off to the mess. I've reached that age when a game of chance has more allure than a woman. I'll tell Marik you'll be coming along to look at the horses."

'Many thanks.'

Nicolai watched the tall figure disappear through the door, frowning a little. He liked Paul, admired him in some ways, but never felt close to him. There was always something held back, something withdrawn about him. He had not expected to find him in Pyatigorsk and could not help wondering what he was doing there, but Paul had adroitly avoided answering his questions.

He took a tray of ices from a passing waiter and hurried back to Anna. He found her with her cousin and sat down beside them.

'Just what I was needing,' said Marya accepting the ice-cream. 'How charming of you to think of it. What about you, Anna?'

'Delicious. Dancing makes one so hot.' Anna dipped her spoon into the frozen cream before she said casually, 'Isn't your friend coming to join us?'

'Oh Paul Kuragin is a strange fellow. He doesn't care much for this kind of thing. He says he's not up to dancing yet.'

'Has he been so ill?'

'He doesn't say much but I gather from Marik, that's his groom, that he had a pretty bad time for a few days.'

She had been aware of his eyes on her when she was dancing with Nicolai and felt a faint irritation that having, as it were singled her out for his attention, he should now decline to be presented to her.

She put the glass dish on the table. 'That was lovely. Thank you. Do you know Paul Kuragin well?'

'I suppose I do in a way. I used to see a great deal of him at one time when I was a child. The Kuragin estates at Arachino are not far from my father's house at Valdaya. Paul was in the Guards then.'

'The Guards? Then what is he doing in the Caucasus?'

'He got into some kind of a scrape. I don't know exactly what it was. It was nine years ago when he was not much more than twenty. The Tsar flew into one of his rages and banished him to the regiment of the Line. He commanded a detachment of Cossacks for a time and when he was permitted to return to Petersburg, refused to leave them. He has been here ever since except for an occasional leave. His Uncle Andrei looks after the family estates.'

'I remember hearing somewhere that the Kuragins were fabulously wealthy,' said Marya.

'Paul still is, I suppose. He was the only son and his father, Count Dmitri, died when he was ten so he inherited everything,' and had run through it before he was twenty-one or so it had been said. Paul for all his air of indifference, indeed perhaps because of it, had always been far too attractive to women. All kinds of rumours had floated back to Petersburg from the Caucasus. Nicolai didn't care for the look of interest in Anna's eyes and had no intention of sharing her with him. A little flirtation, he had decided, was just what he needed to pass the tedious wait in Pyatigorsk. The fact that she was married only added spice to the affair. If what Nina said was true, that fellow Prince Gadiani had been a bit of an outsider anyway. He leaned towards her. 'I forgot to tell you. I have found where I can obtain horses, good ones.'

Her face lit up. 'How clever of you. When can we ride?'

'Any time you like. Tomorrow if you wish.'

In actual fact a spell of spring rain held them up and it was several days before they set out one morning, a little party of them, riding south of the town into the foothills of the mountains. Anna was delighted with her dappled grey mare. The Kabardan was small but compactly made, fiery-eyed but easily controlled. A love of horses had been one thing she and Gregory had shared from the beginning. The girls had been allowed to ride at the Smolny but only the quietest and most reliable of hacks. Gregory kept a magnificent stable and encouraged her to ride fast and furiously with him. Sometimes she wondered guiltily if it was that which had contributed to the loss of her baby. She had loved the riding so much and had been so anxious never to fail him. Occasionally he had spoken of Kumari, of the hundred horses his father had kept, of the leopard that was allowed to wander from room to room like a dog in the great house where his ancestors had lived in lavish splendour. One day, she had supposed, she would go there with him. It felt strange that now she would go alone.

She was so silent riding beside Nicolai that he rallied her on it. 'You are very quiet. Are you sorry you came?'

'Oh no. Could anything be more beautiful? What a pity that Marya did not feel well enough to come with us this morning.'

They rode first along the ravine. Above their heads a torrent leaped from ledge to ledge in an icy sparkling stream and the freshnesss of the morning was filled with the perfume of the white acacias and the tall grasses that clustered beside the track.

Presently they passed a small lake of the boiling medicinal mud which formed an important part of the cures at the spa and smelled it long before they reached it so that the ladies were riding with their noses buried in lace handkerchiefs.

At noon they stopped on the grassy bank of the river. Yakov with Nikolai's servant spread the rugs at the foot of the beeches, a little apart from the others, and unpacked the picnic lunch from the baskets. After they had eaten, Nicolai poured another glass of the light wine and put it into her hand, moving closer beside her. She sipped it dreamily, leaning back against the trunk of the tree, eyes half closed. The breeze stirred her hair and a long loose strand blew across his face. He put up a hand and let it run through his fingers.

'It is fine as silk and smells of lime flowers.'

She smiled but did not answer and with a quick look around, he leaned forward and lightly kissed her cheek.

She sat up abruptly, the peace of the morning suddenly broken. 'No,' she said quickly, 'no, please, don't do that.'

'Have I offended you?'

'No.' Half embarrrassed at her swift reaction, she got to her feet. She enjoyed his company but had never intended it to become intimate. She looked around her. 'No one seems to be moving yet. I think I'll walk a little.'

'I'll come with you.'

'No, Nikki, please . . . I would rather you didn't.'

'Are you angry with me?'

'No, of course I'm not.'

'Very well, if you're sure . . .' He drew back, a little hurt at her rejection. 'Don't go too far. You might get lost.'

She walked quickly along the river bank and then turned up a path that rose steeply through a belt of eucalyptus, the stiff grey-green leaves sharply scented in the hot sun. It was a hard climb but the view when she came out of the trees at last was breathtaking. She was standing on a little ledge of rock. The narrow gorge stretched in front of her winding through the mountains, dark and mysterious. On each side the lower slopes were furred with deep green foliage, oak and ash and birch mingled with larch and pine, rising into a dazzle of light to the brilliance of snow-capped peaks. Here and there were patches of wild flowers glowing like a Persian carpet in the sunlight. It was a world of which she had never dreamed, immutable and unchanging, with a grandeur that thrilled and at the same time filled her with awe. All everyday things, all worries and troubles seemed suddenly trivial and of no significance in this ancient rockstrewn wilderness going back to a time when God had created the universe.

Then a cloud momentarily obscured the sun and out of the shadows of the valley came a black horseman riding dangerously fast across the stony ground, a man wearing the narrow-waisted Circassian coat banded with silver, the full breeches tucked into soft leather boots and the *Papakh*, the tall white sheepskin hat on the dark hair.

Gregory had worn that dress once at a Court ball and for

an instant seeing him come at a gallop out of the ravine, she felt a tingle of fear and then with a little gasp of relief recognized Paul Kuragin. He came directly towards her, reined in his horse and sat looking down at her.

'Did I frighten you? I apologize. The truth is that this is a comfortable costume for riding in this kind of country.' He glanced around him. 'You surely have not ventured all this way alone?'

'Prince Astrov is not far off. We lunched beside the river. I climbed up because I thought I might be able to catch a glimpse of Mount Elbruz from here.'

He dismounted, throwing the reins over his horse's head and moving closer to her on the narrow path. 'It's only rarely that you can see the summit. More often than not it is veiled in cloud just as it is now.' He looked at her quizzically. 'Do you know what they say about Elbruz? On the highest peak there stands a gigantic cock crowing and flapping his wings to salute the sun and attacking with beak and talons any intruder rash enough to steal the treasure he guards.'

She glanced at him doubtfully. 'Have you just invented that?'

'No indeed. You only have to ask the peasants.'

'Has anyone ever climbed up to find out?'

'Not to my knowledge. Think how disappointing it would be to discover only rock and snow. There are legends attached to most of the mountains. On Kazbek for instance we not only have Prometheus in his chains, but there is also a crystal castle and a temple in the midst of which there hovers a golden dove.'

'I think that's charming. I hope no one ever goes up to disprove it.'

'You would prefer to keep your illusions?'

'Wouldn't you?'

'My dear young lady, I lost mine a long time ago.' He smiled suddenly and she saw that the brown eyes had a luminous quality, a kind of golden light. He said, 'Here we are talking like old friends and I have not even introduced myself.'

'I know who you are, Count Kuragin.'

'I am honoured,' he gave her a little bow, 'and you are Anna Stepanovna Crispin. Nikki has been our go-between it seems. I met your father once in Moscow, a very remarkable man.'

She gave him a quick look sensing sarcasm but his expression was quite serious. 'I think so too.'

A scurry of wind came racing up the valley, whirled around them and blew the silk scarf from her neck. She reached out to recapture it at the same time as he did so that they laughed as their hands met. Then he was looking down at the broad gold ring on the third finger.

'Forgive me bit was not aware that you were married. Nikki failed to mention it.'

'I asked him not to. I am travelling under my father's name.'

'I see.'

She took the scarf from him twisting it in her hands and conscious of a slight embarrassment. 'My husband is Gregory Gadiani. I am going to Tiflis and then to Kumari.'

He stared at her for a long moment before he said brusquely, 'But surely you know . . .'

'Know what?'

'They must have told you.'

She swung round on him, her eyes wide, and he noticed that behind the silky fringe of dark lashes, they were a deep violet blue. 'Count Kuragin, what is it that I ought to know? It's nearly two months since I left Moscow.'

'There still should have been time for the news to have got through to you.'

'What news?'

'Prince Gadiani is dead.'

In one way she had expected it and yet it still had the power to shock. 'No, it can't be true. I won't believe it.'

'I am afraid you must.'

'Are you sure?'

'As sure as anyone can be.'

The realization turned her dizzy. She swayed a little and put out a groping hand. He took it and after an instant drew her towards him steadying her with an arm around her shoulders.

'What a fool I am. I should have broken it to you more gently.'

She drew a deep breath. 'It's all right. You weren't to know.' She disengaged herself. 'How did it happen?'

'You are looking very pale. I think I should take you back to your party.'

'How? I want to know. I have a right to know.'

He hesitated, looking away from her. 'He went out one

morning riding towards Kumari, it was believed, but he did not return. You may not know but it is wild country. Later they found his horse and the cloak he was wearing, nothing else.'

'I know that already. That does not mean that he is dead,' she said passionately. 'He could have been captured and still in time be released.'

'No. I wish I could hold out that hope, but I cannot.'

'Why are you so sure? Why?'

'If it was true, there would have been demands for ransom by now, perhaps an exchange of prisoners. Shamyl and his henchmen are hard bargainers.'

'Why did Gregory ride out alone that morning if it was dangerous? Why should he be so foolish?'

'I am afraid I can't tell you that. I was never in your husband's confidence.'

There was a curious note in his voice that alarmed and angered her. 'I believe you can and for some reason you want to hide it from me. Why? What have you against him?' In her vehemence she put her hand on his arm and he stood quite still for a moment before he said quietly, 'I am hiding nothing and am only sorry that I should be the one to cause you so much pain.'

'I shall go on to Tiflis. I shall find out for myself.'

'I think you might be very ill advised to do so. Remember what you said just now. It is sometimes better to keep your illusions. You are very young. Life still has a great deal to offer you.'

'No. I want the truth and if you won't tell me, then I shall look for those who can.'

'You are a very determined young woman.'

'Is there anything wrong in that?'

'There may be more problems to be faced than you imagine.'

'Perhaps. I shall overcome them.' She paused and then went on more quietly. 'There are other reasons too. Gregory's grandmother, the Princess Gadiani, has asked me to stay with her at Kumari.'

'The estates will now be yours, I presume.'

'I don't know.' She looked very young and troubled. 'Until Gregory's death is proved, there is still uncertainty. The lawyers tried to explain but it is confusing.'

He watched her for a moment. He had been expecting a storm of tears, but after that brief weakness she had recovered her balance. She had a look of fragility but he suspected that beneath it there was a steely strength. He wondered if she had any notion of the kind of society into which she was venturing so innocently. The viceregal court at Tiflis was a melting pot of nationalities, Russian, Persian, Georgian, Turkish, all fighting one another for power and privilege. He knew it only too well from his own experience, but he doubted if she would heed him if he tried to explain.

She moved away a little. 'I think I should return to the others.'

'Yes, of course.'

He walked beside her, leading his horse. Once as she slipped on the rocky path, he took her arm but she shook herself free. As they came through the trees and on to the river bank, Nicolai came hurrying towards them.

'Wherever have you been, Anna? I've been worrried about you.' Then his eye fell on her companion and he stiffened. 'I didn't realize you had company.'

'We met by chance,' said Paul calmly.

'Indeed. When I asked you this morning if you cared to come with us, you said you preferred not to ride.'

'I changed my mind. I find it easier than walking just now and as a general rule, I like to ride alone.'

The whole party was now on the move and Yakov brought the horses. Paul gave Anna his hand to mount and then stood for a moment, his arm along the neck of the horse.

'How do you like my Kabardan?'

'Yours?'

'Didn't Nikki tell you?'

'No.' She felt angry because it had somehow put her under an obligation to him. 'I am very grateful,' she said stiffly.

'Think nothing of it. I am always happy to oblige a friend.'

He swung himself into the saddle and moved up beside her. In another moment Nicolai had followed and she rode back between the two young men when she would have infinitely preferred to be alone.

They left her at the gate of the cottage and she slipped from the saddle quickly before either of them could alight to help her. She watched them ride away, the tall erect figure in the black coat with the heavy silver belt clasping the narrow waist and the slim boy beside him.

In the sitting room Marya greeted her cheerfully. 'Did you have a good day?'

'Yes, very interesting. Is your headache better?'

'Quite gone. I believe it's all that mud. I shall give up the treatment for a day or two.'

'I think perhaps we shall be moving on soon.'

'Why?' Marya looked up at her. 'Did you hear something new today?'

She avoided a direct answer. 'I shall go and see Captain Gorsky again. It is absurd to go on waiting like this.' She moved away impatiently. 'I'm rather tired. I think I shall go up and change and then lie down for a little.'

'Aren't we due at a concert this evening?'

She paused in the doorway. 'I'd prefer to stay at home. Do you mind?'

'Not at all. Is anything wrong?'

'No, of course not. It's only that a day's riding when you are out of practice can be a little fatiguing.'

She escaped up the stairs aware that she should have told Marya what Paul Kuragin had said about Gregory and feeling quite unable to do so. It was something she had to come to terms with first.

In the tiny bedroom she threw her hat on the bed, unbuttoned the tight-fitting jacket and went to the window pushing it wide. The evening sun slanted in and a drift of petals from the cherry tree had blown along the sill like snow. She felt the cool air on her hot face and wished that she could weep. What had happened to her that she could not feel as she should? What had put out the fire of love that had once blazed in her heart so that now it was only dead ashes, only the bitter after-taste of regret for dreams and illusions lost for ever?

—— 3 ——

It was a few days later when Nicolai inadvertently let slip that a company of Cossacks had been ordered to proceed immediately to Tiflis and that he would be travelling with them.

He was sitting with Anna outside the little pavilion that held the Aeolian harp and the wind music had formed a sweet melancholy background to their conversation. Abruptly the peace was broken. Anna set down her coffee cup and rounded on him.

'Why didn't you tell me before? I thought we were friends and that when you left Pyatigorsk, Marya and I were to go with you.'

He looked a little crestfallen. 'I know . . . only . . . well, the truth is, Anna, that I don't think Paul will take kindly to the suggestion that ladies should travel with us.'

'What has it to do with Paul Kuragin?'

'A great deal. The men will be under his command.'

And he had given no hint of it when she had met him in the town only the day before. He had been all charm and pretty compliments, but not a word had been uttered about his intentions, and he knew how important it was to her. She said stormily, 'I shall go and see Captain Gorsky at once.'

'I will come with you.'

'No, I don't need anyone. I can manage my own affairs.'

He rose when she did. 'Anna, I'm sorry . . .'

'It's all right, Nikki. I know it's not your fault. Will you be kind enough to tell Marya where I have gone? She was to meet me here.'

'Yes, of course.' He watched her go rather unhappily, only too well aware that Paul had warned him to say nothing, had in fact made quite a point of it.

The fiery wave of indignation sent Anna hurrying down the hill to the town and then through the narrow streets towards the garrison outpost. It was near to midday and the sun was blazing. When she arrived, hot and out of breath, the

36

young lieutenant on guard in the doorway tried to bar her way but she swept him aside.

'I'm afraid the Commander is engaged,' he said hastily, following after her and putting a restraining hand on her arm.

'In that case, I'll wait until he is at liberty,' and she sat down firmly on the wooden bench.

'He may be some time.'

'I am in no hurry.'

The young man looked at her doubtfully. He was proud of the way in which he controlled his peasant soldiers, but was quite unaccustomed to dealing with fashionable ladies with a will of their own. After a second he retreated rather sheepishly to the window.

The door of the inner room was ajar and it was obvious that some kind of a strong argument was going on inside. The voices rose and fell but she could not hear what was being said. A bee buzzed lazily about her head and as she waved it away, her agitation began to subside. After all perhaps she was being foolish. Nikki could easily have been mistaken. Maybe it was just that there were military mattters to be settled before she was approached. It was very warm and she leaned back, still determined to wait, when suddenly she heard Maxim Gorsky say quite clearly, 'Really, Colonel, is it so much to ask? It may be a matter of months before another suitable escort passes through.'

'I don't care if it is a year,' was the abrupt reply and she sat up. The lieutenant opened his mouth to say something and she silenced him with a gesture.

'The young lady was very insistent,' went on the Commander.

'More than likely, but the suggestion is utterly ridiculous.' That was Paul Kuragin's voice, she was sure of it, strong, incisive and brooking no opposition. 'I have been held up here long enough and now I intend to ride hard and fast. There is no time to be wasted and it's a devilish journey as you know only too well. I refuse to be hampered by a frivolous and obstinate young woman who won't listen to reason or good advice, to say nothing of her sick elderly relative . . . what in God's name am I going to do with the pair of them?'

Anna's anger boiled over. Without stopping to think, she got to her feet, crossed the room and had flung open the door before the lieutenant could prevent her.

'I am neither frivolous nor obstinate,' she said loudly, 'as you both know perfectly well, neither is my cousin sick or elderly, but as fit and healthy as myself. I have no intention of waiting here for month after month when there is absolutely no reason why I should not travel with your company.'

Both men had turned in astonishment. The Commander looked a little amused, but Paul Kuragin, arms folded, was regarding her with a frown.

'My dear young lady,' he said ironically when she paused for breath, 'didn't your nurse ever tell you when you were a child that listeners never hear any good of themselves?'

'Don't dare to make fun of me!'

'I wouldn't dream of such a thing. Now listen to me,' he went on firmly when she would have interrupted him. 'I can give you any number of good reasons why it is impossible to take you with me. My men are not courtiers, nor are they well-bred gentlemen accustomed to fine society. They are Cossacks of the Line, tough soldiers, hard-living, hard-drinking, hard-swearing. Do you expect them to put up a tent for you each night, cook you dainty meals, bring you boiling water whenever you ask for it, watch their habits, their manners and even their tongues in case accidentally they offend your pretty ears . . . ?'

'Why not?' she said coolly. 'Have you no authority over your men? Don't they obey your commands?'

Captain Gorsky stifled a smile. 'She has a point there, Colonel.'

Paul Kuragin scowled at him. 'It is not only my men of whom I am thinking, Princess Gadiani,' he said sharply, 'but of you and the hardships you and Marya Petrovna will have to endure. Believe me, it will be no picnic. It will be extremely hard going.'

'I am perfectly well aware of that.'

'Well then, there is really nothing more to be said.'

'But there is . . .'

'Indeed?'

She raised her eyes to him pleadingly. 'You know why this is so vitally important to me, Count Kuragin, better than anyone. I swear that we will not hold you up. Yakov will look after our comfort and see to our needs just as he has done on the journey from Moscow. Won't you help me please? Is it such a great deal to ask?'

He hesitated. Damn her for a witch! It was ten times more difficult to resist when she looked at him like that and knowing what he did. He had tried to smother the feeling of guilt but it had persisted. She was not aware of it but he did after all owe her something.

He said gruffly, 'I suppose if I still refuse, you will take it into your head to set out alone.'

She lowered her eyes. 'I'm afraid I can't do that. The Commander holds our papers and will not give them up.'

'Is that so?'

Gorsky nodded. 'I thought it wise in the circumstances.'

'Very wise.' Paul sighed before he said wryly, 'Well, now you can hand them over to me.' He frowned at Anna. 'I know I'm every kind of a fool, but how quickly can you be ready?'

'Tomorrow if you wish.'

'The day after tomorrow will be soon enough,' he replied dryly. 'And pack your baggage into as small a compass as possible. I can't spare a team of mules for your finery. Are you and your cousin prepared to ride?'

'Yes,' she said joyously because she had won. 'Don't be afraid. We are not weaklings, either of us, and we'll be no trouble to you.'

'I hope to God you are right,' he said a little sourly.

'And thank you, Count Kuragin, thank you with all my heart.'

The face she turned to him was radiant, the velvet eyes filled with light, and there was a curious tug at his heart when he looked at her. Well, he had done his best to warn her off and now she must face what was coming to her. He said, 'You had better wait to thank me until we have reached Tiflis.'

'You are very fortunate, Madame,' remarked Gorsky cheerfully, relieved to be rid of the responsibility. 'Colonel Kuragin is a brave man and his Cossacks are all picked soldiers. I only hope you will not regret your decision.'

'Why should I?'

He glanced at Paul. 'I think that you have not yet fully realized that we live here in the midst of violence and no one can be sure where it will strike next. Now if there is anything further I can do for you, perhaps you will let me know.'

'I am grateful, very grateful.' She gave them a beaming smile and then went quickly before they could change their minds.

'God damn it!' exploded Paul as the door closed behind her. 'You were no help at all. You let me in for that.'

'I don't see how you could refuse. Besides,' he gave Paul a

swift sly look, 'several days in the company of a pretty woman, what could be more delightful?'

'A great many things,' said Paul wrathfully. 'I'd hoped to do the trip in a week, now it is likely to take a fortnight, even a month, and don't call me Colonel. I am no longer entitled to that rank.'

'But why? Surely when you were here a year ago . . .'

'That was a different matter. The Tsar has since seen fit to strip it from me. I am a simple Captain like yourself.'

'May I ask why?' enquired Gorsky opening the drawer and taking out Anna's papers.

'I killed a man or caused him to be killed. It amounts to the same thing.'

'In a duel?'

'I suppose you could call it that,' said Paul curtly. He looked down at the papers the Commander handed to him. 'Did you ever meet Gregory Gadiani?'

'How could I? I have never been lucky enough to be invited to the viceregal court.'

'You've not missed anything, my friend, believe me. Prince Gadiani was handsome enough to take any young woman by storm, but wild and reckless as a hawk and with some of a hawk's more unpleasant qualities. The Gadianis are old Caucasian aristocracy, Princes of Kumaria, charming, devious, ambitious and utterly ruthless. I wonder what she made of him.'

'Isn't she going to Tiflis to join him?'

Paul gave him a swift glance. 'Hasn't the news reached you yet? He was murdered some months ago. She doesn't realize yet what a nest of vipers she is venturing into. Oh well, it's none of my business. I'll get her to Tiflis safely. After that it will not be my responsibility. There are Gadanis enough to take her under their wing. Can we get back to business? I want to know about provisions, horses, weapons, mules . . .'

They began to discuss the practicalities, but Maxim Gorsky who had dealt with Paul Kuragin before on some of the other unorthodox missions he had undertaken thought that the young man was not as single-minded as usual in his attention to detail, and was not entirely surprised. A few weeks of enforced companionship, sharing pleasure and hardship with a disturbing young woman like Anna Gadiani, could be unnerving and produce some unexpected results. Then he mentally shrugged his shoulders and got back to the work in hand.

* * *

Afterwards when she looked back on it, Anna thought that some of the days during the long and often painful journey to Tiflis were among the happiest in her life and reluctantly she had to admit that it was largely due to Paul Kuragin though at first she would never have believed such a thing possible.

It was true that once he had agreed that they should travel with him, he was scrupulously courteous. Indeed, Marya, who had been prejudiced by Anna's description of him as arrogant beyond bearing, was agreeably surprised when he paid them a polite call on the morning before they were due to set out, making useful suggestions as to how they should travel and advising them on what they might need to make the journey tolerable.

'I don't know why you dislike him so much, Anna,' she said after he had gone. 'I think we're fortunate to have him as our protector. We might have fared much worse. After all he is a gentleman of very good family. He is extremely thoughtful for our comfort and he speaks so well of your father.'

'I don't dislike him. It's just that . . . oh I don't know . . . I have a feeling that he despises everyone and that includes us.'

'He doesn't strike me as a particularly happy man,' said Marya thoughtfully, 'but that is not really our concern.'

Perhaps it was because of what he had said about Gregory that made Anna uneasy. She was sure that he knew something which he was deliberately keeping from her and it irritated her. But all the same she went about her preparations with a feeling of relief that now at last they were actually on their way.

The party started out soon after dawn when the air was still cool and fresh. The newly risen sun was already gilding the high peaks but the valleys were in deep shadow. The detachment of Cossacks was drawn up on the outskirts of the town waiting for them. In their narrow-waisted caftans, their shaggy lambskin caps, with their glittering weapons and the *bourkas*, the cloaks of heavy felt, strapped to their saddles, they looked a villainous group, nothing at all like the trim lines of handsomely turned out soldiers whom Anna had watched the Tsar review on the Field of Mars. At their head was Paul dressed like his men with nothing to mark his rank except the splendid black horse, the jewel-studded hilt of the dagger in his belt and the silver-mounted pistols in his holsters.

'Did you ever see such a company of brigands?' murmured Marya with amusement as twenty pairs of eyes watched curiously as they trotted up the road. 'I feel as if I were living in the midst of one of those Gothic novels which were so popular with the English.'

She called a gay good morning to Paul and he nodded, running an appraising eye over them. Thank heaven they had had the good sense to dress sensibly in neat riding habits and not in the fashionable falderals he had half expected.

He looked over his men. Everything was in order, the mules with the baggage bringing up the rear under the command of Marik and Yakov. He glanced irritably at his watch. Where the devil was Nikki? He barked a command and the Cossacks split up, two riding ahead. He motioned to Marya and Anna to take up position in the middle, soldiers in front and behind with a rear-guard to follow the baggage animals.

The horses were stamping impatiently, the Cossacks glancing at one another and then at their frowning Captain when at last Nicolai came up at a gallop, magnificent in his Hussar's uniform, his groom following behind him with two mules loaded with luggage.

'You're late,' snapped Paul, 'and where the hell do you think you're going dressed up like a tailor's dummy? We're not in Petersburg now.'

The young man flushed at the rebuke. 'There's surely no need to look like scarecrows. We are Russian officers,' he said stiffly, 'and we do have ladies in our company.'

'We're not going on a pleasure trip nor are we attending a garden party at the summer palace,' went on Paul ironically, 'and for God's sake, cover up that gold braid when we reach the mountains. We want to look inconspicuous, a very ordinary party, not worth a kopek. Some of these tribesmen would slit your throat for just one of those fancy gold buttons of yours. You'd better ride in the centre with the women.'

'No. I won't do anything of the kind,' protested Nicolai violently. 'Do you take me for a coward?'

Paul cut him short. 'I hope not, but that's hardly the point, is it? Now don't argue. Do as you're told. We're already an hour later than I intended.'

Nicolai joined Anna and Marya fuming. 'Who the devil does he think he is? I am not under his command.'

'You are for the present,' said Marya placatingly. 'We all are. If you fuss, you will only make it worse. Count Kuragin has a great deal on his mind.'

He was certainly efficient, thought Anna, during the next few days when everything seemed to work perfectly and run to plan. Travelling along the river bank and then into the foothills of the mountains, she had a sense of freedom, an elation and a gaiety she had not experienced for many months. Laughing and talking with Marya and Nikki, healthily hungry at the end of the day, she did not mind the burning heat of the midday sun or the simple food and primitive conditions. Only sometimes at night she would feel ashamed that she was enjoying it so much. She should have been grieving for Gregory and instead found days slipping by when she hardly thought of him at all.

Paul was seldom with them except to enquire if there was anything they needed. He would be either riding ahead or at the rear or talking with his second-in-command, a giant of a man, grey-haired and heavily bearded, who treated his Captain with a mingling of respect and easy familiarity which would never have been permitted in army circles in Petersburg.

'Varga has been with me since I first came to the Caucasus,' he said once when Marya remarked on it, 'when I was as much of a greenhorn as Nikki is now. Without him I could have died a dozen times over.'

The resthouse at Vladikavkaz was the most comfortable they had stayed at since they started out. After supper had been served to them in their room, Anna took off her blouse and washed her face and neck in cool water. Then she put on a fresh silk shirt and vigorously brushed the dust and grit out of her hair. She tied it back simply with a ribbon and examined her face in the mirror. Already she had acquired a light golden tan which would have earned a stern rebuke from her grandmother. She was free of that now, free as air to do as she pleased. A widow . . . how strange that seemed. In some ways it liberated her, made her free of the conventions and strict behaviour required from a young unmarried girl.

'You look about sixteen,' said Marya smiling at her. 'Where are you going?'

'I thought I'd walk a little by the river.'

'Are you going to meet Nikki?'

'Certainly not,' she said sharply. 'Why should I?'

'Only that you seem to enjoy his company and it is a lovely evening.'

'Marya, you're nothing but an old romantic! Don't read more into things than are there. Anyway this is a garrison town and I saw a number of officers downstairs. Nikki is probably spending the evening playing cards with them. I shan't be long.'

'Take care and don't go too far.'

'I won't.'

The town had been built half a century before as a jumping-off ground for the conquest of the Caucasus and boasted only one main street. The Alexandrovskaya was lined with pretty pink and white stucco houses where the officers of the garrison lived and was shaded by an avenue of limes smelling sweetly in the cool of the evening. It opened into a public garden with a winding path running alongside the river. She followed it for a little way and then sat down on a fallen log beneath a great beech. The water flowed swiftly, so clear that she could see the brown stones of the river bed. On the opposite bank the flag flew from the tower of the fortress and she could hear the barked commands as the soldiers marched to relieve the sentries. From somewhere near at hand there came the low melancholy wail of a pipe. She listened dreamily, lying back with her eyes closed, letting the strange barbaric music flow over her and she started when a hand was put on her shoulder.

'That is an Ossetian bagpipe. Do you know they dance reels to it like Scottish highlanders?' Paul Kuragin had dropped down on the log beside her.

'What do you know of Scotland, Count Kuragin?'

'Nothing, except what I have read in books,' he replied lazily. 'Perhaps all mountain folk have similar tastes.' He was more relaxed than she had ever seen him, his face for once without the taut wary look it wore so often.

'I thought you would have been spending the evening with your friends in the garrison.'

'Drinking and gambling?' he said lightly. 'Do I detect a note of disapproval? You must remember, Anna Stepanovna, that more often than not, it is the only relaxation a soldier enjoys if he is stationed in the Caucasus.'

'Why do you stay here then? Nikki said you could have returned to Petersburg any time you wished in the last few years.'

'Nikki talks too much,' he stretched himself. 'There are

times when I too find pleasure in drinking and gambling, but not tonight.'

'Why not tonight?'

He shrugged his shoulders and turned to look at her, his eyes frankly examining the shining red-gold hair, the slim white neck, the swelling breasts under the thin silk. 'I've been watching you for some minutes. You look no more than a schoolgirl with your hair like that. I find myself teased by a memory. Are you sure we have never met before?'

'Not that I know of.'

He stared at her, frowning, then suddenly thumped his knee. 'I have it. Why didn't I think of it before? My Uncle Andrei's party on the Neva. It must be three . . . no, more than four years ago now.' In a flash of memory he saw the young girl as he had seen her then in her white dress, unbelievably innocent and fresh among that jaded sophisticated company, a passing glimpse that had aroused his pity and then been forgotten in his own weariness and boredom. He leaned forward. 'Were you there?'

'Yes.' She met his eyes and looked away. 'I don't remember you among the guests.'

'Probably not. I didn't stay long. Were you with Gregory Gadiani?'

'Yes.' Her eyes were on her clasped hands. 'It was because of that evening that we married. I had played truant from the Smolny. It was a crazy thing to do and it was discovered. Gregory smashed the carriage on our way back to the Convent . . .'

'And so they found out. Damned young fool!'

'No, don't. It was an accident.'

'I'm sorry. I didn't mean to remind you. You must have been very young.'

'Nearly nineteen.'

No more than a child and probably forced into marriage with that headstrong young rake for the sake of convention. The Tsar had a passion for arranging other people's lives, he thought savagely, including his if he would have let him.

'Were you very much in love with him?'

'I don't think you should ask that.'

'Did he make you so unhappy?'

'Count Kuragin please . . .' It was absurd but she felt her eyes fill at the memory of that wildly foolish, wildly happy evening.

'Forgive me. It's not for me to ask.'

He touched her hand in apology and through a blur of tears she saw the large square green ring . . . it was not Gregory's ring, though it was so like, and suddenly she remembered the road and the beggar at her feet and the blood. She turned to look at him, the question trembling on her lips, but he had already risen and was glancing around him.

'It's late and growing cool . . . besides this is a border town.'

'Surely we're safe enough here.'

'Yes, of course, all the same I think we should go back.'

He did not tell her that nowhere was it completely safe. He had known a party of Shamyl's horsemen to come unexpectedly out of the night, sweeping through the streets, even once through a ballroom, leaving ravage and death behind them. Instead he said quietly, 'You should get some rest. I am afraid it will be another early start tomorrow. We've a very long day before us.'

They walked back along the street, full of people hurrying home, and she said nothing about the ring but was curiously aware of a link of sympathy between them. In some odd way she couldn't explain, there had been a feeling of comfort in the momentary pressure of his hand on hers, and then it was gone.

The following day they entered the mountains and were climbing all the morning up the steep stony track. At each side rose wooded limestone hills and above the tree line were bare rocky cliffs, some of them streaked with snow. Now and again through the side valleys they had glimpses of villages with their watchtowers and clusters of black huts clinging like swallows' nests to the high precipices.

When they stopped to eat at midday, the sun blazed down beating off the rocks relentlessly and there was little shade. Anna pulled off her jacket, pushing back the damp hair which she had left loosely tied back for comfort and coolness. They were all glad of the fresh food they had bought in the town, creamy goat's cheese and crusty wholemeal bread with tomatoes and cool refreshing cucumbers. Paul did not allow them long to rest. He himself had eaten with his Cossacks sprawled beside their horses and he came across to them as Yakov was about to unpack the samovar.

'No time for tea,' he said abruptly. 'Leave it until we camp this evening.'

'Damn it, Paul, do you have to play the slave-driver?' said

Nikki lazily. 'Anna and Marya are tired and thirsty. It is as hot as an oven. Wouldn't it be easier to ride on when the sun goes down and it is cooler?'

'And cross the Daryal gorge in the dark?' remarked Paul witheringly. 'Don't be such a fool. At least give me the credit of knowing what I am doing.' He shouted to the soldiers and they began to saddle up.

'Come on,' said Marya wearily, 'no use arguing.'

Nikki looked mutinous but he gave her his hand to help her up. The horses were brought and they mounted while Yakov and Marik repacked the luncheon baskets.

'Now remember . . . you must keep together. No straggling,' urged Paul. 'The road is narrow and dangerous and I don't want any accidents. I should be particularly glad if you would take note of that, Nikki.'

'You say it so many times, I'm hardly likely to forget it,' snapped the young man, his mouth tight as he flung himself into the saddle.

Anna looked anxiously from one to the other. The friction was growing and at any moment there would be an explosion between these two young men. She longed to ask Paul to be more tactful, more forbearing, to remember that the little boy he had once known was now a young man with all the uncertainty, all the touchy pride of youth, only somehow she had not been able to summon up the courage.

Up and up they mounted, the path growing more and more narrow until they were following a shelf cut out of the rock face above a raging torrent. Anna dare not look down in case she should be overcome with vertigo. She stared straight ahead keeping her eyes fixed on the straight back of the Cossack in front of her in his sweat-stained caftan. They were riding now in single file, Nikki immediately behind her, then Marya and the rest of the soldiers. Where Paul was, she did not know. On both sides vertical walls of granite rose five or six thousand feet above them, shutting out all but a thin ribbon of sky.

This was the entrance to the Daryal gorge, an eerie and sinister place. No sun reached them here, the wind blew cold and their ears were filled with the incessant roar of the river. The road went down and up again, winding through towering cliffs, and then slowly descended once again and she saw the narrow bridge across the torrent, foaming and creaming far below. On the opposite bank perched on the high precipice and almost indistinguishable from the rocks were the ruins of

Tamara's castle, the famous and evil Queen of Georgia, whose discarded lovers, so legend said, had been hurled to their deaths in the black water. In this savage place it was easy to believe anything and she shivered as she paused on the brink of the bridge. Involuntarily her tight grip on the rein relaxed, her horse took a false step, for an agonizing moment she teetered on the edge, too terrified even to scream, then felt herself jerked back.

'My God, can't you keep your mind on where you are going? Do you want us all to be drowned in the gorge down there?' Paul was white with anger.

Shaken she muttered an apology and Nicolai behind her said fiercely, 'Don't speak to Anna like that!'

'I shall speak how I like if I consider it necessary,' was Paul's sharp reply.

He began to lead her horse across the bridge. Varga followed, his hand on Marya's bridle, then Nicolai and the rest of the party. It was nearly nine miles before they were through the gorge and Paul kept Anna close beside him all the way until slowly the road began to widen out and unbelievably alpine meadows opened up before them. He left her then, riding back to the rear where the baggage animals were giving trouble. The road widened still more. She gasped with relief from tension as Nicolai cantered up beside her.

'Phew!' he mopped his face. 'What a devil of a track. I'm not sorry to be through that. What do you say, Anna? Shall we ride on a little?'

'Should we?' she said doubtfully. 'Paul was very insistent that we should keep together.'

'To perdition with him! He is not our god even if he thinks he is,' he said impatiently. 'My horse and I need to stretch our legs.' He dug in his heels and galloped forward.

It was tempting after the long hours crawling nose to tail and she took a deep breath and followed after him. They were flying along the first level piece of road they had met that day, her hat falling back, her hair streaming behind her, the cool wind fanning her hot face. They passed the two outriders who shouted to them, but they paid no heed. The pounding of hooves behind them did not deter them from their crazy gallop until Paul swept past, wheeled his horse and straddled the road in front of them. Panting and dishevelled, Anna pulled up while Nicolai unable to stop galloped by, then turned and came back, his horse rearing, his excitement dying in face of Paul's grim expression.

'Are you both out of your minds?' he demanded dryly, 'or do you find it amusing to ignore everything I say? I thought I told you to keep together with the men.'

'We've come through the gorge. What's all the fuss about?' said Nicolai defiantly.

'There's the reason, twenty good reasons, perhaps more,' and Paul pointed with his whip. Across the valley on a little rise stood a group of black horsemen, motionless and sinister, outlined against the golden sky.

'What of them?' asked Nicolai insolently.

'They are Shamyl's horsemen. They have been keeping pace with us most of the day. If they had come across and cut you off, I could have done little to save either of you, your head could now have been swinging from a saddle bow and Anna be on her way to the slave market or worse.'

Startled she said, 'I didn't realize . . .'

'Perhaps in future you will believe that I do have your safety in mind,' said Paul sarcastically.

Nicolai frowned. 'Why didn't you warn us?'

'I didn't want to alarm you unnecessarily.'

'Surely I had a right to know,' he protested hotly. 'I'm not a child.'

'Then don't behave like one.'

'Damn it, Paul, I'm not going to be spoken to like that. You presume on our old friendship. At any other time . . .'

'At any other time you'd call me out, I suppose, shoot me at dawn,' said Paul with an aggravating smile.

'Oh please,' broke in Anna, 'isn't it stupid to quarrel over nothing?'

'It is a question of honour,' said Nicolai haughtily. 'If Paul questions my courage . . .'

'I agree with Anna. It is ridiculous. Don't be afraid, my dear, I don't fight with boys,' said Paul acidly.

Nicolai flushed scarlet. He raised his riding crop but with a swift movement Paul had seized his wrist in an iron grip so that after a moment it fell from his numbed fingers.

'Now that was extremely silly,' said Paul reprovingly. 'If Varga saw you threaten me, you could be very sorry indeed. Keep your temper till we reach Tiflis, then you can horse-whip me at your pleasure.'

By this time the soldiers had caught them up with Marya looking anxious and alarmed. Nicolai bit his lip and Paul said crisply, 'Varga, pick up Prince Astrov's whip, he accidentally dropped it.' He looked around at them. 'We need to ride fast if we are to reach Kazbek by nightfall. I know we have all had an exhausting day, but may I say,' and he smiled at them suddenly with a charm that Anna found quite maddening, 'you have come through it with flying colours, particularly the ladies. It will be easier tomorrow I promise you.'

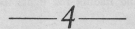

—————— 4 ——————

The resthouse at Kazbek was crammed with soldiers, most of them drunk already, delighted to be on their way home to Russia after a long stint in the Caucasus. Paul took one look at the crowded rooms and decided it was no place for ladies. He made up his mind to move on and camp in the open. Nights at this altitude could be cold and the ground would make a hard bed, but better that than being poisoned by bad food and suffocated by the reek of animals and unwashed humanity. The great mountain loomed above them, dark and forbidding, but the fields glowed green in the evening light with young oats and barley. He chose a spot carefully, not far from the bank of the river, flowing quietly on its long journey to the Caspian Sea. He posted sentries and disposed his men with some care while Yakov and Marik set up a small tent for Marya and Anna and began to unroll the bedding rolls and fur rugs they had brought with them for this very purpose.

They were tired but it was pleasant to wash hands and faces in the bowls of water brought to them and then lie back on the piled cushions watching the soldiers light their cooking fires.

Nikki, still smarting from Paul's sharp rebuke, was the only one who grumbled. 'Why couldn't he ask us what we felt about it?' he muttered to Anna and was annoyed because she smiled at him teasingly.

'Marya and I don't mind so why should you? You're a soldier, aren't you, accustomed to bivouacking?'

'That's hardly the point,' he said stiffly and walked away from her.

Yakov, who was never at a loss, was blowing on the charcoal in the brazier until it glowed red and presently began to grill the last of their fresh meat, juicy chunks of lamb on long skewers. Soon the air was fragrant with the smell of the roasting *shashliks* while Marik spread the white cloth and set out the plates with the rest of the food.

They had already begun to eat when Paul strolled across, a bottle in each hand, and stood looking down at them, the glow of the fire highlighting the high cheekbones under the flaring eyebrows and finding red lights in the dark curling hair.

'May I join you?'

'Of course.' Marya looked up in surprise. She moved a little to one side indicating a place on the rug between her and Anna.

'Thank you.' He sat down and held up the bottles. 'Champagne. I thought we deserved it after the long day we've had. Varga has had it in the stream for the past hour so it should be cool enough.'

Marya clapped her hands with pleasure. It was one of the endearing qualities that made her such a good travelling companion, thought Anna, the fact that she rarely grumbled and took a childish delight in the simplest things.

'Never in my wildest dreams,' she was saying to Paul, 'did I imagine I would find myself drinking champagne at the foot of Kazbek with a hero of the Caucasus.'

He smiled and raised his glass to her. 'You do me too much honour. In my turn may I say I've never yet met a lady with such a cheerful courage in very trying circumstances.' Marya giggled at the compliment and they clinked glasses while Anna bit her lip staring down at the brimming goblet in front of her.

Paul glanced at her over his shoulder. 'Drink up,' he said lightly. 'It will take the ache out of your bones.'

Piqued she swallowed the wine at a gulp and immediately choked over it. Nikki patted her on the back as she coughed and Paul quietly refilled her glass.

'Take it more slowly next time,' he said kindly.

'I am not a child,' was her tart reply.

He raised his eyebrows, turning back to Marya and accepting the food she pressed on him. He made no apology for the curtness of his manner during the afternoon, but talked so well and so amusingly while they ate that after a little even Nikki forgot his ill humour. The second bottle was opened and Anna leaned back among the cushions, her momentary annoyance forgotten, the wine suffusing everything with a golden haze. She was very conscious of Paul, lounging beside her, his tunic unbuttoned, the white linen shirt open at the throat, the half-emptied glass in the strong brown hand.

It was Marya who asked about Shamyl. 'Have you ever seen him, Count Kuragin?'

'Paul please. I think we've been through enough together to dispense with formalities. Yes, I have seen him . . . twice.'

'What does he look like? One hears so many different tales about him.'

He sat up, putting down his glass and staring into the leaping flame of the fire. 'He is exceptionally tall, always dressed in black, with a lean pale face, deep smouldering eyes and his beard stained red with henna. Wherever he goes, he is followed by his executioner, a huge fellow carrying a long-handled axe, ready to gouge out an eye or lop off a hand or even a head at his master's bidding.'

'Oh come,' said Nikki, 'that can't be true. It sounds remarkably like some traveller's fabulous invention.'

'In the mountains of the Caucasus, one begins to believe in fables,' said Paul quietly. 'I have seen it happen and it was not a pleasant sight, but it inspired terror and instant obedience in those who watched and that was his purpose. To his men he is Allah's mouthpiece placed on this earth to execute his will, and they die willingly if he asks it of them.'

'You turn him into something of a hero.'

'And so he is among his own people. Don't underestimate him, Nikki. That's the mistake our Generals have made during the past ten years. Prince Vorontsov now knows better. Shamyl and his black horsemen, his Naibs as they are called, are utterly ruthless. Vengeance is their creed and violence is part of their life. They will fight for their independence to the last man without pity for their enemies or for themselves.'

'How do you know all this?'

Paul did not answer immediately and Anna had the notion that he was holding something back, then he went on quietly. 'I was at the siege of Akhulgo seven years ago. It was my first real campaign when I was not much older than you, Nikki. We had fought our way over miles of impossible precipices to his stronghold in the mountains. It took us from June to August to conquer it. When their ammunition ran out, the men flung themselves on to our bayonets and their women slaughtered their children and then threw themselves to death rather than surrender. This is the kind of people we are trying to conquer.'

There was a momentary silence at the horror of the picture

he had conjured up. Then Anna said slowly, 'You sound as if you admire them.'

'In some ways I do. It always pays to know your enemy and they do have some qualities. They are immensely brave, fanatically loyal. They ask no quarter and give none. I prefer them to the turncoats, the renegades, the cowards, like some of the native Princes who intrigue and betray and murder each other out of a greed for power and wealth.'

There was a suppressed anger in his voice and for some reason Anna shivered as if an icy wind had blown off the mountain. She said in a stifled voice, 'Was Gregory one of them?'

He evaded her question. 'Why should you ask that? The Gadianis are Princes of Kumaria and their loyalty has always been to the Tsar.' Then he smiled. 'You shouldn't have got me started on the subject. All old Caucasians are the same and will bore you to death with their experiences if given half a chance. It can be very pleasant in Tiflis. Vorontsov keeps great state. There are balls, concerts, horse racing, the opera, plenty to keep you amused.'

'While the men are away on a campaign.'

'Some of them,' he said dryly. 'There are still a great many left behind to partner you in a quadrille.' He got to his feet. 'Come along, Nikki, it's late. We mustn't keep the ladies from their beds. We all need sleep.'

They strolled away together amicably enough, Paul's hand on the younger man's shoulder. Marya began to roll up the rugs.

'It's growing cold. We're going to need these.' She grinned up at Anna. 'Who would have thought it? Paul Kuragin has decided we're worthy of his company after all.'

'I don't think it's that at all.'

Marya paused in her task. 'That's a sudden change of heart. All along it has been you who have complained of his churlishness.'

'Yes, I know.' Anna bent down to gather up the rest of the cushions. She pushed the bundle into Marya's hands. 'You go in.'

'Aren't you coming?'

'In a minute.' She watched Marya duck under the flap of the tent. Despite her fatigue she was restless.

Darkness fell early in the mountains. The moon had not yet risen but the black velvet canopy of the sky was spangled with brilliant stars. She stood irresolutely for a moment and then walked down towards the river bank. Some of the Cossacks were already sleeping wrapped in their *bourkas* but a few still lounged around the dying fire, singing quietly. She paused trying to distinguish the words . . .

> The haunting sound of evening bells
> That brings back my dreams
> That brings back my love to me—my dear dear love
> And then no more, no more . . .

The melody was filled with sadness, a painfully sweet nostalgia for home and dear ones. She thought of her dead love. He seemed so far away now, part of another life, and she forgot the bitterness and regretted only the lost happiness. On the brink of the river she leaned against a great tree looking up to where a star trembled on the highest crest of the mountain. She saw the tiny glow of the cigar, smelled the fragrance of the scented smoke and was aware of his presence before he spoke.

'What are you dreaming of?' he said quietly. 'The golden dove in the crystal temple?'

'Yes, in a way. The mountains are so remote, so lonely . . . they seem to cast a spell.'

'So that anything, however fabulous, becomes not only believable, but probable.'

She turned to look at him. 'Do you feel that too?'

'They make me realize my own unimportance in the Almighty's scheme of things.'

'I wouldn't have thought that anything could do that.'

He smiled. 'Touché. I'm sorry if I spoke brutally today.'

'You had every right. We had behaved foolishly.'

'True enough, but I could have put it more gently.' He didn't tell her that it had been the thought of the red-gold head flung across a saddle bow, the slender body ravaged and broken that had prompted his anger.

She said impulsively, 'I wish you would be kinder to Nicolai. He is so young.'

'And so spoiled. Nikki has to learn. There are too many gilded darlings like him at the viceregal court.'

'That is very harsh.'

'Perhaps, but life out here is not a bed of roses. He reminds me of myself and the fool I was when I first came to the Caucasus.'

'Why did you come?'

'Hasn't Nikki told you?'

'He said something about the Tsar.'

Her eyes were growing accustomed to the darkness. She could just make out the lean profile, the straight nose and firm chin. He threw his cigar into the river and the glowing tip vanished with a tiny hiss.

'It was not for anything heroic or romantic, not a political squib, a love affair or even a duel. It was one night in the mess. We were all pretty drunk and I improvised a lampoon on the Tsar. Unfortunately it reached his ears. It was meant as a joke but it misfired badly. He has no sense of humour and he was outraged.'

'How did he know it was you? Did someone give you away?'

He shrugged his shoulders. 'Everyone has enemies.' He began to laugh. 'It really was rather funny . . .'

'Tell me about it.'

'I don't dare. Most of it was not fit for a lady's ears, but one verse did compare him to a camel. You've seen him—you know the way he stands, his head flung up, that long upper lip, that icy contemptuous stare, damning to hell everyone who opposes him.'

It was so true . . . the Tsar in a rage condemning her and Gregory, frightening but ridiculous too if you had the courage to defy the terror . . . she began to laugh with him.

'I wish I could have seen his face when he read it.'

'I did. He went quite purple. Someone had obligingly written it out and he tore the paper into little pieces before pronouncing judgment. I was rather proud of myself, but my uncle who was my guardian then, was furious with me for ruining my career. Oh dear, what an utter idiot one is at nineteen!'

'Yes, what an idiot . . .'

'That's not true of you, I am sure.'

'I'm afraid it is.'

'Idiot or not,' he said thoughtfully, 'I've never really regretted it.'

'I have . . . often.'

He gave her a quick glance. Then a voice said something and there was the sound of footsteps. 'That will be Varga, wondering where I am. I was on my way to look around my sentries.'

'Are we in danger here?'

'You can never be too careful in the Caucasus. You should get some rest. Goodnight, Anna.'

'Goodnight . . . Paul.'

She felt his hand reach out and touch hers for an instant, then he had disappeared into the darkness. She walked slowly back to the tent, uncertain of herself, a little confused, still not sure if she liked or detested him, only knowing that in some inexplicable way he disturbed her.

In the days that followed a comradeship developed between them, something Anna had never experienced before. She had never known a brother, had never had a man as a friend except her father. Gregory and she had been lovers, there had been ecstasy mingled with pain, wild happiness and tormenting jealousy, but never the quiet ordinary joys of every day. Paul did not pay her compliments or make pretty speeches or attempt any physical approach as other men had done. He could be aloof and uncompromising at times as he had been from the start, but now he would occasionally invite her to ride ahead with him and more and more he joined them when they sat down to eat at midday and in the evening. He had not wasted his nine years in the Caucasus and Nikki was jealous because so often Anna listened to him spellbound.

He told them once about a mission he had undertaken to the Caspian Sea where the naphtha buried in the earth sends up towering jets of flame, where in the temple of the Persian fire-worshippers the light has burned since Noah's Flood.

'When we took a boat out on the water, we floated in fire, the pale golden flames were as volatile as burning brandy,' he said, 'and the mountains are haunted by legends of lovely winged creatures, half woman and half bird.'

'It is a land of magic,' said Anna wonderingly.

He smiled. 'Perhaps. At any rate a land of extremes where the impossible becomes reality. In Ghimri where Shamyl was besieged among the precipices there are sudden black storms and rushing whirlwinds and the peasants say it is the passing of Simurg, the gigantic white bird of Solomon, who looks with one eye at the past and with the other at the future. Only two of the Tartars escaped that massacre and one of them was Shamyl himself.' He paused looking down at the golden wine in his glasss.

'Go on,' urged Marya, 'what happened?'

'He was seen quite clearly outlined against the rocks and the men were preparing to fire when he leaped clean over their heads, came up behind them, sword in hand, and killed three before he was bayoneted in the chest. He wrenched the blade free and with another superhuman leap had disappeared into the night.'

Nikki stirred restlessly. 'Do you believe tales like that?'

'It is not a drunken fantasy, it is the sober truth,' said Paul sombrely. 'Our men are as brave as troops anywhere in the world, but he has created a legend and legends are very hard to destroy.'

There were other times when, riding ahead of the others, they would talk of pleasanter things, arguing about books and poetry. Paul had a man's scorn of the romantic Byron she loved, reminding her of her father's cool judgment. Again and again she thought how different he was from Gregory and the young men she had known in Petersburg, who never seemed to think of anything but racing their horses, indulging in a love affair or gambling the night away. He rarely spoke of himself and when one day she asked him about his home at Arachino, he adroitly changed the subject. She felt as if she lived in a kind of timeless present with the past forgotten and the future too far off to trouble her.

So the days passed, sometimes under a blistering sun, sometimes in rain, and once in the high peaks swept by a snowstorm. Frequently when the going had been hard, she and Marya were so tired and saddle sore that their limbs ached intolerably, but at other times the grass was soft and green as velvet, there were flowers everywhere, the shepherd boys sang as they pastured their long-haired sheep and in the tiny villages there would be stalls heaped with early fruit and vegetables.

They were lulled into a feeling of content and security so that the attack when it came was unexpected and terrifying. They had stopped to eat their midday meal where the twin rivers, the black and white Aragvi, met and they really were black and white, Anna noticed with delight, bizarre and fantastic like everything else in this fascinating country. Paul had been amusing them with the tale of a Princess of the Aragvi who had once lived in the ruined castle they could see high up the mountain. While out hawking one morning she had been kidnapped by her husband's most bitter enemy. Later she was returned to her Lord, but alas, without her pink pantaloons which were hung like a triumphant banner from the highest point of her captor's battlements.

'What happened?' asked Marya with interest.

'Naturally her husband was furious at the slur on his honour. He gathered his men, besieged his enemy's castle and slaughtered him and his garrison to a man. They say the pink pantaloons are still preserved as a grim warning among the family heirlooms.'

'It sounds remarkably like a fairy tale to me,' remarked Anna sceptically.

'Not at all, I assure you. It really happened not much more than a hundred years ago in this very spot. Passions in the Caucasus are apt to be sudden, violent and bloody.'

He was interrupted by one of his Cossack scouts coming back to report that a mile ahead the road was completely blocked by a massive landslide.

'Oh no!' Paul was on his feet at once and went to inspect for himself taking Nikki with him. He returned looking grave. 'It's only too true. It's impossible to take the horses through. It's a question of either staying here until it is cleared or taking a track that bypasses the highway but which is extremely narrow and steep.'

'How long will it take for them to clear the road?' demanded Nikki.

'God knows. You could see for yourself what little progress has been made. It looks as if it could be at least a week.'

They glanced at one another in dismay. 'A week! In this damnable place!' exclaimed Nikki.

'What are we going to do?' said Marya appealing to Paul.

It was an awkward situation. There was no resthouse, only a few peasant huts. They argued about it briefly deciding in the end, and much against Paul's inclination, to risk the mountain track rather than spend days in conditions that would be primitive in the extreme.

They set out shortly after midday and at first, though the going was slow, it was not too troublesome. But then they entered a pass where on one side the wall of rock rose sheer above them and on the other was broken by giant boulders. They were picking their way with care, the horses stumbling on the stony ground, when suddenly there was a warning shout ahead. The Cossacks halted and closed in around Marya and Anna while Nikki spurred ahead to join Paul. Peering round the broad backs in front of her, Anna could just see the black horsemen strung across the road. She had no idea of how many there were, only that they were a great deal more frightening at close quarters than they had been from a distance and that, hemmed in as they were, there was no escape. Then with blood-curdling yells, the horsemen charged.

The next moment Varga and Yakov were beside them urging them out of the road and into a hollow cave behind one of the tall boulders.

'What is happening? What are we to do?' whispered Marya.

'Ssh, don't speak.' Varga was helping them to dismount. 'Stay hidden and keep as quiet as you can. Above all they must not see you.'

There was scarcely enough room for them to push themselves into the hollow space.

'Keep guard over them,' went on Varga hoarsely to Yakov. 'It could be the women they want. I'm going back to the Captain.'

They crouched in their hiding place shivering, unable to see anything and terrified at the yells, the thud of horses' hooves, the clash of weapons, the sharp report of a gun.

Yakov, desperate to join in the struggle, bent down to Anna whispering in her ear. 'Stay there, Barina, don't move whatever you do. I'll be back in a moment.' He moved out of their sight.

It was agony to know nothing. What was happpening to Paul and Nikki? Would they all be murdered? Paul's grim stories of the savagery of the Tartars went through Anna's mind until she could endure it no longer.

'I must see,' she muttered.

Marya clutched at her. 'Don't move, for God's sake, don't move. Remember what Varga said.'

'I must . . . I must know . . .'

She edged her way round the rock, holding her breath in terror at the spectacle that met her eyes They were fighting on horseback, sword against sword. She saw Nikki lean over to parry a thrust and fall sideways as he lost a stirrup. Then Paul had driven his own horse between him and his opponent. One of the black horsemen had something dangling from his saddle bow that looked horribly like a human head. She backed against the rock shaking and at that moment felt the arm go round her waist. She struggled violently, twisting round to see a dark hawklike face grinning down at her.

'Gadiani!' he muttered. 'The Princess Gadiani . . . yes?' and he threw back his head and laughed triumphantly.

She was pressed against his chest in an iron grip and

Marya cried out in fright. He held her with one arm and had the other on the bridle of his horse. He swung her round. In another instant he would have been on its back galloping towards the mountains when there was a shot. The Tartar dropped his arm with a howl of pain. She tore herself away from him and he flung himself onto his horse. Dazed she watched the stream of black riders go racing down the track at an unbelievably reckless speed. She felt her knees give way and sank to the ground shaken by reaction. Then Paul was kneeeling beside her.

'My God, I was afraid I had hit you. Are you all right?'

She nodded her head, unable to speak, and he lifted her to her feet. 'I thought Varga told you to remain hidden.'

'He did.' She leaned against him, still trembling. 'I couldn't bear not to know what had happpened to you.'

'Thank heaven there were not as many of them as I feared.'

'He knew me,' she said looking up into his face, the shock and fear still with her. 'He spoke my name.'

'You must have been mistaken.'

'No, no, I am sure of it . . .'

'It is just possible,' he admitted slowly. 'They have their spies and a Gadiani would be worth a ransom.'

'Oh God!'

'Don't be afraid. I doubt if they will try again.' He held her close to him for a moment before he said gently, 'Can you stand? Will you stay with Marya while I find out what has happened to my men?'

'I'm all right now. Don't worry about me.'

He smiled at her briefly before he went back to the Cossacks. Despite the frenzy of the fighting, the skirmish had lasted barely fifteen minutes and casualties were few; cuts, bruises, one of the soldiers severely wounded in the leg and one baggage animal stolen.

'Damnation!' exclaimed Nikki. 'That's my best uniform gone.'

'Better that than your head,' commented Paul unsympathetically. 'You can re-equip yourself in Tiflis.'

'Can I do anything to help?' asked Marya, pale but calm.

'No need. We have some experience of first aid. It's a necessity in this mountain warfare,' said Paul grimly. He supervised the binding of his soldier's leg and ordered his comrade to ride close beside him and make sure he did not fall from his horse. It was not until, shaken but resolute, they were preparing to ride on that Anna saw Paul's blood-stained sleeve.

'You are wounded,' she exclaimed.

'It is nothing, a dagger thrust.'

'You can't go on bleeding like that. Take off your coat and let me see it.'

'We should not delay,' he said impatiently.

'We shall be still further delayed if you faint from loss of blood,' said Marya crisply.

'Nonsense,' but he shrugged off his coat with Marik's help and Anna took a quick breath at the long savage slash from elbow to wrist. Bandages were in short supply but with the help of linen handkerchiefs and a long frill ruthlessly torn from the hem of Anna's petticoat, Marya effectively staunched and bound the wound.

'Anna, give me your silk scarf,' she said.

Despite Paul's protests that they were making too much fuss over nothing, Anna tied it round his neck into a sling.

'Men!' remarked Marya tartly. 'They've no more sense than rabbits. What would we do without you, I should like to know? Now keep your arm in that. It will help to stop the bleeding. Can you ride with one hand?'

'I think so,' he said meekly, 'and now, Marya Petrovna, if you are quite done with me, I think we should be on our way.'

The rest of their journey was uneventful and they were thankful to rejoin the military highway and ride on to the next resthouse. They were late in arriving but there were rooms of a kind available and after supper Anna and Marya went to bed early, Paul promising them a later start than usual the next morning to give them time to recover from the stress of the day.

Anna slept badly. She kept dreaming and waking with a jerk, haunted by the dark grinning face of the Tartar who had so nearly carried her off to unimaginable horror. For the first time she realized that what had happened to Gregory was real and could happen to her, to anyone. Soon after six she was so wide awake and restless that she decided to get up. Marya was still sleeping soundly so she dressed quietly, tiptoeing around the room, dipping her face in the cool water and tying back her hair with a ribbon. She slipped out closing the door gently behind her and went down the stairs.

It was a lovely morning, the sky like pearl faintly tinged

with pink and a sharp breeze chasing the white clouds. They were on one of the high green pastures where she was surprised to find familiar shrubs, azaleas and viburnum and mock orange blooming among the more exotic flowers. A small torrent tore down the mountainside in a white stream to widen out and meander across the meadow, ice-cold and clear as crystal over its stony bed.

She breathed the fresh morning air gratefully. Far above her as she walked by the stream a great white-tailed eagle swooped and soared up again with a mighty rush of dark wings. She came upon Paul unexpectedly. He was sitting on a rock, naked to the waist, his hair damp as if he had recently dipped it in the water. He did not move as she came quietly up behind him across the grass and she saw the blood-stained bandage bound round his arm and then the brown back seamed by the scars still raw and ugly as if not long healed. She stared at them wonderingly. They did not flog men of his rank whatever they might have done, so why . . . ? She stood for a moment uncertainly and he glanced over his shoulder smiling up at her.

'You're awake early. I thought I told Yakov that you were not to be disturbed.'

'I couldn't sleep.'

'Neither could I.' He held out his hand. 'It's a beautiful morning. Come and talk to me.'

'May I ask you a question first?'

'Ask away.' He bent down plucking one of the long grasses and chewing on it lazily.

'On our way to Pyatigorsk we stopped overnight half a day's journey from the town. I took a walk up the road and saw what I thought to be a beggar in native dress. He was badly hurt and bleeding. I sent Yakov to help him but by then he had vanished.'

'That was a kind thought on your part.' He threw away the blade of grass, not looking at her. 'To tell the truth I don't remember much about that night.'

She took a step towards him. 'So it *was* you. Why, Paul, why?'

'Believe it or not,' he said lightly, 'but I had been acting the spy.'

'Spy?' she repeated incredulously.

'It helps, you know, if we can find out what the feeling is among the tribes. Some of them are very easily swayed to us, and then just as easily turn back to Shamyl. I have a certain facility with the language and with disguise.'

'Isn't it terribly dangerous?'

'No more so than the chance of a bullet or a sabre thrust on campaign.'

The casual manner with which he dismissed it did not deceive her in the least and she guessed he would tell her little, but she was still curious. 'Where were you making for that night?'

'I was on my way to a rendezvous with Marik and nearly missed it.'

'And this?' With one finger she gently touched the scarred back.

'Oh that. I apologize . . . not a pleasant sight, is it?' He reached for his shirt and pulled it over his head, emerging to grin at her. 'I am afraid I rather overdid my role as horse-dealer. They thought I was cheating them and dealt with me accordingly. It was a damnable nuisance. It held me up for weeks in Pyatigorsk.'

'So that was why . . .' It was a side to him she had never once suspected and it explained a good deal. 'And I thought . . .'

'What did you think?'

'I thought it might have something to do with Gregory.'

'Now why should you think that?' And when she did not answer immediately, he held out his hand again. 'Come and tell me why.'

'It was foolish, I suppose.' He moved up and she sat beside him. 'It was that ring you sometimes wear. It was so like one that belonged to Gregory . . . I thought . . .'

'That I was he.'

'Only for a moment.'

'I'm sorry if I disappointed you,' he said dryly. 'The ring is an old one belonging to my grandmother. All these tribesmen wear trinkets, usually stolen.' He paused for an instant. 'In one way you *were* right. Gregory was part of it.'

She turned on him like a flash. 'How?'

'We had heard rumours. It was possible that he was being held prisoner. Part of my mission was to find out where.'

'And rescue him?'

'Not alone, but we could have mounted an expedition.'

'And did you find out?'

'It was too late. He was dead.'

'How could you be sure? Did you see him?'

'No.' He looked away from her. 'I have told you I was sure. Isn't that enough?'

'No, it is not,' she said passionately. 'If you knew he was there in the power of those savages, why didn't you help him? There must have been something you could do.'

'There was nothing.'

'Why?' And when he did not answer she went on pleadingly, 'Please, Paul, please. I want to know.'

'A Tartar chieftan numbers the heads of his enemies as battle trophies,' he said grimly. 'Gregory's was one of them.'

'Oh no, no . . . how horrible!' The thought was almost too much for her. She buried her face in her hands, sickened and distressed.

'I'm sorry . . . you shouldn't have pressed me . . . I didn't want you to know.'

'Poor Gregory,' she murmured in a stifled voice.

He had a great desire to put his arm around her, to stroke the red-gold hair, to comfort and protect, a feeling that in all his turbulent life he had never yet felt for any woman. He was trying to find the right words when she looked up at him, the velvet eyes swimming with tears.

'Why should they do that to him? Why?'

'It happens from time to time. Gregory's cousin, Daniel Gadiani, is high in the council of Prince Vorontsov. They may have believed that Gregory could tell them something of our future plans.'

'And when he would not . . .'

'I doubt if he knew anything of value.'

'They murdered him.' She stared in front of her thinking of her young husband as she had first seen him, gay, handsome, charming . . . and now . . . his head swinging from a saddle bow. It was unbearable.

Paul said gently, 'Did he ever write to you about his life here?'

'No, not really.' She could not bring herself to tell him about the last day when Gregory had walked out of her life leaving her with nothing. She said slowly, 'There was one letter. He must have written it just before that day. He asked me to go to Kumari . . . it was almost as if he knew he might be going to his death.'

'And that was what brought you here?'

'It was one of the reasons.'

He hesitated wondering if he should tell her what he knew and then drew back, painfully aware of his own part in it. It would only distress her further, he told himself. Later she might have to know, but not yet.

She got to her feet and he rose with her. 'I must go back,' she said. 'Marya will be wondering what has become of me.'

'I must go too. It won't be long now. Very soon we shall be in Tiflis. What will you do when you reach there?'

'I am not sure. Gregory's grandmother wants me to go to Kumari but first there are people I must see.'

'There is a great lack of suitable accommodation in Tiflis. It is a poor place for ladies alone. I have a house there. If you and Marya Petrovna care to be my guests before you go to Kumari, you would be very welcome.'

'Oh no, I couldn't . . .'

'You needn't be afraid that I shall be there,' he said with his ironic smile. 'I do not expect to be in Tiflis longer than a few days and most of that time will be spent with my men.'

'It is very kind of you, but . . .'

'Not kind at all. The house is empty most of the year except for the servants.'

'It would be quite impossible,' she said with sudden decision.

'Nothing is impossible.' He took her hand and after a moment dropped a kiss lightly on the palm and closed her fingers over it. 'Think about it.'

With a tiny gasp she drew her hand back and almost ran away from him. He looked after her, not sure if he had done a wise thing, but knowing himself not mistaken in her. On a journey such as this, you come to know a great deal about your fellow travellers. She had courage and resilience, dignity too. The attack in the mountains had been terrifying, but she had conquered her fear. He wondered how Natalie would have reacted in similar circumstances. Damn her for what she had done to him with her seductive beauty and her betrayal, embittering him, sending him on a suicidal venture, not caring whether he lived or died. And what was he going to do about her? It was six months since he had left Tiflis afraid of his own savage anger and he had still not made up his mind. He shook the unwelcome thought away from him and went off to find Varga. There were other and more pressing problems to be dealt with.

——— 5 ———

Anna had no intention of accepting Paul's offer of hospitality even though Marya saw nothing against it.

'After all, my dear, we are two lone females in what is to all intents and purposes a foreign country and inhabited by the most barbarous of people if all we hear is true. I can see no harm in accepting Count Kuragin's protection for a few days until you contact Gregory's family and find out how the land lies.'

Anna could not say exactly why the idea disturbed her so much. 'It puts me under an obligation to him,' she said obstinately.

Marya shot her a keen glance. 'He has not taken any liberties, has he?'

'No, of course not.'

'Has Nikki said something?'

'No, and I wouldn't pay any heed if he had. In any case Nikki will be occupied with his duties at the palace.'

'Well then, I thought you liked Paul.'

'That has nothing to do with it.'

Marya said no more, aware that argument was only too likely to harden Anna's determination to remain independent and Paul, having repeated his offer and been firmly refused, did not press it.

In actual fact Nikki had been strongly against it. 'Paul is not married, Anna. I don't think it is at all the proper thing.'

Curiously enough that nearly made her change her mind. 'I'm not exactly a child,' she replied tartly. 'You seem to forget that I am a widow and that I have Marya with me.'

That had been on the morning before he left them to ride ahead. 'We shall see one another again,' he said earnestly, taking her hands in his. 'Promise me, Anna.'

'Of course. I shall not be going to Kumari for a while.'

He was a dear boy and she saw him ride away with a sense of loss, but in a day they would be following after him. The long journey was at an end and with relief there was also a feeling of regret. For weeks she had been living in suspended time, now she would have to face up to Gregory's death and all that was linked with it.

They reached Tiflis in the late afternoon. The town lay in the valley of the Kura surrounded by high hills and after the cool mountain air, the heat was almost overwhelming as they rode across the vast fields of vines and Indian corn. Anna was tired and thirsty, her hair damp with sweat, her thin blouse sticking to her. On the outskirts they passed a huge caravan-serai surrrounded by a low stone wall and she stared in aston-ishment at the noisy colourful scene. In and out of the narrrow gate were men of every race and nationality, leading camels, horses, donkeys and pack mules, jostling one another in the clouds of dust and gabbling in a dozen different tongues.

'Where do they come from?' she asked.

Paul shrugged his shoulders. 'Tiflis is still one of the main centres for trade routes from the East. There are caravans carrying Chinese silks, Indian spices, Persian silver and car-pets, jewels, perfumes . . . you can buy it all in the bazaars if you are interested.'

It was a town of astonishing contrasts. Presently entering through the gate they found themselves riding down the Govolinski Prospect past fine shops and the magnificent viceregal palace as elegant and fashionable as anything to be seen in Russia and she looked up at Paul triumphantly.

'I thought you told me that Tiflis was a meanly built city.'

He smiled but said nothing because in no time at all they had left the broad street behind them and were threading their way through narrow cobbled alleys where the gutters ran with filth, refuse lay in evil-smelling heaps and tattered garments fluttered from high windows and broken balconies. The road was crammed, camels stretching their long thin necks, donkeys pulling ramshackle carts, ragged children darting in among their horses' feet and holding up grimy hands with shrill cries, the inevitable beggars displaying crippled limbs and hideous sores, all of them slow to shift though the soldiers riding ahead shouted at them, wielding their whips vigorously.

Instinctively Anna moved nearer to Paul and he put a hand on her bridle. 'Keep close. Tiflis is an ancient city, you know. During the last thousand years it has been fought over and looted by Mongols, Persians, Greeks and Turks and now we are here. We are not always popular.'

At the end of the street he drew rein outside a dilapidated building with a swinging sign. Men lounged on the steps, some of them asleep in the sun, others fingering greasy packs of cards, Armenians, Turks, hook-nosed Egyptians, handsome black-haired Georgians in soiled silk pantaloons. They looked up at the cavalcade and one of them rose slowly to his feet. He stretched out a hand and put it on Anna's reins.

'Are you wanting a bed, mistress?' he said leering up at her. Paul's whip came down smartly on the dirty hand. He drew it back with a curse and spat disgustingly. Then he went up the steps and flung the door wide.

'The Hotel Marama,' said Paul. 'Do you wish me to enquire what accommodation he has to offer?'

Anna looked around her in dismay, biting her lip. 'There must be better places.'

'I'm afraid not,' he said dryly. 'The Hotel Orient is as yet only a project in the air, not even the foundations laid. There is always one of the caravanserais if you don't mind the fleas and the bed bugs.'

'How can you be so aggravating! You knew all the time.'

'I did warn you,' he said mildly, 'more than once. You didn't choose to believe me.'

There was a glint of amusement in the brown eyes which she found quite infuriating. 'If this is meant to be a jest, then it is a very unkind one,' she said angrily.

'No jest, I assure you.'

Marya saw the mutinous look on Anna's face. Out of sheer obstinacy she was capable of landing them in this filthy place where they might well be robbed or murdered or both. She interrupted quickly.

'We cannot possibly stay in a house of this kind,' she said decidedly. 'Count Kuragin, if your offer still holds, we shall be most grateful for your hospitality for a few days.'

He gave her a little bow. 'My house is yours. Permit me to lead the way. Varga, take the men to their quarters and report to me this evening. Yakov, bring up the baggage animals.'

They followed him up and down steep narrow alleys fascinated in spite of their weariness by the sights, smells and sounds so different from Petersburg or Moscow. When they emerged at last, it was like coming out of a dark tunnel into sun and light. Tall white houses with fretted stone balconies and pillared porticos were built along a high bank overlooking the rushing river.

Paul stopped at the far end and dismounted. 'Here we are at last.' He gave them his hand to alight. They went up the steps and the door was opened by a blue-robed Circassian bowing low. They went through a wide cool hall into a large airy room, striped awnings over the open windows shading it from the glare of the sun.

The next moment a stout elderly woman dressed in black with a starched white cap came hurrying in from the hall, going at once to Paul and seizing his hand excitedly, pressing it to her ample bosom, laughing and crying at the same time.

'So you have come back to us at last. We have been waiting and waiting and hearing such terrible news of you.' She exclaimed at the arm he still carried in a sling. 'What have you done to yourself?'

'Now, now, Anfisa,' he said affectionately patting the old woman on the shoulder, 'I am perfectly well, never better. Don't you see we have guests? This is the Princess Anna Gadiani and her cousin Marya Petrovna. I want you to make them as comfortable as you can. We have had a long and tiring journey. You have rooms prepared, I suppose?'

'The house is always ready for you and your friends,' she said with a look of reproach. Anna felt the shrewd old eyes run over her briefly before she curtseyed. 'You are very welcome. No doubt you would like to wash and rest. I will tell the maids to make all ready for you.'

She bustled out and an elderly white-haired man took her place at the door. Paul waved him in.

'Is everything in order, Ivan?'

'Yes, your excellency.'

'See to the horses and have the ladies' baggage taken up to their rooms.'

'At once, your excellency. May I say how very happy I am to see you returned safely?'

'Now why on earth shouldn't I? Go along with you, man.'

Ivan bowed and went out. Paul grinned a little apologetically. 'You must forgive all this fuss over my return. Anfisa was once my nurse and is now my housekeeper. She likes to believe that I am still six years old. Ivan served my father and came with me from Arachino.'

Then Anfisa was back again. 'Will you be supping with your guests, Paul Dmitrivitch?'

'No, I have too much to do. I'll be returning later.' He

turned to Anna and Marya. 'You will forgive me, I'm sure. Please make yourselves at home. Ask for anything you require. No doubt you will be glad to retire early so I will say goodnight.'

He bowed and went quickly from the room. Anfisa looked after him, a frown on her plump peasant face. 'He asks too much from himself. He always has since a boy.' Then she recalled her duties and turned to Anna. 'If you will come with me,' and she led the way through the hall and up the stairs.

Anna was not sure what she had expected, a bachelor establishment perhaps, small and comfortless. In all the weeks she had known him he had made no show of wealth or luxury; he lived as simply as his men, making less fuss than Nikki over hardship and inconveniences. But the house was rarely beautiful, not lavish or extravagant, but everything of the finest quality and taste. The rooms to which Anfisa took them were spacious, opening off one side of a corridor and with a linking door. The floors were tiled for coolness but covered with Persian rugs in deep rich colours, soft and luxurious as velvet. The walls were white and hung with panels of Chinese silk embroidered with flowers in exquisite shades of pink and lilac and in one corner hung a jewelled icon of the Virgin with a small lamp burning in front of it that she guessed was Anfisa's doing.

She had stripped to her petticoats when there was a knock on the door and a bevy of maids came in carrying a hip bath between them and jug after jug of steaming water. They filled the bath with quick sidelong glances at her and then stood, offering sponge and soap, ready to help her bathe.

'Thank you,' she said, 'I think I can manage for myself,' and sent them scurrying and giggling from the room.

Oh the absolute bliss of stepping into water scented with some subtle eastern perfume and feeling it soak away the weariness, the sweat, the grit and dust of weeks of travel. In a mood of recklessness she washed her hair, revelling in the unexpected luxury, and then stepped out on to the huge soft towels they had spread around the bath. When she was dry, she slipped on her thin silk dressing gown and began to brush her damp hair.

The maids returned to clear away the bath and one of them in halting Russian asked where she wished supper to be served.

'Oh in here please,' she said. 'Bring it for both of us,' and she waved a hand to Marya's room.

The girl nodded, but still hesitated, the black eyes sparkling and curious.

'What is your name?' asked Anna.

'Darinka. Shall I brush your hair for you? I have never seen such colour. It is like the fire.'

Anna smiled. 'It is clean at least. Will you tell Marya Petrovna when supper is ready?'

'Yes, Madame.'

When the girl had gone, Anna crossed to the floor-length window and went out on to the balcony. Like many eastern houses, it enclosed a stone courtyard with one-storied rooms running all round the other three sides. That must be where the servants slept, she thought. A fountain bubbled in the centre spilling into a small basin and giving a delightful feeling of coolness to the evening air. At one corner was a lime tree with a bench around the base of the trunk. A great borzoi lay sleeping beside it, head on paws, and everywhere there were stone pots filled with flowers, roses, syringa, lilies and other more exotic plants flowering in purple, crimson and white.

The fiery heat of the sun had gone and she was leaning against one of the slender pillars, dreamily content, when the quiet was broken by a burst of childish laughter. A small, dark-haired boy, no more than two or three years old, came running out of a door at the far end and behind came Paul in shirt and breeches. Shrieking with mock terror the child ran in and out of the pots pursued by the young man until he caught him up in his arms, tossing him into the air and then catching him again. A girl had come to the far door, very young and slender, dressed in some native costume of red silk banded with gold, her long hair hanging like black silk to her waist. Paul sat on the stone bench lifting the child on to his knee and the girl sat beside him laughing as the boy struggled to snatch at the box held above his head. He grabbed it at last delving inside to find the sweetmeats and leaning over to give one to the dog that had come to join them.

It was a simple domestic scene. Many young men, marooned for years in the Caucasus, took a native girl as a mistress. Anna knew that as everyone did, so why not Paul Kuragin? Why this fierce reaction as she watched him turn to the girl, saw the way she looked up at him and the tenderness he showed to the child. After a few minutes he put the boy down, touched the girl's cheek with a gentle caress and strolled across the garden and into the house with the dog at his heels.

Anna went back into her room, picking up her brush and attacking her hair with short, hard strokes. She liked him as a friend, as an amusing companion, as a man who had shown her courtesy and consideration and that was all, she told herself angrily, so why should she resent his declining to sup with them and then going to join his mistress, if she was indeed his mistress? Why should it trouble her? She was not in love with him. She had made one foolish mistake and was not going to make another. Hadn't Gregory caused her enough pain and heartache to last a lifetime?

Six weeks ago she had not even known that Paul Kuragin existed. The days they had spent together when they had grown so close were over and done with. He had his own life just as she had hers. She put down the brush and stared at her face in the mirror. She thought of the baby who had only lived for an hour, the son Gregory had wanted so badly. Would everything have been different if he had lived, running and laughing with his father like that small boy in the garden . . . Paul Kuragin's son? With a sharp stab of envy she shut her mind against it. It was time to forget the past and think of the future. She was here now but in a few days she would be leaving the house and beginning a new life. She tied back her hair and was glad when Marya knocked and came in with Anfisa and the maids bringing their supper.

Anna did not see Paul for several days. Anfisa brought his apologies. 'He is in and out of the house like a whirlwind,' she said disapprovingly. 'He takes no care of himself and that arm of his has been giving him trouble.'

'He is not sick, I hope,' said Marya with concern.

Anfisa snorted. 'I had Ivan fetch the doctor to him but he paid him no heed. "I am well enough," he said and scarcely gave him time to treat the wound. He begs me to tell you that you are to stay as long as you wish.'

'I trust we are not causing too much trouble.'

'To tell you the truth,' said Anfisa confidentially, 'I am glad of it. It keeps the servants busy and they have too little to do. In the past two years the Count has only been here for a few weeks at a time.'

Marya, who could get on with anyone, soon struck up a friendly relationship with the old nurse and so it was from

Anfisa that they heard about the house at Arachino, the vast estates and the lonely boy who had spent his childhood there with only his uncle as guardian.

'I wonder that he has never married,' remarked Marya.

'There's many a young lady who would give all she has to become the Countess Kuragina and he's no saint, far from it. There was this one and that before the Tsar sent him off to the Caucasus, but none that took his fancy. It is high time too if all he owns is not to go to his Uncle Andrei's children. There was a time last year when we all believed . . .' she broke off as if she had already said too much.

'Was there an engagement?'

Anfisa shook her ample shoulders. 'Yes . . . and no. Some said one thing and some another. There have always been tales about him. It came to nothing and I for one was not sorry. It wouldn't have been right. There is no one good enough for him in this place. He should have gone back to Russia years ago.'

It seemed an imposition to stay on in his house but the first few days were spent in recovering from the rigours of the journey and after that it was difficult to know what to do for the best. They had been there nearly a week when Nikki came one morning bringing a message from the palace. The letter was from the Viceroy's secretary. In formal and guarded terms it conveyed the compliments of his excellency Prince Michael Vorontsov inviting Anna to the palace one day in the following week when he would have the pleasure of welcoming her personally and presenting her to his wife.

She read it slowly, frowning over it, and then glanced up to see Nikki watching her anxiously.

'There is to be a ball,' he said. 'You must accept, Anna, you must do as he says. It is like being presented to the Tsar. Everything here centres round the viceregal court. I have learned that already. Society here will not accept you without his approval.'

'But why?' she said rebelliously. 'I'm not anyone of importance. I don't care very much for society. That was not my purpose in coming here. I only wanted to find out about Gregory and go to Kumari to see his grandmother. What harm is there in that?'

'None, but you don't understand. The Gadianis are very important people indeed. They are Princes of Kumaria, they still have tremendous influence. Even Vorontsov himself prefers to keep on good terms with Daniel Gadiani and you are

Russian. It is vital for you that you should be accepted by him otherwise there could be difficulty over any inheritance your husband may have willed to you.'

'I'm not concerned with that. I can live without it,' she said proudly. 'My father is not rich, but neither are we beggars.'

'Of course not, but you can't help yourself,' he went on earnestly. 'You are Princess Gadiani, wife of the last hereditary Prince of Kumaria.'

She had known that from the beginning of course, but a thousand miles away in Petersburg it had not seemed to matter very much. She had a feeling that without realizing it, she had become involved in a world in which she was lost, a devious eastern world of intrigue. It was like being caught in a silken net when she wanted only to be free, and for some reason in the warmth of the room she shivered. She would have liked to ask Paul's advice, but he never seemed to be in the house and she did not want to make too much of it. It was after all not his responsibility. Then she smiled at her own stupidity. Nikki had probably got it all wrong. What was there to be afraid of? This was 1846, not the middle ages, and Georgia was a civilized country under Russian rule. In the meantime she supposed she must do what was required of her and if there was a ball to be attended, she must think about clothes.

'What should I wear?' she said despairingly to Marya. 'It is so difficult to know what is correct. If I attend at the palace, should I wear mourning now that I know Gregory to be dead?'

Marya considered for a moment. 'White,' she said at last. 'You're so young and the circumstances are so unusual. White with no colour except perhaps a black shawl or black ribbons.'

Their gowns had suffered badly from being folded into small valises on the backs of the pack mules. She looked in dismay at the crumpled white satin and limp lace.

'Whatever am I going to do with it? There is no time to have a new gown made.'

'It is so beautiful,' said Darinka admiringly as Anna held it up. 'You could ask Bela. She is wonderfully clever with silks and laces. She will make it like new for you.'

'Bela? Who is she? One of the serving maids?'

Darinka grimaced. 'She wouldn't like to hear you call her that. She is proud, that one, a Tartar, but she is good with her needle. She looks after the household linens and embroiders the Count's shirts. Shall I call her for you?'

'Thank you, I should be most grateful.'

The girl ran off and in a few minutes while Anna and Marya were still looking over the dresses, shawls and mantles laid out on the bed, there came a tap at the door and a young woman in a red silk dress with a light scarf thrown over her dark hair came quietly into the room.

'You wish me to do something for you, Madame?' She spoke Russian but hesitantly.

'Yes.' Anna turned round and then, taken by surprise, stared at her for an instant, noting the charming oval face, the downcast eyes. Then she held up the white gown. 'It has become soiled and creased from the heat and the packing.'

'Let me see.' The girl touched the delicate lace and ran her hand down the rich silk. 'The material is very fine. It can easily be restored. Give it to me and I will make it as good as new. I have done it before many times for Count Kuragin's guests.'

She took the dress and was turning towards the door when Anna stopped her.

'Haven't I seen you in the courtyard with your little boy?'

'Possibly.'

'Have you lived here long?'

'Ever since Mitya was born.'

Mitya, the pet diminutive for Dmitri, the name of Paul Kuragin's father. 'And your husband? Does he live here too?'

The girl looked up with a flash of her dark eyes. 'My man is dead.'

'I am sorry . . .'

'It was some time ago . . . in the war,' she said evenly. 'Is there anything else, Madame?'

'No, thank you.'

'Then I will bring the gown back when it is ready.' The girl went out as quietly as she had entered.

Marya said, 'Some of these native girls are really quite attractive. What were you saying about the child?'

'I have seen him playing in the garden with the dog. Marya, do you think . . . ?' Then she stopped, unwilling to voice her suspicion.

'Do I think what?'

'Nothing really . . . it's just that I find I need so many things and so do you if we are not to look like scarecrows. Why shouldn't we make an expedition to the shops?'

'Why not? I think it a splendid idea.'

Anfisa would not hear of them leaving the house unattended. 'It is not safe for ladies alone. You must take one of the men with you.'

'Surely it is not necessary,' protested Anna, but Anfisa insisted backed up by Ivan so in the end, declining the carriage, they set out armed with parasols against the blinding sun and with Yakov following at a discreet distance behind them.

After they had explored the shops in the Govolinski Prospect, Anna was eager to go on to the old quarter of the city where the craftsmen lived and displayed their wares, but it was only after a great deal of persuasion that Yakov, who had a knack of finding out everything about a place immediately he arrived there, reluctantly led his ladies through one of the cobbled alleys.

In the space of a few minutes they had left behind them the fashionable tree-lined boulevard and were plunged into an entirely different world, an oriental world, hot, crowded and noisy. Here there were no fine shops, only open booths where the goldsmiths, the silversmiths, the coppersmiths plied their trades amid an incessant tapping and hammering. There were dark-skinned men in white robes, Persians with scarlet-painted fingernails, veiled Moslem women in shapeless garments, bargaining and arguing in shrill excited voices while stallholders slapped shrieking children away from their precious goods and the drivers of carts and baggage animals cursed one another as they fought their way through the centre of the market.

There was jewellery of every kind temptingly laid out among the dishes of beaten silver and the ewers of finely ornamented copper. The subtle scents of the perfumiers mingled with the reek of roasting meat and the rich cloying smell of the confectioners, Turkish delight stuffed with pistachios, sugared almonds and delectable sweetmeats artfully fashioned into the shapes of flowers.

Anna wandered from one stall to the next, more and more fascinated, hardly noticing that she had outdistanced Marya and Yakov. She stopped at the table of the weapon-maker admiring the daggers with jewelled hilts, the curved scimitars in velvet sheaths studded with turquoise. Under the shade of the awning a man was handling a sword, running his finger down the slender blade of blue steel. His face was half hidden but suddenly she was aware that the black eyes were fixed on her watching her intently. It disconcerted her so much that she dropped the dagger she had picked up and walked on quickly. In a few minutes, ashamed of her panic, she paused to take breath at an open shop where materials were piled in great bales, silks and satins shot with silver and gold, gauzes in every colour of the rainbow lovely enough to be worn by Scherezhade in the *Thousand and One Nights*. She took up a scarf of filmy black powdered with silver stars, so gossamer thin as to be almost transparent. It was just what she needed with her white gown. The tradesman was bargaining with another customer at the back of the booth and as she waited to enquire the price, the scarf still in her hand, she heard someone near her call out imperiously, 'Paul!'

Instinctively she stepped back a little, shading her face with her parasol. A few yards away, with her back half turned, was a young woman in a dress of lilac muslin. Anna could not distinguish the face under the straw hat with the long ribbons of violet velvet, but she saw the gloved hand extended, saw Paul Kuragin halt and turn back.

'Paul! So you are back at last,' went on the voice. 'Where have you been that you have not come to visit us?'

'My dear Natalie, you know well enough how it is. There has been scarcely a moment.'

'Not even for me?'

'Not for anyone except the Commander-in-Chief. What in heaven's name are you doing in this quarter of the town?'

'Looking for something different. The shops on the Govolinski are so boring, nothing in the latest style. How I long for Petersburg!' She leaned towards him, her whisper richly seductive and intimate. 'I hear that you were obliged to escort that little English girl whom poor Gregory was forced into marrying.' She put a hand on Paul's arm. 'All those weeks on the road . . . how tiresome for you. Tell me, darling, was she so unutterably dull and bourgeois as he told us?'

'I did not find her so,' he answered stiffly.

'Oh don't be so pompous! You remember how he used to make us laugh with his tales about her, so commonplace, so ordinary. It was so unfair on the poor boy. No wonder he ran away from her.'

'That is unjust.' He made an impatient gesture and Anna drew further back praying to escape his notice. 'Natalie, where is your carriage?' he went on.

'At the end of the alley, *mon cher.*'

'Let me escort you to it.'

'But I haven't finished looking at everything . . .'

'I think you have.'

He took her by the elbow threading his way purposefully through the crowded lane, leaving Anna feeling sick and wretched at the careless malice which had struck so unmercifully at the frail self-confidence she had built up during the last few weeks. Then Marya, who had been examining the goods in an adjacent booth, came to join her.

Anna put down the scarf she was still holding. 'Shall we go?' she said abruptly. 'I think we've seen enough for one morning.'

'I thought you were enjoying it.'

'So I was, but it is so hot in these alleys. I'm tired and thirsty and it is quite a long way home.'

'Very well, my dear, if that's what you want.'

Marya took her arm and they turned to walk back up the lane with Yakov going ahead. They had reached the end and had begun to climb the hill to the upper bank of the river when they heard the hurried steps behind them and Paul Kuragin caught them up.

'I thought I caught sight of you in the market. I've been intending to apologise for my neglect during the past week.'

'You mustn't concern yourself on our account,' said Marya warmly. 'I'm sure you have many duties to occupy you.'

'It is true and I have been out of the city for a day or so,' he replied, but his eyes were on Anna. He carried a small parcel and he held it out to her. 'I wanted to give you this.'

'What is it?' she said icily. 'A peace offering?'

'So you did hear what she said. I'm sorry but you mustn't mind Natalie. She often speaks without thinking.'

'So I gather.'

'And it is not a peace offering.' He smiled suddenly and charmingly. 'It's a replacement. You remember the scarf you so kindly loaned to me. Well, Anfisa has done her best, but I'm afraid it is irretrievably ruined. Will you accept this in its place?'

'I would much rather not,' she said and walked on, unable to explain how she had been carried back to all that misery and humiliation that she had tried so hard to put behind her, made even worse because now she realized that he must have known Gregory, heard all that had been said about her long before they met and had never once mentioned it. He was left frowning down at the package still in his hand.

Marya said placatingly, 'Give it to me. It is most kind of

you. You must forgive Anna. She is not quite herself this morning.'

'I am sorry if I have offended her. It was not intentional.'

'No, of course not. I will tell her.'

A little embarrassed Marya took the parcel from him and hurried after Anna. 'Really,' she said, 'did you have to be so insulting, especially after he has done so much for us?'

'I know, I know . . . it's just that . . . oh, you don't understand,' and she quickened her pace. She would have liked to leave his house now, this very minute, go to Kumari, fulfil her promise to visit Gregory's grandmother and then go back home, away from this disturbing place which had promised escape and seemed now to be turning into another prison, only of course it was not possible. To run away would be childish.

Back at the house Marya unwrapped the little parcel. 'Oh Anna, look! It is the loveliest thing! How did he guess?' She threw the flimsy black scarf around Anna's shoulders. 'It is exactly right.'

He must have noticed her after all and returned to buy it. She was touched by the gesture and at the same time a little afraid. To accept was in some way to commit herself.

'I can't possibly take it from him.'

'Of course you can. What nonsense! You are eating his food, aren't you? It is just his way of saying thank you and a very charming way.'

'Well . . . perhaps . . .'

Not sure of herself she looked in the mirror. It was like a moonlit cloud of gossamer. It emphasized the red-gold hair, the creamy skin, giving her an unexpected allure. 'It is lovely,' she said reluctantly. She heard again the sweet mocking voice and knew a surge of anger. Her courage came flooding back. She would not let them humiliate her as Gregory had done. She would show these Caucasian beauties that the bourgeois English girl was as good as any of them.

—6—

'A land of magic,' Anna had said wonderingly of the Caucasus listening to Paul round the camp fire under the stars, but it was an oriental magic as old as time and shot through with intrigue, with sudden violence, with a *frisson* of fear. She had been aware of it ever since the attack by the black horsemen. It was in the eyes of the man who had watched her that day in the market, an air of secrecy, even among the blue-robed servants who went silently about Paul's house and the girl Bela with her veiled look of some hidden knowledge as if she could have told her something but did not dare.

She felt it again on the night she went to the viceregal palace. The Vorontsovs were said to be wealthier even than the Tsar himself and the ballroom was magnificent. Under the crystal chandeliers there were pillars of flowers, orchids frail as butterflies, lilies, roses from palest pink to velvety purple, branches of creamy orange blossom, brought from the shores of the Black Sea, doomed to bloom and die in a single night, as exotic and colourful as the thousand guests; staff officers in their brilliant uniforms, the Caucasian beauties, curled, painted and bejewelled in their gorgeous crinolines, Princes and rulers from outlandish places, their lean dark faces curiously at odds with their striped silks, their diamond rings, their earrings and collars of pearls and rubies. Servants in the Vorontsov colours of scarlet and white moved among them with trays of golden wine and frosted glasses of lemon or sherbet for those who followed Mahomet and drank no wine.

When she paused on the threshold, when the usher's stentorian tone announcing her had silenced the gabbling voices, she felt that every eye was turned towards her. Paul, standing among the other army officers around the Viceroy, was struck by the contrast. She looked like a dove, he thought, a snowy dove among a collection of gaudy screeching peacocks. There was something pure and untouched about her though God knows what kind of hell she must have lived through with Gregory Gadiani.

He saw a gleam of interest in Prince Vorontsov's eyes. They had been discussing her in a private interview that very morning.

'The English girl may well serve our purpose, Kuragin,' he had said.

'She knows nothing, your excellency, I am sure of that.'

'Very probably not, but she may provide useful bait to lure the fox into the trap.'

'There could be danger.'

'No, we will make sure of that.' He shot Paul one of his keen glances. 'She is staying in your house, I understand. You are not going to make a fool of yourself over this young woman, I hope.'

Paul stiffened. 'You need have no fear of that.'

'Good. We don't want a repetition of last year's folly,' he went on dryly. 'The Tsar has seen fit to reinstate you as Colonel. Another affair like the last and he may demote you to the ranks.'

'I know that, your excellency.'

'And what would your damned Kuragin pride have to say about that, eh? Not that I always agree with the Tsar's decisions, but I am forced to carry out his orders. Now tell me more of this harebrained scheme of yours. It interests me.'

Paul aroused himself from his thoughts to see her coming towards them, heels tapping on the parquet floor, the bell-like crinoline swaying, the silver stars in the filmy cloud around her shoulders shimmering in the candlelight, camellias at her breast and in the red-gold hair. Who had given them to her? Nikki probably. The boy liked to think himself in love and he felt a stab of unreasonable jealousy and at the same time an absurd pride at the impression she was creating because they had come through danger together and he felt he alone knew her strength and resilience beneath the flower-like fragility. She had sunk into a deep curtsey. Prince Vorontsov leaned forward to take her hand and she looked up at him, saw the handsome cynical face, the fair hair greying, the blue eyes shrewd and penetrating.

'My dear Anna Stepanovna,' he said graciously. 'I wish that you had come to see us in a happier time. We have felt your husband's cruel fate very deeply. We must do our best to help you forget.' He passed her to his wife and the

Princess Elizabeth smiled vaguely and touched her cheek with her ivory fan.

Then a man stepped out from those close to the Viceroy and for an instant to her dazzled eyes it was as if Gregory had come back from the dead.

'Let me be among the first to welcome my cousin's wife,' he said, his voice smooth as silk, sweet as honey. He was older than Gregory, a narrow brown-skinned face, a thin dark moustache. His black full-skirted Circassian coat was embroidered heavily with gold. He bowed over her hand and then drew her towards him, the shaven cheek touching hers, a subtle perfume strange in a man. 'We must see more of each other, my dear Anna, there is much to discuss.'

'Yes, of course.'

This must be Daniel Gadiani. He was smiling but the piercing black eyes held no warmth and she felt a shudder of recognition but where, when? She was given no time to remember. Others came forward to greet her, staring at her curiously, asking questions, confusing her, until Paul took her hand.

He touched the black scarf. 'I see you have forgiven me.'

For a moment she clung to him, feeling him to be her only friend among these strangers, then he too was obliged to leave her, following the Viceroy who had summoned his officers and led them away to his own private sanctum, leaving her feeling desperately alone.

Elizabeth Vorontsov held out a languid hand. 'Come and talk to me about England, my child.'

'But I have never been to England,' she protested.

'Never, how strange. Michael told me you were English.'

'It is my father who is English.'

'Indeed, how fascinating,' murmured the Princess and went ahead so that Anna had to follow with the other ladies, all of them glancing at her out of the corner of their eyes, whispering together, not daring to raise their voices unless the Vicereine spoke to them first.

In the scarlet and gold salon the Princess stretched herself on the sofa, ostrich plumes trembling in her hair, a great pearl on her forehead. A little negro boy dressed in silver brought her a *tchibouque*. She took one or two puffs of the Persian pipe, the scented smoke curling above her head. With a screech a tiny monkey in a gold jacket raced down the velvet curtains, scuttling across the laces and the crinolines, startling the ladies into little screams, and then leaping on to the

Princess's lap where she caressed his velvet head, feeding him with grapes from the dish at her elbow.

It was a scene straight out of the book of eastern fairy tales which Anna's father had once given her. The room was stiflingly hot. She had a feeling of being trapped and looked around her desperately, longing to escape. It was with infinite relief that she saw Nikki come in with some of the younger officers. He bowed to the Princess and after receiving her gracious nod, took Anna's hand and led her into the ballroom.

'Oh Nikki, I am so glad to see you,' she murmured gratefully.

'I thought you might be.' He grinned at her boyishly. 'I have had to dance attendance on the Princess more than once.' The orchestra had begun to play a waltz. He slipped an arm round her waist. 'Shall we?'

'Oh please.'

It was a long time since she had danced with such gaiety, with such a sense of freedom from restraint. The young men were soon crowding around her and Marya, sitting with the other ladies, watched her with affection, wanting her happiness and yet at the same time a little afraid for her. Once, long ago, she had loved Stephen Crispin passionately, would have followed him anywhere if he had asked,but it had not happened. She had never had the grace or beauty of her cousin and when he married Nadia, she had learned to swallow her bitterness, her regret that Anna was not her daughter, and make the best of what she had.

Later in the evening Anna came to sit beside her, breathless, her eyes shining and Marya smiled at her.

'Enjoying yourself?'

'Yes, far more than I thought. Is it very wicked of me, Marya?'

'No, of course not.' Be careful, she wanted to say, wait, be sure, don't let yourself be hurt a second time, but warnings are never any use. Only experience teaches.

The centre of the room had been cleared now, the guests seated or standing around the walls. Prince Vorontsov and his wife had come out to watch. The musicians were playing, strange undulating rhythms, insidious and disturbing, and then came the long files of dancers, the women in white gliding across the floor, their veils floating behind them and the men, startlingly like Shamyl's black horsemen, advancing and retreating, slow, powerful, compelling.

'It is a dance of courtship,' said a voice close to her and she looked up to see that Paul Kuragin had come to stand behind her chair. 'It goes back to the days when the tribesmen chose their women by the light of the camp fires.'

The music was subtle, insistent, the men leaping, stamping, the women always eluding them, the beat quickening until Anna held her breath. It was intensely sensual and yet they never touched one another. She felt the rhythm vibrating deep within her and Paul's hand resting lightly on her bare arm seemed to burn into her flesh.

She moved a little, trying to break the tension, to be calm and matter of fact. 'What have you been doing all the evening?'

'Have you missed me? You will never guess,' he said smiling. 'We've been discussing where we can open new strata of coal for use on Black Sea steamers and reporting on experiments with growing cotton imported from America.'

'At a ball?' she asked incredulously.

'It is true, I assure you. The Prince is a dedicated administrator.'

'And the war?' she said ironically. 'Did you discuss that too?'

'Of course.'

She had never seen him in full dress uniform. He looked very splendid. She noted the epaulettes, the gold-fringed sash.

'Colonel Kuragin,' she said, 'no longer Captain. You didn't tell us.'

'I go up and down like a Jack-in-the-box at the Tsar's whim,' he answered lightly.

The performance had come to an end, the dancers bowed to their applause and withdrew. The orchestra began to play again and the guests surged back on to the floor.

'Are you hungry?' he asked. 'There is an excellent buffet in the salon, lobster, truffles, soufflés, ice cream . . .' She shook her head. 'In that case will you trust yourself to me? It's a year since I danced but I'll try not to walk all over your feet.'

She laughed and let him lead her into the gay whirl of the mazurka. The music played faster and faster and they kicked higher and higher until at last she leaned against him, breathless but very happy.

'How I enjoyed that!'

'So did I.' He smiled at her. 'You are looking particularly lovely tonight, did you know?'

'I thought you never paid compliments,' she said teasingly.

'It is not a compliment. It is the simple truth.'

Then she saw his face change. The laughter died as Daniel Gadiani came purposefully towards them.

'Ah there you are. I've been looking everywhere for you. I want you to meet my sister. Natalie, my dear, this is Anna, Gregory's little wife.'

She was instantly aware that it was the woman of the market place and that she was beautiful, no doubt at all about that. A small queenly head crowned with silky black hair. In her golden dress she was slender as one of the tawny lilies in the great jar beside them. Long almond-shaped eyes were gazing into hers before she leaned forward to kiss her cheek.

'Dearest Anna, we must have some long talks together. Gregory and I grew up together, you know, until he was taken to Petersburg. I was ten and I cried for a whole week, just fancy!' She had a little silvery laugh. 'I want to hear all about your trip from Pyatigorsk. So brave of you to come all the way alone. Paul tells me nothing.'

'There is nothing to tell.'

'That's what you say,' she tapped him with her fan. 'Anna will have quite a different tale, I am sure. Where have you been all the evening, mon cher? We've scarcely seen you.'

'The Prince detained me.'

'I don't believe a word of it. You have been trying to avoid us. Daniel, take Anna away. I have a serious bone to pick with Paul.' She had created an air of bantering intimacy between them to which her brother instantly responded.

'Certainly, my dear. Command and I obey,' he said smiling and drew Anna's arm within his own. 'We must leave these two to settle their differences, mustn't we?' He led her away, speaking of Kumari. 'When do you go there, my dear Anna? My great-aunt is very old now, but she is still an autocrat, quite feudal, you know, commanding her servants like an empress. She forgets that things have changed and lives in the past. She is deeply eccentric, maybe even a little mad.'

It was vaguely alarming, but at least she didn't have to face that yet. Listening to him, she was more and more convinced that he was the man she had seen in the market. His were the black eyes htat had watched her every movement. Why hadn't he spoken to her then? She would have liked to challenge him on it but he was too daunting a figure. He would deny it and she would be made to appear a fool in his eyes. He was charmingly attentive and amusing. She answered him appropriately while part of her thoughts remained with Paul and the woman whose hand had rested so possessively on his arm.

The two who had been left alone together were silent for a moment, then Paul said quietly, 'What is it you want from me? Do you wish to dance?'

'No, I do not. How can you speak to me like that?' The eyes that he had once thought so soft, so melting with love for him, shot him a glance of pure hatred. 'Why are you treating me like this? Are you jilting me? Throwing me over for the sake of that fool of a girl who ruined Gregory's life and now thinks she can come here, calling herself Princess Gadiani, taking precedence of me, robbing Daniel of what should be his. What happened during all those nights you spent together in the mountains?'

Her voice had risen shrilly and he seized her wrist. 'Natalie, for God's sake! Not here. What are you thinking of? Do you want everyone to hear you?'

'Why not? They will know soon enough.'

'Know what?'

'How you have betrayed me.'

'Isn't it you who have betrayed me?'

For an instant they stood glaring at one another, then he moved through one of the curtained alcoves, taking her with him, into a small anteroom where guests could rest between dances. With a swift glance he saw that it was empty and closed the door, leaning back against it.

'That hurt,' she said resentfully, rubbing her wrist. 'Were you so brutal with her?'

'Natalie, stop playing with me.'

'I don't know what you mean.'

'I think you do.'

'All I know is that you went away six months ago, without a word, without a promise, went away on some stupid mission, volunteered for it when there was no need. Oh don't deny it. Daniel told me. And now you have come back and it is as if I never existed.'

'Do you really need me to explain?' He moved away from the door, crossing to the window which had been opened against the heat. He swung back the heavy curtain. Beyond the roofs of the town he could see the shape of the mountains faintly outlined in the moonlight and he took a deep breath of the clean night air.

'I went because if I had stayed I might have killed you.' She gave a gasp and he turned round to face her. 'Why did you lie to me, Natalie? Lie over and over again. Gregory was your lover, wasn't he? All the time I was away on campaign. Even when I came back. All those weeks, coming to me from his bed, with his kisses on your lips. I didn't believe it at first, I refused to listen to anyone until I realized how they were laughing at the trusting fool who would have sacrificed everything, career, ambition, friends, for the sake of a whore, a faithless bitch . . .'

'It's a lie,' she said passionately, 'a wicked lie.' She hit at him viciously and the ring on her finger clawed across his cheek leaving a streak of blood. He seized her by the shoulders.

'I wish to God it were, but it is the truth. Admit it, damn you, or must I shake it out of you?' His fingers dug into the naked shoulders until she cried out.

'Yes, yes, yes . . . Gregory was my lover.' He still held her in his grip. She was staring into his face and what she saw there frightened her. Her eyes widened. She said in a whisper, 'So that was why . . .'

'That was why. God forgive me. I did what I did.'

'Oh no!' She collapsed on to the sofa. Tears were running heedlessly down her face. 'Oh God, what will become of me?' She was as beautiful when she wept as when she laughed and once her tears would have taken him to her feet, his arms round her, begging for forgiveness, imploring her love, but not now, never again. The woman he had worshipped had never even existed. He had created her out of his own hunger and loneliness.

He said wearily, 'Don't pretend to what you don't feel, Natalie. You never cared, did you? You used me because it suited you and because for all your pride, you and your brother, you are ambitious and poor. A Kuragin would have been a feather in your cap, wouldn't it?' He laughed mirthlessly, 'I have never cared much for my name or my wealth but you did. I could have bought you like any of those poor creatures offering themselves for a few Russian roubles in the bazaar.'

'Like the women you keep in your house with her child . . . your child . . .'

'Leave Bela out of it,' he said savagely, 'she has never been my mistress.'

'I don't believe you.' Then she stretched out her hands to him, her voice soft, tremulous, beseeching. 'It is true, all true, except that I did love you, Paul, I swear it, only when Gregory came you were so far away . . . how can I make you understand. If Father had not died, if it had not been for Gregory's grandmother . . . she always hated me . . . we might have been married . . . then the Russians came and took him away. They gave me to that old man against my will . . . you know that . . . I was so unhappy until you came here . . .'

He stood looking down at her. 'You could have made a great success in the theatre, Natalie. Every man would be fighting mad for you. Perhaps you are right. Who am I to judge? But it is too late, it is finished. I loved you. If you could have obtained a divorce from General Krylov, I would have given up everything to make you my wife, but you couldn't wait, could you? You wanted Gregory, you wanted other men . . . how could I ever be sure of you again?'

'It's different now, Paul. The General is dead and I am free. You will have to give up nothing.' With one swift movement she had risen and come close to him. She slid her arms around his neck, pressing herself against him. 'Have you forgotten, darling? It could be like it was.'

The lovely face was only a few inches from his own. He could smell her perfume, feel the old enchantment, and for an instant he wavered. Then he took her hands and put her firmly away from him.

'It is too late, Natalie, we can't go back. You will have to find another rich fool to torment and beguile.'

'It's that girl, isn't it? She has changed you. Did you tell her about Gregory so that she would come weeping into your arms?'

'No, it is not Anna. She has problems enough without grieving over her husband's infidelity. She knows nothing.'

'I'll not accept it, Paul. You owe me something. I'll make you pay, I swear, and so will Daniel.'

'Do what you please. In a few weeks I shall be gone from here.'

'Where? Where are you going and for how long?'

'Months . . . a year . . . perhaps for ever.' He shrugged his shoulders. 'That is not your concern.'

'Have you no pity for me?'

'A great deal . . . but pity is not love.'

'Go,' she said turning on him passionately, 'go, leave me alone.'

'Very well,' but he still lingered torn by conflicting feelings, knowing her for what she was and yet unable to forget the love they had shared and that he knew now to be nothing but a sham. Then he turned and went out of the room.

The door closed and Natalie stared at it for a moment and then took up the costly vase on the table and threw it with all her strength across the room. It hit the wall and splintered into fragments. Her rage appeased, she crossed to the mirror. She was dabbing her eyes with her handkerchief when she heard the door open again and saw her brother's face reflected in the glass beside her own.

'Well, my dear, how did it go? Did you play him carefully? Paul Kuragin is not a fish to be hooked so easily.'

'I know what I am doing, Daniel.'

'I hope you do.' His hand on her shoulder gripped suddenly. 'You lost him once. He won't be gulled a second time.'

She was frightened of him, but would not show it. 'Leave me alone. What are you going to do about the girl?'

He released her, sauntering away, one hand fingering his moustache. 'I've not decided. It depends on what happens when she goes to the old woman at Kumari. I might even marry her.'

'You can't be serious.'

'Oh yes I am, perfectly serious. There's only one snag. Is she really a widow?'

And while she stared at him, he said banteringly, 'You had better come back to the ballroom with me, my dear. They are going to wonder what you and Paul have been doing shut up together for so long. Come,' and he hooked his arm in hers and took her with him out into the hall.

It was three o'clock in the morning before Anna and Marya returned from the palace. Ivan opened the door to them and handed them their bedroom candlesticks. They went slowly up the stairs. Outside Anna's door, Marya kissed her.

'Sleep well, my pet. It was a fascinating evening, wasn't it?'

'Yes, fascinating.'

'Goodnight.'

Marya disappeared into her own room and Anna stood for a moment, yawning, her head whirling with so many different impressions, so much excitement, so much dancing, that she wondered if she would be able to sleep a wink. She had put out a hand to open her door when she noticed the light that flickered across the passage and realized that the door opposite to her own was half open. She did not know who slept there but it was very late and for some reason she felt alarmed. She tiptoed to the door and peered into the room. The candles in the three-branched candelabra on the table by the bed were flaring dangerously and even while she watched one of them toppled over and fell with a faint plop to the carpet.

Whoever was in there must have fallen asleep and forgotten to blow them out. There was a smell of scorching. In another moment the whole place could be set alight. She hesitated no longer but pushed open the door and went in. She blew out the guttering wax and stooped to pick up the candle from the carpet. She was stamping out the small smouldering patch when she saw the white and gold tunic discarded on the floor and realized that Paul was sprawled across the bed in shirt and breeches, his dark hair tousled, his face flushed. She was no child. She had seen Gregory drunk more than once, had even helped Yakov put him to bed. It was only that somehow Paul had never seemed the kind of man to give way to such indulgence. Still it was no concern of hers.

She was moving quickly towards the door when the toe of her satin slipper struck against something and she bent to pick it up. It was a small portrait miniature framed in gold but cracked and split as if someone had ground it under his heel. For an instant as the light of her candle fell on it, she thought it was Natalie, the same delicate features, the same black hair and smouldering eyes. Then she realized that the style of dress was of a much earlier time, twenty or thirty years at least. She went to place it on the table but accidentally dislodged a heavy book balanced on the edge so that it fell to the ground with a thump.

Paul grunted and half sat up. She would have fled out of the room but it was too late. He raised his head.

'What is it?' he said thickly. 'What is the matter? Is that you, Anfisa?'

'Not, it is not Anfisa.'

'Who then, for God's sake?'

'It is Anna.'

'Anna!' He pushed himself upright. 'What the devil are you doing in here?'

She was acutely embarrassed, conscious that she still held the miniature in her hand.

'Marya and I have just come home. I . . . I was going to bed when I saw your candles guttering and smelled burning. I . . . I thought I had better put them out.'

'Oh hell, I must have forgotten them. Damned careless of me.'

He was looking at her in a curious way and she came back a step, holding the miniature out to him.

'I . . . I found this on the floor. It's badly damaged, I'm afraid.'

He swung his legs off the bed and stood up, swaying a little as he took it from her. He stared down at it before he spoke.

'It's my mother. She died when I was six. They told me she had been thrown from her horse. She loved to ride above all things.'

'How terrible . . . I am sorry . . .'

She knew she ought to go at once, but she still stood there and he went on almost as if he were talking to himself.

'She was so lovely. I worshipped her. Ridiculous, wasn't it? I used to think of her like the saint in the icon that hung in my nursery . . . until I found out the truth. She had killed herself, ridden her horse over a ravine because the father of the child she was carrying was her husband's steward, his bastard half-brother who had already tried to murder him. And she had other lovers, any man could creep into her bed, even my uncle, a man I had loved and respected. Sometimes I've wondered if I am really my father's son,' he went on broodingly. 'It's a damned unpleasant thought to live with, wondering if you are some filthy peasant's by-blow!'

She stood there, shocked and distressed, very sure that she was hearing something that any other time he would have died rather than confess. He threw the miniature on the table seeming to notice for the first time that she was still in the room.

'I'm talking like a damned fool. You had better go to bed.'

Blood oozed from a long scratch on his cheek. He had such a distraught look that she still hesitated. 'Are you sure you are all right?'

'I'm drunk,' he said savagely, 'that's all that is wrong with me. Don't you want to go to bed alone, is that it?' and he reached out an arm and pulled her to him so that the candle fell out of her hand and went out. The room was plunged into darkness and he was kissing her, his mouth on hers, hard, searching, the fierce male strength that so often in her loneliness after Gregory went, had haunted her dreams. Then she was resisting him, struggling to free herself, and he released her so suddenly that she staggered and nearly fell.

'Go to bed, Anna, for God's sake, go to bed,' he said harshly and she ran out of the room and across the passage, slamming her door and leaning back against it, trembling, frightened, because despite the shock, there had been a sweetness, an immediate response. She had wanted him to make love to her.

Presently she recovered herself a little. She had no candle and dared not go in search of one. She went to the window, pulling back the curtains. There was already a faint lightening of the summer sky and as she stood there, she saw Paul come out into the garden. He paused for a moment, the morning breeze blowing the dark hair across his forehead. He is going to her, she thought with a stab of pain, going to the bed of his mistress. But he did not cross the courtyard to Bela's room. Instead he went through the arch that led to the stables and though she called herself every kind of fool she knew that she was glad.

—— 7 ——

It was eleven o'clock before Anna awoke the next morning when Darinka knocked and came in with her coffee and a great armful of velvety white roses. He must have bought the entire stock of the flower-seller in the market, she thought, smiling at them and at the message scrawled on the card.

'I owe you a debt for saving me from the fiery furnace.'

Darinka was looking at them admiringly. 'Shall I put them in water for you, Madame?'

'No, I'll do it myself when I get up.'

She lay sipping the scalding coffee and thinking of the night before, wondering how much he would remember of the revelation about his mother, sensing the bitterness, the disillusionment of the boy who had idolized her and trying not to think of her own reaction when he had briefly held her in his arms.

Presently when she was dressed, she went into see Marya who was still drowsing happily in bed. She had meant to tell her about what had happened and then abruptly changed her mind. Better not to make too much of it, both for his sake and for her own, better to put it out of her mind and let it be forgotten.

She arranged the roses in a Persian vase of a deep rich blue which Darinka brought her and on impulse took one of them and pinned it in the bosom of her morning gown. Soon now she must leave here and go to Kumari. Daniel Gadiani had spoken of it last night when he took her away from Paul.

'It is a full day's journey and through pretty wild country,' he had said. 'I have to go there myself very soon. Perhaps you will give me the pleasure of escorting you.'

It was only sensible to accept his offer and thank him for it even though obstinately she would have preferred to go there alone.

'I am afraid Gregory's death has left our affairs in a sorry state of confusion,' he told her with a charming air of apol-

ogy, 'especially as it has only just been confirmed. We must
discuss your future and where better than at Kumari with my
great aunt, though,' and he smiled wryly, 'I fear she does not
altogether approve of me.'

It was a moment she had long dreaded, but now that it had
come, she must be prepared to face it. She opened her writing case and took out Gregory's last letter that she had not
looked at again since she had left home. It was very short
and would appear to have been written in haste.

'My dear Anna, I know only too well you have much to
forgive me, but the future is uncertain and in case there
should be no other opportunity I want you to know that
there has been regret in my heart for what we did to each
other. But one thing I ask of you most sincerely. When you
receive this, come to the Caucasus and go to Kumari. It is
asking much, I know, but it is important' (and here he had
underlined it so heavily that the pen had dug into the paper) 'and if it should so happen that I am not there, then
my grandmother will tell you why. I know I have no right
to beg anything from you, but because you are you and
you did once love me, I implore you to come.'

She looked at the dashing signature with a pang at her
heart. She had wept over the note when it had come and
wondered if in his reckless way he had decided to go on campaign with the army. Within two weeks of receiving it she
knew he had disappeared. Reading it again and knowing now
so much more about the Caucasus and the tensions of the
people who lived there, pulling this way and that, she suddenly realized why he had written so vaguely. Maybe he had
been afraid that somewhere it might be intercepted and for
that reason put her into danger.

She shivered a little, not sure if she was letting her imagination run away with her and reading into it more than was
actually there. Many people had spoken to her of Gregory at
the ball, some pityingly, some evasively, and all the time she
had felt there was something hidden, something deliberately
withheld from her. She had asked Daniel Gadiani outright
and he had shrugged his shoulders turning the question aside.

'I wish I could help you, Anna, but I myself was not in Tiflis when it happened. I know only what I was told on my return.'

She folded the letter and put it carefully away. The sun

was streaming in through the windows. She felt tired after a
restless night and the garden looked so inviting, she thought
she would sit out there for a little until Marya was up and
they could lunch together.

When she came into the courtyard, the little boy was playing with a ball, rolling it along the paths and trying to persuade the big dog to run after it. She sat on the bench under
the lime tree amused by their antics. The borzoi had flopped
down, head on paws, refusing to be tempted to run any more
in the heat though the boy tugged at his collar. The boy
stamped his foot at him, then picked up the ball and threw it
away from him in temper. It bounced to Anna's feet and she
tossed it back.

'Mitya,' she called, 'don't take any notice of him. Come
and play with me.'

The child looked at her shyly, then suddenly giggled and
threw the ball back to her. Presently tiring of his game, he
ran off and came back pulling a wooden cart piled with other
toys, putting them on her lap, animals of all kinds, obviously
from a Noah's Ark. He jabbered excitedly in a mixture of
Russian and some incomprehensible tongue.

She began to range the animals two by two on the seat and
the child danced about laughing and clapping his hands.

'Mitya, come here to me at once.' Bela had appeared at the
door and the boy glanced up startled at the stern note in his
mother's voice. Then he shook his head and took refuge behind Anna's skirts. With a little impatient sound Bela crossed
to him and took his hand. 'You must come when I call you
and not annoy the lady.'

'He is not annoying me and it is my fault,' said Anna
quickly. 'I was playing with him.'

'It is time for him to eat and then sleep a little. It is too
hot out here in the afternoon.' Bela began to walk away dragging the reluctant child with her.

'Bela, wait a moment. I want to thank you for what you
did with my dress. It was wonderful. You made it look just
like new.'

'I am glad you were satisfied with it. Come now, Mitya.'

'Won't you stay for a few minutes and talk to me?'

'Why?' The girl paused looking at her resentfully. 'If you
wish to ask whether I share the Count's bed, then the answer
is no.'

Taken aback, Anna said, 'But I was not going to ask any
such thing.'

'I think you were,' said the girl with angry pride. 'All the ladies who come here want to know that though they may not say it.' The black eyes flashed. 'They do not like to believe that a man can be kind and not want payment.'

'I think I do,' said Anna gently. 'Won't you tell me about it?'

Bela hesitated, still holding Mitya by the hand. 'I don't know . . . why should I?'

'Oh please. Count Kuragin has been kind to me too, very kind. I should like to hear more about him. You did tell me that your husband was killed during the war.'

'He was not my husband, he was my man.' She took a step nearer and Mitya pulled away from her, running off to kick at his ball. 'You must know it is not easy for a Tartar to marry a Russian,' she said reluctantly, 'and my father, he hates them. He wants only to see all Russians dead.'

'Did he forbid your marriage?'

'He would kill me first. He beat me often . . . but my Sergei, he loved me and I loved him before he went away.'

'And then he was killed?'

'Far away in the mountains. My father, when he knows the baby is coming, is very angry. I had disgraced my family, he shout at me, calling me whore, bitch, terrible names, and my brother too. He push me from the house and tell me never to come back.'

Anna leaned forward. 'What did you do?'

'I come to Tiflis and find work in the bazaar,' she shivered, 'it was terrible. You do not know what it is like there for a woman like me . . . the men, they never leave you alone. I thought I would die.'

'What happened?'

'When the Count come back, he go to my father. They shout at him, calling him bad names, but he find out a little about where I go and he searched the market till he find me and bring me here and ask nothing from me, nothing at all, not like the other men.'

Anna felt ashamed of her suspicions. 'It was generous of him.'

'More than you think,' said Bela warmly. 'Because I am Tartar, they call me spy, even the Prince, the Viceroy, try to persuade the Count to send me away but he refuse . . . that black-haired one who come here so often last year, she accuse me in front of him, but he only laughed at her. She wants him that one, but I think she make him very unhappy.'

Could that have been Natalie? Anna wondered.

Bela took a quick look round and then moved closer. 'Count Paul has been so good to me,' she whispered, 'but sometimes I am frightened for him.'

'Frightened? Why?'

'My brother is very angry because he brought me here.'

'Angry? He ought to be grateful.'

'He believes that . . . that the Count . . .'

'Is your lover?'

'Yes. I swear to him that it is not so but he is sure that I lie. One day, he says, he will make him pay.'

'Have you told Count Kuragin?'

'Yes, but he takes no heed. He says it is nothing but foolish talk. It is many months now since Kamil has come, but I still worry.'

'I am sure there is no need. I think Count Kuragin knows very well how to take care of himself.' Anna touched Bela's hand. 'Thank you for telling me about yourself. Perhaps some day you will find another man you want to marry.'

'I want no one. I am happy with Mitya. Now I must take him in and your luncheon will be waiting for you.'

'Yes. I suppose it will.'

Anna watched the girl call the child again and take him into her room. The boy waved to her and she waved back before she returned to the house. So Bela was not his mistress. But what of Natalie? She had been married to Prince Krylov (were they all princes in this country, she thought with exasperation) a man twice her age and General of the Georgian Grenadier Guards until his death. Had Paul been her lover? Last night there had been a sharp dislike in the black eyes even if the voice was honey sweet. Then she thrust the thought away from her. She must not even think of it. It was no concern of hers.

In the days that followed she was given little time to brood on anything. The Prince's favour was like an accolade and an invitation to one of his wife's soirées set the seal on her acceptance into viceregal society. She was showered with requests for her company which she and Marya accepted sparely. She saw Paul only fleetingly, exchanging a few courteous words as he came and went in the house until one morning when she met him in the garden with Mitya.

He was looking down at the boy, both hands behind his back, while the child pummelled him with two tiny furious fists.

'Choose,' he said teasingly.

Mitya hesitated and then pointed. He opened the empty hand laughing at the crestfallen little face.

'There,' he said, 'don't cry,' and brought round the other hand holding the pink striped box. 'Run away and share them with your mother.'

'You spoil him,' said Anna and he swung round with the look of a boy caught out in mischief.

'Mitya has a passion for Turkish delight.'

'Which I'm not at all sure that you ought to indulge.'

'Why not if it makes him happy? You see, I was brought up very strictly.'

She smiled at him. 'Bela told me the other day how kind you have been to her.'

'It was little enough. Sergei was a good soldier, one of my serfs from Arachino. I knew he wanted to marry the girl but the Prince frowns on any "fraternization with the enemy". I had to do something to protect her when he was killed.'

'You're aware of what they say?'

He gave her a quick glance. 'So that tittle-tattle has reached you. Do you believe it?'

'No, I don't think I do.'

'Thank you for your good opinion of me,' he said ironically. 'Most of my acquaintances are only too ready to assume the worst. I regret it but what the devil could I do? To set her up in a lodging of her own would only provoke still worse scandal. To bring her here seemed the best solution to the problem.'

'Bela also told me that her brother has sworn vengeance on you.'

'Oh Lord yes. She came to me with that tale some time ago. She even offered to go away so as not to put me in danger.'

'Is it a serious threat?'

'Good God, no. Kamil is a young hot head, always waging war against someone or something. If I took any notice of ravings like that, I'd never stir outside the house. It is her father who is the real bully. Now that she has regained her looks and has a fine son, he wants her back.'

'But why when he turned her out?'

'You don't understand, Anna. To a man of his kind, daughters are so much merchandise. He would sell her to some wretch like himself who would beat her and turn her into a household drudge. I'd not condemn anyone to a life like that. If some decent man wants her, I'll give her a dowry. That means a great deal to a young woman in her position. It will make her feel of value.'

With his wealth, money mattered little to him, she knew that, but all the same the thought behind it was generous and she warmed to him.

'That's enough about Bela,' he said lightly, taking her arm. 'Have you a moment to spare? I'd like to show you the two mares I have just bought.'

They walked together through the archway to the stables and paused by the stalls. A handsome narrow head thrust forward and snuffled at him.

'Oh how beautiful they are,' she exclaimed, 'both of them.'

'I thought you might be interested. They have Arab blood. Would you like to try one of them?'

'If you're sure you could trust me.'

'You forget how often I have seen you ride.' He felt in his pocket for sugar and held it out on his palm. 'When do you go to Kumari?'

'I don't know exactly. Not for a week or two. Daniel Gadiani has offered to take me there himself.'

He frowned. 'You surprise me. I understand that he is not on good terms with the old Princess.'

'Why?'

He shrugged his shoulders. 'Some ancient family feud probably. Don't trust him too far, Anna.'

'Why should you say that?'

'No particular reason except that I know the Gadianis better than you do.'

'You forget that Gregory was my husband,' she said stiffly.

He looked directly at her. 'I don't forget it at all. Did you learn nothing from him?'

She knew what he meant, the charm that was so unpredictable and could change in a moment to blazing anger, the promise made one day that would be ignored the next, the jealousy if she as much as smiled at another man. She did not answer and he went on.

'In a few days I hope to have some free time. Would you care to ride with me?' She hesitated and he smiled wryly. 'Oh come, I think we know one another well enough by now, don't you?'

The faint irony in his voice made up her mind for her. 'I should like it very much.'

'Good. That's a promise. I shall hold you to it.'

But before that promise could be fulfilled, something happened that disturbed her greatly. It had surprised her a little that Paul did not attend any of the concerts or evening parties to which they were constantly invited though once or twice his name was mentioned and some of the ladies eyed her curiously. But there had always been something about Anna that did not encourage gossip. It had been the same in Petersburg. She held herself aloof from it so she was not aware of what was being said until one morning when she went walking in the Prince's new botanical gardens with Marya. They had persuaded Bela to go with them and bring the little boy. The flower beds were a riot of magnificent colour, soon to be burnt brown by the fierce sun. The child had run ahead with his mother, pulling his toy cart with the dog racing after them when they met Natalie with Nikki in attendance and a bevy of other young officers. In her cream muslin dress with a lace parasol she looked particularly lovely. It was little wonder that the boy was gazing at her with obvious admiration.

She greeted Anna effusively. 'We've not yet had that long talk we promised one another,' she said sweetly. 'You and Marya Petrovna must come and spend a whole day with me.'

'Thank you, but we are rather occupied at the moment.'

'Yes, of course, anyone coming from the capital is sure of a welcome in our narrow little group here.' The black eyes darted from one to the other. 'What have you done with Paul? I was quite certain that he would have been escorting you everywhere.'

'I'm afraid we rarely see him,' said Marya quietly. 'He is far too busy.'

'Really! How strange. Last year when he was on leave he kept open house. I believe he's up to something. What do you think, Nikki?' She leaned on the young man's arm looking up at him familiarly. 'Find out for me. You are aide to the Prince. It should be easy.'

'I'm afraid they don't tell me anything.'

'I don't believe that. I know you men. You all stick together and don't tell us a thing. I can see you have a great deal to learn. I shall have to take you in hand. Now be a dear boy and take me back to the carriage. Goodbye, Anna, don't forget. Come and see me soon.'

They watched them go, Natalie clinging to Nikki's arm, and Marya said dryly, 'That young man is riding for a fall.'

'Oh I don't know. She is very attractive.'

'And unscrupulous, I should say. Someone ought to warn him.'

'He's young but he's not a fool. She is only amusing herself with him.'

She liked Nikki but refused to worry over him until he called a few days later. She came down to the salon to see him waiting for her and at first he spoke of so many trivialities that she could not think why he had taken the trouble to come. Then abruptly he came out with the purpose of his visit.

'You shouldn't take that girl and her child about with you, Anna. It is not decent. You know what they say about her.'

'What do they say?'

He looked uncomfortable. 'I don't care to repeat it.'

'Oh Nikki, for goodness sake! Do you take me for a child? And anyway it's a tissue of lies. I know all about Bela. She told me, herself.'

'And you believe her?'

'Why shouldn't I? You ought to be ashamed to come here with such ridiculous scandal. If that is all you have to say, I think you had better go.'

'It's not all.' He hesitated, looking away from her. 'Anna, I warned you before you came here. You should not go on staying in this house. They are talking already . . . about you and Paul.'

'What!' She was furiously indignant. 'I don't believe you.'

'It is true. Natalie told me . . .'

'Natalie. What is it do with her?'

'She is concerned for you, Anna, and she knows everyone here. She knows Paul too, has known him much longer than you have. Anna, you must listen . . .'

'Why should I listen to such detestable gossip?'

'She means well, Anna. She is Gregory's cousin after all.'

'And does that give her the right to tell me how I should behave?' She was swept by a blaze of anger. 'If anyone wants to say such vile things, then let them come and say them to Paul himself. He will have an answer for them.'

'You trust him too far, Anna.'

'I have good reason to trust him and I will not listen to lies about him.'

'Anna, please . . .'

'No,' she put her hands over her ears. 'I've heard enough. Please go now.'

'Very well. I'm sorry. I didn't mean to offend you.'

'Oh heaven,' she said with exasperation, 'I know you didn't, but it's so unjust. I thought Paul was your friend.'

'So he is . . . but . . . I do feel responsible for you.'

'You don't need to feel like that. I can take care of myself.'

'You're not angry with me?'

'No, I'm not angry, but I still think you had better go.'

He took her hand and kissed it. 'All right, I will.'

She let her hand lie in his for a moment. 'Nikki, you're not falling in love with Natalie?'

'Are you jealous?' he asked with a touch of mischief.

'No, of course I'm not.'

'Well then, I am not so foolish.'

'I'm glad.'

'Anna,' he paused before he said slowly, 'Anna, there is one more thing that I think you ought to know.'

'What is that?'

'Now don't jump down my throat again, but I have heard that a year or so ago there was a great deal of talk about Paul and Natalie . . .'

'Why not?' she said calmly. 'She is a very beautiful woman.'

'You don't mind?'

'Why on earth should I?'

'No, of course not, only . . . oh well, I've said it now,' he gave her a grin and impulsively she held out her hand to him again.

'Dear Nikki, it is sweet of you to be so anxious about me, but I am all right, really I am.'

She meant what she said but all the same after he had gone she couldn't help wondering how much truth there had been in what he had told her and if Paul had been deliberately avoiding Natalie during the past weeks. She was shocked by her malice and angry that she should spread such tales about her. In her indignation Nikki's well-meant advice had the opposite effect to what he had intended. When Paul appeared a morning or so later while she and Marya were breakfasting and asked if she would permit him to show her something of Tiflis and its surroundings, she agreed readily. Let them say what they liked of her. She was independent of them. She could do as she pleased.

All that week and the next she saw him every day. It was quite unplanned but somehow one thing led to another. Once or twice Marya accompanied them, but she tired easily in the

sultry summer heat so more often than not, they went alone.
Because she pressed him, Paul took her to parts of the ancient city where she would never have dared to venture
alone; narrow cobbled streets between tall ramshackle houses
where the Armenians lived, the Jews, the Turks, with crazy
wooden staircases climbing up to balconies and where even in
the poorest quarter there would be pots of flowers or a
brightly coloured shawl draped on the railing.

He took her across the rushing torrent of the Kura into the
old Persian quarter and bought her a handwrought rope of
silver studded with turquoise from an old man sitting cross-
legged outside his tiny booth.

She protested that she could not accept anything so valu-
able and he said, 'Don't spoil it, Anna. He is happy and so
am I. Give it to Bela if you don't like it.'

The old man grunted as Paul fastened it around her neck,
raising his hands in admiration and mumbling something she
did not understand. She looked at Paul questioningly.

'He says the light of your face is like the splendour of the
moon and that you must be my solace and my jewel, my
water of life.'

'Heavens, why should he say all that about me?'

'He is quoting from *The Knight in the Panther Skin*. It is
the great medieval epic of the Caucasus. He probably can't
even read and yet he can reel off whole passages from it.' He
gave her his ironic smile. 'May I say I rather agree with him?'

'Oh Paul, you are laughing at me.'

'Not at all, I assure you.' He drew her arm through his.
'And now I'm thirsty. Shall we find some refreshment?'

In the market with the sun pouring down on them, he
bought slices of melon, the flesh a deep orange, cool and so
juicy that it ran down their chins as they ate it and they
laughed as he mopped her face and his own.

Walking around the Sioni Cathedral he told her of the Sul-
tan Jelal-eddin who had built a bridge from his palace to the
Cathedral so that whenever so inclined, he could personally
trample on the hated Christian temple. The church was cool
and shadowy, the massive stone walls towering above them.
They looked at the cross which St Nino had plaited from
vine stems and bound with her own hair.

'She lived in the fourth century and converted the people
to Christianity. Some say she was martyred for it.'

She shivered a little in her thin muslin dress and looked up
at him leaning against one of the mighty stone pillars, the

rather stern lines of his face relaxed and she asked the question that had long been in her mind.

'Paul, will you tell me something?'

'If I can. What do you want to know?'

'Not about the Caucasus, about you.'

He glanced down at her, eyebrows raised. 'What is there to know about me?'

'You are not like Nikki or the other army officers, are you?'

'No,' he admitted after a moment. 'I was for several years, obeying orders, doing exactly as I was told.' He took her arm as they paced slowly along the aisle. 'This is not quite an ordinary war, Anna, you must have realized that. We are fighting in mountain country, the strategy has to be different. There are pockets of resistance everywhere. If Shamyl were to unite the tribes against us, he would become almost unbeatable so certain detachments are formed from time to time to search them out.'

'Is that what you were doing before you came to Pyatigorsk?'

'Not exactly, but the information I picked up then and sent back to headquarters enabled the Prince to prevent the Tartars from uniting the whole of Kabardia and splitting the Caucasus in two, cutting our supply lines from Russia.'

'And this time?'

'I can't tell you about that, not yet at any rate. The fewer who know, the better. If I'm lucky, it could greatly help our cause, if not . . .'

'You could be killed.'

'I hope nothing as final as that.'

'Why Paul, why do you do it?'

He shrugged his shoulders. 'I don't know. Why does one do anything? I like to be independent, to act on my own initiative, make my own decisions, so when the chance came, I seized on it. Back home in Petersburg, we are forced to live like the Tsar's slaves. Here in the mountains men are free as eagles.'

There was an anger in his voice that reminded her of her father and the fights he had had with authority before he was forced to submit like everyone else. Then Paul smiled wryly. 'It doesn't lead to a comfortable life, but at least it is an interesting one, but why on earth are we talking like this? We are supposed to be enjoying ourselves and I am hungry. Will

Marya Petrovna bite my head off if I take you to eat in a favourite restaurant of mine?'

'Marya is not my keeper and I too like to be independent.'

'The liberated English, eh? It is perfectly respectable but you won't find the fashionable there. Do you mind?'

'Not a bit.'

It was a great smoky cavern of a place in the old quarter but clean and well kept. The proprietor obviously knew Paul well. He came bowing to them, leading them to a table set apart in one of the alcoves and spreading a snow-white cloth.

'They serve the best *shashliks* in the whole country,' whispered Paul, and he was right. The cubes of lamb grilled on skewers over the charcoal brazier were delicious and so was the crusty wholemeal bread still warm from the oven. There were stuffed aubergines with tomatoes and cucumber, roasted kid and wine served in tall slender-necked jugs cool and damp from the stone cellars. Beside her plate the waiter laid a rose, deep red and perfect.

'That's Ahmed's way of saying how much he admires my choice of companion,' said Paul.

Blushing a little she tucked it into her dress. 'How many other women have you brought here?'

'You may not believe me but you are the first.'

She raised her eyes to his. 'Not even Natalie?'

'Most certainly not Natalie,' he replied shortly.

They were still eating when the figure of a man appeared in the doorway, dark against the glare of light outside. Then when he came across to them, she saw that it was Nikki.

'I've been looking for you everywhere,' he said frowning down at Paul. 'I went to the house and Anfisa told me you had taken Anna to the old city. I had the devil of a job finding you. The Prince wishes to see you at once.'

'Damnation! All right, Nikki. Thank you.'

The young man looked around him with distaste. 'Do you think you should bring Anna to a place like this?'

'Why? What's wrong with it? The food is excellent. Sit down and join us.'

'I have to return to my duties,' he said stiffly.

'Please yourself,' said Paul carelessly. 'Tell Vorontsov that I'll be with him this afternoon.'

'His order was to come immediately.'

'I shall finish my meal first and then take Anna home.'

'Very well, it's your decision.'

Nikki gave her a little bow, nodded to Paul and strode out of the restaurant.

Paul smiled. 'I'm afraid he disapproves of me. Nikki likes to be very correct.'

'Paul, do you think you should go? I can go back to the house alone.'

'I am not running like a scalded cat for anyone.' He raised his glass. 'We'll drink a toast, shall we? To independence.'

He refused to be hurried. He finished eating, drank a last glass of wine, insisted on coffee, thanked the bowing landlord when he paid him and then leisurely took Anna's arm. They strolled up to the main street where he hailed a hackney carriage to take them to the house.

At the door he took her hand for a moment. 'Tomorrow we'll take the horses and go out into the country, that is if you can still put up with my company.'

'I would like that very much but what about the Prince and your orders?'

'My orders can wait. I don't intend to be sent anywhere,' he said lightly, 'not for another day at any rate.'

He kissed her fingers and she watched him run down the steps and leap into the waiting cab before she went into the house.

Marya said, 'I was anxious about you when you did not come back at midday.'

'Paul took me to a wonderful place where the food was simply marvellous.' She went on describing it all in detail, her cheeks flushed so that when she came to an end, her cousin looked at her quizzically.

'You certainly seem to have been enjoying yourself, but don't you think you are seeing rather too much of him?'

'Why should you say that? It has not been so often and you have been with us for a good deal of the time. Anyway he is going away soon.'

'Did he tell you that?'

'We met Nikki with an order from the Prince. Paul has gone to the palace now.'

'You will be careful, won't you?'

'Careful of what?'

'You know what I mean. Paul Kuragin is a fascinating man, charming, attractive, different from others, I grant you that, but we don't really know very much about him.'

'I thought you liked him.'

'So I do, but I'm not falling in love with him.'

'Neither am I.'

'Are you sure?' She leaned forward, taking Anna's hand. 'My dear, you had a bad time with Gregory . . . no, don't deny it, I know. I'm not quite a fool. Don't be trapped on the rebound from it.'

'Oh Marya please . . .' she pulled herself away.

'I mean it. He could be just amusing himself.'

'You don't understand,' said Anna turning on her passionately. 'Paul has never shown me anything but perfect courtesy and friendship. I enjoy his company and I think he enjoys mine. I'm not a young girl hunting for a husband. Isn't it possible to be on terms of friendship with a man?'

'Quite possible, in moderation, and as long as you're wise to what you're doing.'

'Oh Marya, don't spoil it. I know the work he's engaged on is dangerous. He may not even come back.'

'That's the trouble,' said Marya dryly. 'Just don't lose your head because of it. You did once.'

'That was a long time ago. This is quite different.' She went down on her knees beside her cousin. 'Don't I deserve a little happiness?'

'Yes, pet, only don't get hurt.'

'If I do, it will be my fault, not his. But don't worry. I won't be.'

And Marya putting a hand on the bright hair prayed that she was right.

—— 8 ——

In the Prince's lavishly appointed study Paul said quietly, 'Those final details complete the pattern. Now we can leave. The men are ready. I shall go the day after tomorrow.'

'Why not at once?'

'There are certain matters I must set in order first.'

'I see.' Vorontsov looked down at the papers on his desk. 'I suppose you realize what a foolhardy task you've taken on. I still think I should have forbidden it.'

'In that case, your excellency, I would have had to go without your blessing.'

The Prince smiled frostily. 'I really believe you would. You're a damned independent fellow, Paul. All the same don't take unnecessary risks. I'd be sorry to lose you.'

'We're all expendable.'

'True, but some are more expendable than others,' he said dryly. 'One other thing . . . when does Anna Stepanovna go to Kumari?'

'In a week or so, I understand.' Paul hesitated and then said abruptly, 'Are you sure it is wise to permit it, sir?'

'The girl is in no danger. It is the child there that is the problem.' The Prince pulled out an immaculate handkerchief and mopped his face. 'The heat in the afternoons is really becoming intolerable. I shall be glad to get away from Tiflis for a few weeks.' He turned to Paul. 'You know as well as I do that for some time now we have suspected that Daniel Gadiani has one foot in our camp and the other firmly planted in that of Shamyl, but we can't prove it. The man is subtle as a serpent. One false move on our part and the whole of Kumaria could go into revolt. They may not care for him overmuch but he is a Gadiani, a member of their hereditary house. Once Gregory's death is established, I presume he will be the heir, and they are loyal. If he takes his people to Shamyl, then we could be cut off from the Caspian Sea, a great deal of fighting will have been wasted and what the

109

devil is the Tsar going to say about it, answer me that!' Paul was silent and the Prince sat back in his chair, tapping the arm impatiently with his fingers. 'The old Princess will oppose him, of that there is no doubt, but she is artful as a monkey. I'm damned sure she is up to something though God knows what it is and these Gadianis are proud as Lucifer and need careful handling. The girl's visit there may bring it to a head and it gives me an excuse to send a small detachment ostensibly to guard against any sudden attack, all reliable men especially briefed to watch and report. One move on our friend Daniel's part and we have got him. You don't imagine that I would risk the life of an innocent Russian girl?'

The Prince is a cold fish, thought Paul, but he would sacrifice anything, even himself, for Russia so why not a young woman of no particular importance whose father is English into the bargain?

Vorontsov was watching him shrewdly. 'Are you interested in this Anna Stepanovna?'

'No more than anyone else,' said Paul carefully, 'but she has in a sense been under my protection and I believe her to be a young woman of character and strength of will. I would not like to see her exposed to Daniel Gadiani's trickery.'

'There is no fear of that. Perhaps it is fortunate for her that she has no son to provide an obstacle to his ambitions.'

'Should I perhaps warn her?'

'I would far rather you didn't except in the most general terms. The least hint and Daniel Gadiani will be on the alert.' The Prince filled two glasses from the carafe of iced wine and pushed one across the desk. 'Now to something more important . . . to your success,' he said smiling.

'To my success,' they clinked the goblets and drank. Then Paul took his leave. He went through the shaded corridors of the palace and out into the intense heat of the streets aware for the first time since he had discovered Natalie's faithlessness that he wanted to live, not die, and that at the same time he had committed himself to a suicidal mission from which he could not now extricate himself with honour and from which he stood little chance of emerging with his life.

It was a golden morning when Anna came down the steps to find Paul waiting for her with the horses. Now in July the sun was so strong that she had left off her jacket. She wore a white muslin blouse with her dark red riding skirt and had tied a silk scarf over her hair.

'You look like a gypsy,' he said as he gave her his hand to help her into the saddle.

Ivan came out of the house carrying the picnic basket and holding out a letter on a silver tray. 'A messenger has just come, your honour, he is waiting.'

Paul broke the seal and read the few lines frowning. Then he thrust it into his pocket. 'No answer,' he said curtly and swung himself into the saddle.

'Is it from the Prince?' asked Anna as he came up beside her.

'No.'

He spurred his horse forward and she caught up with him. 'Where are we going?'

'Didn't I tell you? To Mtskheta. It is the old capital of Georgia. I think you will like it.'

Their route lay to the north and once out of the close confines of the city and riding towards the foothills, the air was fresher. Paul glanced questioningly at her and she nodded. He touched his horse's flank with his crop, it leaped forward and then they were riding neck and neck past fields of maize already ripening, through acres of sunflowers raising their enormous black and golden heads to the sky. It was wildly exhilarating and when Anna pulled up at last, panting, the scarf fallen back from her hair, they laughed together and she was filled with a great surge of happiness.

It was cool and dark in the cathedral church where the Kings of Georgia had been crowned and lay buried since the fourth century. High up on the wall was the carving of a single hand holding a set square, grimly commemorating the master builder who dared to vie with his king for the love of a young woman and had lost his right hand for his audacity.

'That's the Caucasus for you,' said Paul dryly. 'Beauty and savagery in a single breath.'

They were standing close together watching the stream of pilgrims, the holy beggars with their rags and long grey beards, cripples hobbling on sticks, well-dressed young women with children, some of them carrying a single flower to lay on the floor.

'Why do they come, Paul?'

'They call it *Sveti-Tskhoveli*, the Life-Giving Pillar.'

'Why?'

'When the church was built way back at the start of Christianity, the workmen were unable to hoist the great central pillar into position and so they prayed to their new God and the next morning when they came, they saw it hovering miraculously in the air before it lowered itself on to its base.'

'And they still believe?'

'It would seem so.'

She saw wonderingly how even the most sophisticated touched the stone reverently as though to absorb some of the sanctity through their fingertips. A small boy hardly more than a baby tripped and rolled to the bottom of the steps, the wild flowers clutched in one tiny hand scattering all over the floor. In a moment Anna had run to pick him up.

Paul looked at the lovely flushed face, alight with tenderness as she comforted the child, dabbing the cut lip with her handkerchief until his mother came hurrying back. There was about her something so fresh and spontaneous, she was so alive, so touchingly eager to know everything that sometimes, he thought wryly, he found himself talking like a guide book and yet always there was the strong awareness of each other that had been there from the first day he saw her in Pyatigorsk though he had fought so hard against it.

Presently when they came out of the church, they left the horses with a peasant boy and walked through the scattered houses of the old town past the stalls heaped with fruit and vegetables. There was a smell of incense and leather and honey. Paul stopped and bought a small jar.

'You must taste it,' he said, 'it is quite unlike any other honey and the people here are famous for it, so much so that bees have become sacred. To kill even one is to commit a crime.'

They had intended to eat their picnic meal on the river bank but Mtskheta was a favourite spot for excursions from Tiflis and a fashionably dressed party was already there with rugs spread on the grassy shore.

'Shall we join them or shall we escape?' said Paul.

Somewhere among them Anna thought she saw Natalie though she could not be sure. 'Escape!' she said quickly and so hand in hand they turned their backs, returning to the horses and climbing the steep hill outside the town to where the Church of the Cross was perched in stark and lonely splendour on the rocky summit.

The climb had been an effort in the midday heat but the view was stunning. Beneath them they could see the glittering silver thread of the river winding its way through fields shimmering in a golden haze so that everything was slightly blurred, colours softened, drowsing contentedly in the warmth of the sun.

'I think I'm tired of churches,' said Anna dreamily. 'Can we just sit and enjoy the view?'

'Why not?' Paul tethered the horses and brought the picnic basket. The great stone arch with its carved angels winging their way to heaven towered above them and Anna leaned back against the sun-baked wall while Paul stripped off his tunic and stretched himself on the grass beside her.

They ate Anfisa's walnut pâté with delicious creamy cheese and dipped the crisp home-baked bread in the jar of honey, pale golden green, warm from the hive, with an elusive fragrance that seemed to hold the very essence of all the flowers of summer.

Anna was to remember those few hours for a long long time though they spoke very little as though they had found a peace and contentment in just being together that neither had known before and did not want to spoil.

For the first time he told her something of himself, of Arachino with its mile after mile of rolling countryside and great forests.

'Every autumn my father held tremendous hunting parties and after he died, my uncle did the same. For a year I had a bear cub that he had captured as a pet and I killed my first wolf when I was fourteen.'

It had been a wealthy aristocratic way of life but she sensed the rebel, the young man who had dared to make fun of the Tsar and been banished to the Caucasus, the man who risked his life in lonely ventures where he was not bound by any rule but his own, the man who had been Natalie's lover. Once she thought of Marya's warning and put it aside. Why think of that now when she was happy? The future could take care of itself.

It was as if a magic was over them that afternoon. They were so close that she found herself saying things that she had never admitted to anyone, speaking of Gregory with regret and sadness but without anger.

The fierce heat of noon had faded when Paul sat up, his arms round his knees. 'How much did you love him, Anna?'

She answered slowly, thoughtfully, her eyes on the doves that pecked lazily at the crumbs they had scattered. 'I thought it was for ever but I was too young. I suppose I loved the image I had created and when I realized that the real man was something quite different, I was so bitterly hurt I could not accept him for what he was.'

'Did he . . . was he unfaithful?'

'I don't know. Sometimes I believed so and we quarrelled. It was so painful, so humiliating to be rejected for another woman. Once after the baby died, I was so lonely, so unhappy that I was tempted to put an end to myself.' He made a move of protest and she went on quickly, 'Oh don't worry. It didn't last. I'm far too much of a coward.'

'What an unfeeling brute he must have been.'

'I thought so once but not now. I blame myself. I should have been more understanding.'

'You are too generous. It is something I could never forgive, never. To be deceived, to live with lies,' he said with so much bitterness that she wondered if it was the betrayal of his mother that tormented him or was it Natalie? Even at this moment of intimacy she lacked the courage to question him about what he had said on the night of the ball and yet the knowledge of it seemed to strengthen the bond between them.

'Anna,' he had turned to her urgently, 'Anna, there is something I must tell you . . .'

At that moment close above their heads an eagle came sailing down the wind with a tremendous sweep of wings. Instinctively they ducked as the black shadow swept over them. The white doves flew up in a snowy cloud. Baffled, the great bird of prey soared up again and Anna watched it flying into the sun.

'Oh wasn't that marvellous?' she exclaimed. 'I'm so glad the little birds escaped.' Then she looked at him. 'I'm so sorry . . . what was it that you were going to tell me?'

'It doesn't matter. It's growing late. I think we should go back.' He picked up his tunic and gave her his hand. They began to walk along the crest of the hill towards the horses.

On one side was a steep drop to the river bank. The short-cropped grass baked hard by the sun was slippery as glass. She turned round to take a last look at the lime-green stone of the cupola and her foot skidded. She stumbled backwards. Paul grabbed at her, dropping the basket, and swinging her round so that she fell against him. Then she was in his arms. For an instant breathless with shock they were quite still. She could see the sweat beading his forehead, feel the heart beating strongly under the thin linen shirt, then he was kissing her and this time there was no resistance, nothing but warmth and a sweetness that seemed to spread through her, flooding her with joy. For a timeless moment they were locked together and then he released her a little so that she was still standing in the circle of his arms.

'It's too soon, Paul, too soon,' she breathed.

'Much too soon, but I have to go away . . . I have to leave you . . .'

'You'll come back.'

'Will I?'

'You must.'

The thought of the danger that was soon to engulf him swept over her so that she could scarcely bear it.

'You must come back,' she repeated and he kissed her again with an urgency that very nearly overwhelemed them. The raucous cry of a bird flying up almost from under their feet jerked them apart. They came back to sanity to see one of the priests of the church, grey-bearded and austere, watching them from the porch in mild surprise.

They rode down the hill in silence, both of them aware that some kind of a barrier had been crossed and nothing would ever be quite the same again. It was not until they were on the road to Tiflis that Anna said, 'Daniel Gadiani is giving a party this evening and Marya and I have been invited. I think we shall have to go. Will you be there?'

'I had not intended it. I must leave at dawn tomorrow.'

He felt the crackle of paper in his pocket and remembered the note that had been driven completely out of his mind during the day. Oh to hell with it! He had never felt like this before, not for Natalie, not for anyone. It was sheer madness but he had to see her again even if it was only for a few minutes. She must know the truth about him before he went away.

'I will come,' he said.

The gypsy dancer, subtle, sensuous and very beautiful, twisted and writhed to the haunting native music in Daniel Gadiani's drawing room. The house where he lived with his sister was just outside the town, set in its own gardens, and lavishly furnished in the Persian style, the walls hung with quilted rosy silk, the perfumed oil in the silver lamps scenting the air. Anna could not explain why she found it so distasteful. Perhaps she was tired from the long day in the sun. She had a slight headache and found the heat and the effort of making polite conversation exceptionally wearying.

The dance ended in a whirl of scarlet skirts and flashing

gold bracelets. The girl sank into a deep curtsey to a storm of applause. There was an interval in the entertainment. The guests began to move about and Natalie slipped into the empty chair beside her.

'I have not had an opportunity to speak to you before. Why didn't you come and join our picnic this morning?' she said sweetly. 'Nikki was so disappointed. Such a charming boy and so fond of you.'

'I wanted to see the Church of the Cross.'

'Really! Climbing that steep hill in all that heat for the sake of a few old stone walls! My dear child, what an enthusiast you must be! And with Paul of all people! I am afraid that was not what everyone was thinking when you turned your backs and ran away from us.'

'I am not very concerned with what other people may think.'

'So brave of you to say that, but you should be.' She put a hand on Anna's arm. 'You are after all a Gadiani. I haven't wanted to say anything up to now, but I do know society here. It is such a small group, everyone knows everyone else and they have been greatly shocked at your being seen so much with Paul . . . and alone.'

She drew away. 'We have not always been alone. My cousin was with us frequently and in any case I am my own mistress. I can surely do as I please.'

'Of course, within limits, and that may be possible in your father's circle in Moscow . . .'

'Please leave my father out of it.'

'I mean no disrespect but it is surely a very different milieu and you would not wish to damage your good name. I know only too well how easy it is.' She sighed. 'Paul can be so persuasive and so thoughtless. I too have suffered at his hands. It is not easy to speak of such things and yet I feel I must. Before he went away last year, there was an understanding between us, a promise. I lived only for his return and then when he did . . .' her voice shook a little. 'I have tried to hide it, to say nothing, to behave just as usual, but my brother has guessed and is very angry. I am afraid of what he may do.'

Anna felt a cramping of the heart. This was what Marya had hinted at and she had refused to believe it. She said in a stifled voice, 'Paul is leaving Tiflis. He is under orders from the Prince.'

Natalie smiled sadly. 'That is what he told you of course.

It is what he said before. He is running away, my dear, running away from his obligations.'

Anna stared at her and then got to her feet. 'He is under no obligation to me,' she said coolly. 'We have been on terms of friendship and nothing more. Whatever debt he has incurred with regard to you is none of my concern.'

She walked quickly away, uncertain of herself in spite of her bold words, and suddenly everything seemed to crowd in on her, the rich room, the heat, a feeling of menace. She felt alone and friendless, a stranger out of step with those around her. She was looking for Marya, hoping to find her quickly and make an excuse to leave, when she saw Paul come in and stand for a moment in the doorway. His eyes roved around the room until they came to rest on her. In an instant she was comforted. They were threading their way towards each other. All around them there were people chatting, taking a glass of wine, eating ices, but they might have been alone. Suddenly it seemed a year since she had seen him and yet it was only a few hours.

He took her arm. 'I must speak to you, Anna.'

She was aware of the urgency in his voice. 'Has something happened?'

'In a way . . . let's get out of here.'

Some of the guests greeted him and he answered briefly as he led her through them and into a curtained alcove where the windows had been opened on to a fretted stone balcony and the night air swept in cool and refreshing. A lamp burned on a low stool beside the cushioned couch.

'Anna, I have only a few minutes. My men are waiting.'

'Do you have to leave now?'

'Yes, there has been a change of plan.'

The light from the lamp threw deep shadows across his face. She could not see him clearly, only that he frowned and there was a taut look about his mouth so that she was afraid.

'What is it, Paul?'

His hand gripped the back of the couch. 'There is something I should have told you a long time ago, something you ought to know . . . I intended to tell you this afternoon but then I couldn't . . . I was too much of a coward.'

She felt her heart miss a beat, half guessing and yet still far from the truth. 'Is it about Natalie?' she whispered.

'Natalie?' he sounded surprised. 'Only indirectly . . .'

Then the curtain was thrust aside and Daniel Gadiani

came in, letting it fall behind him, isolating them from the crowded room.

'I had not expected to see you here, Paul, not after the note I sent you this morning.'

'I would not have come, but I had to see Anna.'

'Is that necessary when she is living in your house?'

'I resent your implication.'

'Take it how you please. It is true, is it not?'

Bewildered Anna looked from one to the other. 'What are you talking about?' she said, but the two men ignored her.

Paul's eyes were on Daniel Gadiani. 'I am under orders from the Prince to leave Tiflis tonight.'

'Indeed. How very convenient. What a splendid excuse to avoid the challenge I sent you this morning. Now I know why my messenger received no answer.' There was a cutting sarcasm in the quiet voice and it provoked Paul to an angry retort.

'I am not fighting you, Gadiani, not for any reason.'

'That was not what you said to Gregory,' was the taunting reply.

'That was different.' Paul turned to Anna. 'I think you should leave us. This does not concern you. It is something between Prince Gadiani and myself.'

'On the contrary, it concerns her very closely. I think it is time she learned the truth. You asked me, Anna, why Gregory rode alone on the morning of his death. It was Paul Kuragin he went out to meet and it was Paul Kuragin who killed him.'

The shock was so great it held her silent for an instant. 'Is it true?' she breathed.

'That we fought a duel . . . yes, it is true,' he said reluctantly, 'but he did not die by my hand.'

'Whether you shot him through the heart or left him to die makes little difference,' said Daniel Gadiani, 'what is undeniably true is that it was a duel without seconds or witnesses and the murder of a Prince of Kumaria by the hand of a Russian officer could have caused diplomatic complications. The Viceroy hushed it up but the Tsar took good care to strip you of your rank and send you on an impossible mission, isn't that so?'

Paul was silent and Anna could not endure it. 'Why, why did you fight? What had Gregory done to you?'

'There was a reason,' he gave her a look of desperate appeal and Daniel Gadiani laughed unpleasantly.

'Men quarrel over a great many things, Anna, especially when they are drunk . . . cards, horses, even a woman.'

'I'm not excusing myself, Anna. It happened and I regret it. I meant to tell you about it, I swear I did. Over and over again. I came here tonight for that very purpose.'

'But all these weeks, from the very first moment we met, you have kept silent. Why did you lie to me? You told me that he had been imprisoned by Shamyl, that you wanted to help him, that you saw him dead . . .'

'I was not lying. You must believe me, Anna, you must trust me. It was not as he says.'

'Then how was it?' she said bitterly. 'How can I believe anything you say?' She felt as if all her hopes and dreams, all her happiness during the last weeks had been shattered like a house of cards wrecked by a careless hand. She turned to Gadiani. 'I would like to go home.'

'Of course.' He opened the curtain, snapped his fingers and said something to a servant.

'Anna please,' said Paul, 'please do not condemn me. Wait until you know everything . . .'

But she turned away from him. 'I believed you and it was all lies. It has spoiled everything, everything. How can I trust anything you say ever again?'

'Anna, listen to me . . .' but then Daniel Gadiani was back.

'Well,' he said in his silky voice with its touch of steel, 'there is still the question of my sister's honour.'

Paul gave one tortured look at Anna before he said quietly, 'I owe nothing to Natalie. She knows that well enough and so do you.'

'I know only what she tells me. There are certain promises a gentleman should fulfil or suffer the consequences. Do you meet me tomorrow or do I brand you coward as well as murderer?'

'You can go to hell, Gadiani,' said Paul with sudden violence. 'At any other time it would have given me all the pleasure in the world to meet you outside the city and put a bullet through your heart, but what I am engaged on is more important than you, more important than both of us. It must wait until I return.'

'If you do return,' was the ironic answer. 'I shall look forward to it.'

For a moment they still glared at one another, then Paul said, 'Take care of yourself when you go to Kumari, Anna.

Remember that there was a serpent even in the Garden of Eden.' He pushed the curtain aside and thrust his way through the crowded room.

'Now what did he mean by that, I wonder,' murmured Daniel Gadiani, 'such a picturesque phrase.'

'I think I know,' said Anna wearily. 'Would you be good enough to find Marya Petrovna for me? I would like to go home.'

Paul had taken his hat and cloak from the footman and gone down the steps, crossing the garden to where Varga waited with the horses. He damned himself to hell for his folly, regretting the opportunities he had let slip, and yet how could he have explained when it was not a stranger, but Gregory, her husband, the man she had once loved. How could he have told her of Natalie's goading, the tormenting jealousy . . . God forgive him, but on that morning when he had faced Natalie's lover, he had wanted to kill and only a miracle had prevented him from becoming a murderer.

He was so absorbed in his thoughts that he did not hear the stealthy footsteps in the shrubbery until his assailant leaped on him from behind, forcing him to his knees. He fought back fiercely. He saw the knife gleam in the moonlight, the glitter of eyes, then he was on his back, desperately holding the dagger away from him while slowly his arm was bent further and further until the cold touch of the steel pricked at his throat. Then it was all over. His attacker was lifted off him, had fought his way free from the grip that held him, vanishing into the night, and Varga was helping his master to his feet.

'Are you all right, Colonel?'

'Yes, a few bruises, that's all, but it was a damned close thing. My thanks, Varga.'

'Cursed slippery rogue escaped me,' growled the Cossack.

'Leave him. He is not important.'

The men were there with the horses and the baggage animals. Paul threw himself into the saddle and they moved out at a sharp trot. He had caught only a glimpse of his assailant's face but he could have sworn it was Kamil, Bela's brother, and it gave him an unpleasant jolt. Was the boy pursuing his own private grudge or had Daniel Gadiani employed him to serve his own purpose since the attempt to involve him in a duel had come to nothing? How much did he know of their plan? It was a teasing problem and it was to be a long time before he knew the answer.

Part Two

Kumari

Who hath not been a lover? Whom hath the furnace not consumed? Who hath not suffered pain? Why should thy spirits flee? Know'st thou that none e'er plucked a thornless rose?

Shota Rustaveli

——— 9 ———

For most of that night Anna lay sleepless. How could she have been so foolish? Had she learned nothing? She had thought herself so invulnerable, so worldly wise, and she had drifted along all these weeks in a happy dream. She had believed in him utterly and he had deceived her, lied deliberately over and over again, as he had lied to Natalie, to others too perhaps . . . how could she be sure of anything any longer? She raged against him and against herself, and yet, despite her anger, she could not prevent herself thinking of a dozen tiny things that were torment to remember . . . his kindness, his ironic smile, the laughter they had shared, a certainty that he too had endured pain and disillusionment which had somehow given depth to their friendship. If only he had not gone away . . . if only there had been more time . . . then she buried her face in the hot pillow because she knew that, whether she cared to admit it or not, she had fallen foolishly into the trap of love and, however painful, had to fight her way out of it.

The warm airless night seemed to press down on her. She could not stay in bed. She got up, crossing to the opened window and going out on to the balcony. The faint breeze stirred her thin nightgown and the tiles were cold to her bare feet. The black arch of the sky was sprinkled with stars but there was no moon. After a moment she saw with surprise a gleam of light in Bela's room and wondered if the child was sick. Then while she stood there, the black shadow of a man slid out of the door. For an instant with a stab of pain she thought it was Paul and then realized that it was someone smaller and slighter. She shrank back out of sight. Perhaps Bela for all her protestations knew the need for a lover and in spite of the warmth of the night, she shivered, feeling desperately alone, thinking of Paul and the kisses they had shared that afternoon that already seemed a century away.

The shadow flitted along the wall and vanished, the light

went out and abruptly she made up her mind. She would go to Kumari tomorrow or the next day and she would go alone, not wait for Daniel Gadiani or for the Prince to supply an escort or for anyone. Yakov could go with her and that would be sufficient. With that decision firmly in her mind, it was possible to go back to bed, to doze a little and get up early with the determination still strong within her.

She had said nothing to Marya about what had happened in Daniel Gadiani's house simply because she could not endure to talk about it and be forced to admit that her cousin's warning had been justified. They were at breakfast on the verandah outside the dining room when she said, 'I am going to Kumari. Tomorrow if possible.'

'Isn't that rather sudden? Did your cousin speak to you about it last night?'

'No, and I'm not going to wait for him, nor for anyone. I am quite capable of making my own decisions and I shall go alone.'

'My dear, is that wise?'

'I'm tired of having that said to me. In all the weeks we have been here, we have not once heard of anyone being attacked or in any kind of danger. It is not as though I were venturing into the mountains. Paul told me that Kumari is only about fifty miles through quite easy riding country. If we set out at dawn with a relay of horses we could reach there by evening.'

'I doubt if I could,' said Marya dryly.

Anna stretched a hand across the table. 'There's no need for you to come. You've done so much for me and it would be an exhausting journey for you especially when you feel the heat so badly. I must go because I promised and because Gregory wished it.' She felt guilty that she had let the days go by forgetting the urgency in that last letter of his. 'I shall stay for a few days,' she went on, 'and then when I return, we shall go back to Moscow.'

'Isn't there a question of inheritance?'

'That will take months. Lawyers can settle that.'

'Well, I don't know,' said Marya doubtfully. 'Wouldn't it be best to speak to Paul Kuragin about it? Ask his advice?'

'He is no longer here. His orders came from the Prince and he has gone already.'

'I thought I caught sight of him last night. Did he come to say goodbye?'

'Something like that.'

Marya had a shrewd notion that there was more behind Anna's decision than appeared on the surface, but she did not press her. 'You know, my dear, I don't think I can continue to stay in his house. It would be trespassing on his hospitality.'

'It will only be for a few days, a week at the outside.'

'All the same, it would not be right.'

Anna frowned. It was a problem that she had not considered and it was Anfisa who put an end to their indecision. She came in with Darinka who began to clear the dishes. She looked from Anna to Marya obviously upset, but trying to hide it.

'Perhaps you know already that Count Paul went away last night, but before he left, he gave me his orders. "The ladies are to stay as long as they wish," he said to me, "and you and Ivan will do all you can to make them comfortable." He would be angry with me if I were to allow you to move anywhere else while you remain in Tiflis.'

'Thank you, Anfisa. It is very good of him.'

'Every time he goes,' she burst out, 'I go down on my knees and pray to God to bring him back safely, but this time I am so afraid.'

'Why this time especially?' asked Marya gently.

'You don't know him as I do. There was a look on his face . . . it was there last year. I was afraid then,' she made an effort to steady herself. 'I mustn't go on like this.'

'He came back, didn't he?' said Marya comfortingly. 'So why shouldn't he return this time safe and sound?'

'Yes, it is true and I know I shouldn't say such a wicked thing but the fact is, Marya Petrovna, his mother never had any care for him. From the very moment he was taken from her, he has been like my own.'

'I understand.' Marya urged the old nurse to sit down and drink some coffee with them and when she had calmed down a little, Anna began to speak about Kumari. Anfisa was shocked at her decision to go virtually alone and it was only after a great deal of argument that she said at last, 'Well, at least you can take Marik with you.'

'Marik? Surely he has gone with his master.'

'No. He left him behind with orders to put himself at your disposal. Marik has been here with him from the beginning. He knows the country well.'

She was forced to acknowledge Paul's thought for her and

be grateful to have someone as steady and reliable as Marik to go with her and Yakov.

'There you are,' she said turning to Marya with a little laugh, 'I shall be perfectly safe and in a little while I shall be back again.'

She spent the day making a few preparations and packing a small valise with a minimum of clothes and necessities. She was in her room washing her hands before supper when there was a knock. She called 'Come in' and after a moment Bela came through the door.

'May I speak to you, Madame?'

'Yes, of course. What is it?'

'Do you know where Count Paul has gone?'

'No, I don't,' she said surprised. 'He is on a special mission for the Viceroy.'

'I thought he would have told you . . .'

'Why should he?' Se put down the towel and turned to look at Bela. The girl was very pale and there was a dark shadow on one cheek like a bruise. Anna felt suddenly alarmed. 'Is something wrong?'

'I don't know . . . my brother came here last night very late. He kept asking questions about Count Paul and about you . . . I didn't tell him anything, I swear I didn't, but he went on and on,' she put a hand to her face.

'Did he do that?'

'Yes, he was angry . . . with himself, I think, and so he punished me. Kamil is like that. His coat was torn. Something had happened to him. I asked him if he had been fighting but he would not answer.'

'What are you trying to tell me?'

'He frightened me. I thought if we could send a warning to Count Paul.'

'A warning of what?'

'I'm not sure,' she sounded near to tears, 'but I think Kamil knows something and the Count could be in danger.'

'It's not possible, Bela,' Anna said gently. 'He might be anywhere in the mountains by now.'

The girl drew a deep breath. 'Perhaps I am being foolish and he would laugh at me for it, but I had to tell someone. If you should see him, will you tell him?'

'I don't think I shall see him, Bela. I am going to Kumari and then back to Russia.'

'Oh I had thought that . . .' the girl stopped and moved towards the door. 'I am sorry to have been so silly.'

'Not silly at all. It is right for you to be concerned for him, but I think Count Paul knows what he is doing.'

'Yes, of course. Goodnight, Madame.'

'Goodnight.'

She tried to dismiss it from her mind. What could this wild boy do to harm Paul or her? It was all so vague, so shadowy, but all the same she was conscious of a quavering of the nerves and a sudden wave of longing for her father, for the ordinary everyday things of home. A few days, she thought to herself, a week perhaps and it will all be behind her.

They left at four in the morning with a sky faintly tinged with pink. She clung to Marya when she kissed her, suddenly feeling very alone. She would miss her cheerful practical good sense. Anfisa and Ivan came to the stables to see her leave, imploring her to be careful. It was not until they had crossed the Kura and were riding north-east up the bare dusty river valley that Anna thought of another dawn when Gregory must have gone out along this same road to meet Paul Kuragin and go to his death.

It was a long ride and far more gruelling than she had antici-pated, but she pressed on doggedly, enduring heat and dust and weariness, glad because it left her no time or energy to brood. They crossed a range of low hills and came into a fer-tile plain riding through villages surrounded by fields of ripe maize and mile after mile of vineyards where the grapes were already being gathered.

'This is all Kumaria,' said Marik, pointing with his whip through a screen of poplars to a line of distant blue moun-tains. 'All this belonged to Prince Gadiani.'

Somehow she had never envisaged it. It was not a mere country estate but a small kingdom where if Gregory had lived, she might have come one day to rule it with him. It was almost dark by the time they reached the handsome park gates so that she saw little as they came up the winding drive except that the house was long and low, built of a pinkish-white stone with windows on the first floor opening on to wide balconies.

They were welcomed with a certain reserve by a butler wearing the Caucasian dress of full black breeches and close-fitting coat. He bowed low when she gave her name, inform-ing her that the Princess had already retired, but a room would be prepared at once and the two men with the horses accommodated.

She was far too weary to take in very much except be grateful for the large airy room to which she was taken. They brought her cool water to wash and food which she was almost too exhausted to eat. She fell thankfully into bed.

Morning brought a maidservant with a tray of coffee, hot buttered rolls, a dish of grapes and an urgent summons to attend as soon as possible on her highness, Princess Gadiani of Kumaria.

Gregory's grandmother was not at all as she had expected. She was tiny for one thing, a mere handful of skin and bone beneath innumerable shawls and veils of deep rich purple edged with gold. But the bright black eyes in the brown wizened face were filled with a lively intelligence. The room was a mingling of east and west, lavish Persian rugs on the tiled floor, handsome painted and gilded furniture, priceless silk hangings on the walls, a silver cage in the window filled with brightly coloured twittering birds and a long slim dog of a breed she had never seen lying beside the couch where the Princess sat bolt upright amidst a pile of brilliant cushions.

'So you are Gregory's wife,' she said sharply as Anna hesitated on the threshold. 'Come here to me. Closer, closer,' she added as Anna crossed the room. She shot out a stick-like arm and gripped her wrist pulling her towards her and peering up into her face for what seemed a long moment before she released her.

'Good bones,' she said at last. 'You'll do. He chose well.'

The room was very hot and rather dark, the shutters partly closed against the morning sun. With her swift darting movements, the diamonds in her ears, the rubies in the head-dress that held the veil on the white hair, the thin fingers loaded with rings, the Princess reminded Anna of the exotic birds she had seen in the Prince's aviary in the Botanic Gardens.

'I am so happy to be here at last,' she said awkwardly.

'Are you? You've taken long enough about it,' was the disconcerting reply. Then the Princess smiled a little. 'Well, well, it's only natural and an old woman is not all that attractive. You may kiss me, my dear.'

The dry papery cheek smelled of sandalwood. The eyes that were so curiously young and bright looked her up and down critically.

'You have a certain beauty, different from others. No doubt that is what caught his eye. We never expected it, you know. He should have married one of his own kind.'

'It might have been better if he had,' said Anna tartly.

The Princess's eyes flashed, then unexpectedly she gave a little cackle of laughter. 'Well, that's honest at any rate. It wasn't all a bed of dreams, eh? Did he treat you badly?' and when Anna hesitated, uncertain how to reply, she went on impatiently. 'Never mind, never mind. The boy is dead and we must think of the future. Did Daniel Gadiani come with you?'

'No.'

'You travelled alone?'

'Yes, except for my two men servants.'

'That was courageous of you, my dear. You have met Daniel, I suppose?'

'Yes.'

'Do you like him?'

'I scarcely know him.'

'He can make himself agreeable, I am well aware of that.' She spoke with an infinite contempt. 'And he will come here, of that I'm sure. He is afraid of what I may say to you.'

'Why should he be?'

'You'll know soon enough. When he comes, I will not receive him. I'll be glad if you will remember that.'

'Of course, if you wish.'

'I detested his father and I detest him, and his sister is a whore.'

'Oh no,' said Anna startled.

'Oh yes. When she was a child, I was obliged to have Natalie staying here for a time. Even then I knew her for what she was and I'm not so shut away that I do not hear things, nor so old that I cannot sift truth from lies.'

Was she thinking of Paul? The black eyes watched her and Anna looked quickly away with the queer feeling that they probed into her very soul reading thoughts that she would have preferred to keep hidden. She began to feel bewildered. Perhaps Daniel Gadiani was right after all. Perhaps the Princess was a little mad. She was grateful when a maidservant came in with a silver coffee pot on a tray. With her came a handsome black-haired child of about five years of age. He ran across the room and then stopped short, staring at Anna, his hands behind his back.

'Where are your manners, Vanya?' said the old lady testily. 'This is Anna, Gregory's wife. You remember Gregory?'

'Yes, Grandmamma. He gave me Suki. I was coming to fetch her.' Shyly the child stretched out a small hand. 'You are welcome to Kumari.'

'That's better, spoken very nicely,' said the Princess with approval. She waved her hand imperiously. 'Go now, my dear Anna. You and I have much to talk about but there will be time later. You can come back this evening and sup with me.'

The child had run to the dog, kneeling down and putting an arm round the silky neck. The servant was pouring the coffee. Abruptly dismissed, Anna went out of the room and down the wide staircase, disconcerted, a little amused. 'Really,' she said to herself, 'it is like being received by royalty. Even the Tsarina is not quite so imperious!' She wondered who the child could be. He had called the Princess grandmamma and yet she couldn't remember Gregory ever speaking about a boy in his old home.

The next few days were very strange. She saw the Princess morning and evening, but they spoke only of trivialities. She would ask probing questions about Russia, about Petersburg and Moscow, about her parents, which Anna answered as well as she could, revealing more of herself than she realized. Then in her turn the Princess would speak of life at Kumari in the old days when Gregory's grandfather ruled his petty kingdom under Russian overlordship. More and more Anna began to understand that the tiny bejewelled figure in the exotic room was the hub of the household around whom everything revolved and not only with regard to domestic matters. She was kept informed of every detail of the grape harvest, which of the barrels of fine wine maturing in the cool damp cellars were ready for sale, exactly how much was being offered in the markets for corn, oil and sunflower seeds. She settled complaints, administered justice and every day spent long hours closeted with her steward.

With nothing to occupy her time Anna was free to explore house and gardens. She wandered through vast rooms, the furniture shrouded in sheets, the candelabra and the gold-framed mirrors thick with dust, a great hall where a hundred could comfortably be seated around the long table and a gallery where once native musicians must have played behind the carved screen through interminable banquets. Servants swarmed everywhere. They stared at her curiously, bowing politely and standing aside to let her pass, but except for the butler and the steward they spoke no Russian.

Kumari was so far from any town that it had to be self supporting. In the vast kitchen quarters there was always intense activity, milk churns being rolled across stone floors, great shallow basins filled with rich yellow cream, eggs being beaten, knives sharpened, meat roasting on spits. There was the cloying sweetness of rose-leaf jam, the sharp tang of apricots, the pungent smell of spices, the bitter-sweet scent of green peppers slowly simmering on a hot stove. An enormous industry and all for the Princess, one small boy and herself.

The gardens were carefully tended. Long stretches of grass stretching down to the river were watered laboriously every day. The rose garden hummed with bees from the straw-thatched hives in the orchard and in the evening, when she sat with the windows opened, the nightingales sang with a piercing heart-breaking clarity in the groves of lime and acacia.

It was then that she found herself thinking of Paul. During the day she could force herself to be interested in other things but sitting late into the night with the moths hurtling themselves against the glass shade around the candles, she remembered how one day he had spoken to her of Arachino, of how in the hot dry summer the frogs climbed out of the lake, their backs iridescent green in the moonlight, how the white peacocks strutted on the lawns, how once as a child he had been thrown from his pony and spent nearly a year flat on his back.

'That was when my English governess came,' he told her. 'You remind me of her, only her hair is a darker more fiery red. I thought she was beautiful. I fell in love at once and made up my mind to marry her when I grew up, but my Uncle Andrei beat me to it.'

'He married your governess?'

'Yes.'

There had been a gentleness in Paul's voice when he spoke of his home and she sensed an aching loneliness beneath the irony that he used as a protective shield. He was smiling as he went on. 'The marriage caused quite a stir, but he had always gone his own way.'

A rebel like his nephew, she thought, and wondered if he was the uncle who had been his mother's lover.

What did the Princess mean when she called Natalie a whore? Had that been part of his bitterness? Had she betrayed his love as his mother had betrayed his father? Why, oh why had he killed Gregory? At that point, she would get up, blow out the candles and go to bed.

Sometimes during the day she would see the child running with his dog with all the grace and beauty of a young animal. He was still shy of her. If she spoke to him, he would mumble a few words and then race away and she would hear him chattering to the servants in their native tongue though to her and the Princess he spoke a careful correct Russian.

The gardens ran down to the little river and there was a small stone summer house on the bank. There in the afternoon she would sit with a book, reading and dreaming. Across the stream lay the blue line of the mountains shimmering in the languorous summer heat or wrapped at sunset in a pearly pink glow, so beautiful that it was almost impossible to believe that beyond the Russian line of garrisons, lay the menace of Shamyl and his black horsemen and that somewhere out there Paul was pursuing his perilous mission.

She was still no nearer to finding out what it was that Gregory had wanted from her. She had a queer feeling that she was here on trial, that the Princess's questions had a purpose though what it was she couldn't imagine. She had been at Kumari for a week when she made up her mind that, delightful though it was, she could not stay indefinitely but must ask the Princess outright what was required of her and that afternoon she received a letter.

'From Prince Gadiani,' the servant said as she took it from the silver salver. She broke the seal.

'I am sorry that you should have decided to go to Kumari alone,' Daniel had written. 'I would have been so happy to accompany you. I hope the revelation I was obliged to make at our last meeting did not distress you unduly.' She ran her eye down the sheet. It seemed that he proposed to call in a few days on his way east. 'I know well that I am not always welcome to the Princess but all the same I would like to be sure of your well-being for Gregory's sake. As I told you, she is not altogether to be trusted.'

Really, she thought impatiently, they are warning me against each other. Are they in love with mystery for its own sake?

That evening after she had supped with the Princess and the boy had been brought in to say goodnight, she said, 'I've had a letter from Daniel Gadiani.'

The bird-like head turned sharply towards her. 'What does he say?'

'Only that he will be calling here in a few days' time.'

'In that case it would be best to move quickly,' said the Princess with decision. 'I would have preferred you to have stayed longer, to win Vanya's confidence, perhaps even his affection. It would have been easier for both of you.'

Mystified Anna said, 'What have I to do with Vanya?'

'A great deal. Did Gregory never tell you about him?'

'Never. In his last letter he asked that I should come to the Caucasus and if anything happened to him, then you would tell me why. That is the reason I am here.'

'He never approved of what his father had done,' said the Princess dryly, 'but he knew what was required of him and what will now be required of you in his place. Go to the door, Anna, make sure no one is listening.'

'Why should they?'

'My dear, where have you lived to remain so innocent, so naïve? The house is full of servants. How can I be sure that all are loyal to me? A large enough bribe can corrupt even the most faithful heart.'

'She really is a little mad,' thought Anna, humouring her by going to the door, peering up the passage and then closing it again. 'There is no one there.'

'Good. Now go to that chest over there. In it you will find a casket.'

The long box of red lacquer was magnificently carved, a bride's dower chest perhaps. When she opened it, there was a faint dry smell of some exotic perfume. She turned over folded silks and velvets, veils and embroidered shawls, until her groping fingers felt the hard outline of a small box. When she lifted it out, she realized it was made of silver dulled with age and very heavy. She carried it to the table.

'Is this it?'

The Princess brought a tiny key from some inner pocket and unlocked it. 'Now open it.'

Anna lifted the lid and gasped. It was filled with jewels: rubies, sapphires, emeralds, ropes of pearls, bracelets, brooches, rings.

'They are yours,' said the Princess.

'Mine? But . . . this is nonsense. I couldn't possibly accept them.'

'Of course you can. They were part of my dowry and I can give them to whom I please. There is no other way I can reward you for what you have to do. They can be sold. I don't know their value but it must be considerable.'

Anna stood back, shaking her head in bewilderment, feeling more and more that she was no longer living in the sane world of everyday but had wandered into some fantastic Eastern fairy tale. 'But I don't need any reward. Whatever it is Gregory wanted me to do, I am ready to carry out if it is at all possible because I was his wife, because it is my duty.'

The Princess sighed. 'You say that now. You may feel differently when you hear what I have to tell you. Sit down, my dear.'

Anna pulled up one of the velvet-covered stools and sat close to the couch. Through the opened window came the breath of the scented summer night. The silver lamp burned on the low table. The room was very quiet, even the birds had fallen silent, their heads tucked beneath their wings.

'It began,' said the Princess, 'many years ago with the birth of twin boys to the reigning Prince of Kumaria. One of them, Alexander, was Gregory's grandfather and my husband. He was born ten minutes before his brother Josef and so rightful heir to the lands and wealth of his ancestors and to a lifetime of jealousy and treachery on the part of his brother.'

'Was Josef the grandfather of Daniel Gadiani?'

'Yes.'

'Is that why you won't receive him?'

The Princess smiled wryly. 'That is a personal matter. I do not care for the way he and his sister live.' She was silent for a moment before she said slowly, 'I have nothing specific against Daniel. I have no proof of his enmity but I know what his father and his grandfather have done to us and so I am afraid.'

'Afraid of what? And what has Vanya to do with it?'

'You will see. Have patience, my dear. There is not a great deal to tell but I must tell it in my own way. By the time Alexander and Josef had grown to manhood, the whole of south Caucasia had come under Russian rule but at first there were many who rebelled against it. We are a proud people and it was not easy to bend the head to the yoke. Alexander was reluctant to give up his independence but he was farseeing and he realized the advantages. You must understand, my dear Anna, that for many centuries we have been under constant attack from Persians, from Turks, from Greeks, ravaging, burning and looting our lands. With the Russians at our backs we could hope for peace and security and so he submitted with good grace.'

'But Josef did not think like him?'

'No. Always from a boy he felt cheated. When he was of age he had been given a house and lands of his own but it was never enough. He lusted for power and now was his chance. He intrigued with the tribesmen in the mountains.

My son, Gregory's father, was only sixteen when Alexander was killed in a skirmish when they came ravaging through our lands.'

'And you were left here alone?'

'It was nothing new to me. Alexander had sometimes been away on campaign with the Russians, but this time it was different. Although it seems so peaceful here at Kumari, we are not far from the border and at that time there was not so strong a line of defence as there is now. Have you any idea what it is like to live in perpetual fear? There was a time when we hardly knew whether we should live through one day to the next and twice we were driven from the house and forced to take refuge in the woods with the servants and the children until the Russians came and drove the invaders from our lands. The second time that happened Gregory's mother died from shock and exposure.'

'How did you endure it?'

'It was not easy and there came a day when I knew we must send the boy away. Gregory went to Petersburg as the ward of the Tsar where he could grow up in safety.'

'How angry you must have been when he married me.'

'Disappointed rather than angry. We hoped for a son.'

'I am sorry . . .'

The Princess stretched out a hand and touched her cheek. 'Who are we to question what God sends us? My son had not the strength or wisdom of his father but he was not a fool. He took precautions. Six years ago he married again, only he kept it secret from everyone, even from me. The girl he chose was a nobody, an orphan on whom I had taken pity and who had grown up here. When I learned she was with child, I reproached him bitterly but still he said nothing and it was only after his death that I knew the truth. Vanya is Gregory's half brother and now rightful heir to Kumaria.'

'Was that when you wrote to Gregory asking him to come back to the Caucasus?'

'I was afraid for him. Everyone believed the boy to be a bastard, a child of no account, but how could I be sure? You see my son had been murdered . . .'

'Murdered! But Gregory told me that his father . . .'

'Died in a hunting accident.' The Princess leaned forward, the thin fingers clutching Anna's wrist, pulling her near to her. 'They called it that but I knew better. He was a magnificent rider and he had known the mountains from a child. When they brought his body back here, they tried to prevent me

seeing him. I knew then that he had been murdered.' Anna
stared at her, shocked, unable to believe and the Princess
drew back reading the doubt on her face. 'You think I exag-
gerate. What do you know of the people here? Not long ago
the three young Princes of Avaria were butchered because
their mother refused to break her alliance with the Russians.
A child is so vulnerable. I wanted Gregory to take him back
to Russia. When he came here, he told me of you. "My wife is
brave," he said, "and loyal. She will care for Vanya. She will
bring him up as you would wish. You need have no fear,
Grandmamma." '

Anna turned away her head, moved because in spite of everything that had happened between them, Gregory could still
speak of her with affection.

'I warned him to take care, but Gregory had been so long
away in Petersburg, he had forgotten the old hatreds, the old
fears. He was to have returned to take the child but he never
came, only the news that he had disappeared, vanished without trace, murdered like his father and his grandfather.'

'No, it was not like that,' said Anna painfully. 'It was a
duel. When I first came to the Caucasus, I was determined to
find out the truth. It took time and I only discovered it just
before coming here.'

'A duel?' repeated the Princess incredulously. 'With
whom?'

'A Russian officer.'

'Why?'

'I don't know. They quarrelled as men do sometimes.'

'No, no, my dear, that is what you have been told, but I do
not believe it. Someone knew what he intended to do and
meant to prevent it. I know he feared something of the sort.'

Anna felt as though she were clutching at straws. Perhaps
Paul had not lied after all, not entirely. Perhaps she had mis-
judged him and he had not been responsible for Gregory's
death, but she must not think of that now.

She said, 'Why didn't you go to Prince Vorontsov, tell him
everything and ask him to take charge of Vanya?'

The Princess lay back amongst her cushions. She looked
very tired. 'There were many reasons. For one thing I am
old. I can no longer make the journey to Tiflis, but above all
I have learned to trust no one, not even the Russians.'

'They would not harm a child,' exclaimed Anna.

'Perhaps not, but they would turn him into one of themselves as they did Gregory. Oh I saw what they had done to

him clearly enough. He had forgotten his heritage. He cared nothing for Kumaria or the people who depend on him. They would do the same with Vanya, pampering him at their Court, a puppet prince, while they ruled here in his place and I will not allow that. Kumaria belongs to us, to the Gadiani. For five hundred years it has been handed down from father to son. Can you understand that?'

'Yes, I think so,' said Anna doubtfully, 'but what can I do?'

The Princess leaned forward. 'I want you to take charge of the boy as if he were your own. I know all about you, my dear, from Gregory and from others. I know about your father, your upbringing, your training, and now I have seen you and spoken with you, I believe I have made a good choice. There will be money enough for his needs and yours, and when the time is ripe, he will come back here.'

Anna stared at her. It was so unexpected. She trembled at the weight of the responsibility that would be placed on her shoulders and yet, at the same time, something in her responded to it. It would give her life a purpose, take away the emptiness, make it worthwhile.

The Princess was watching her. 'Are you afraid?'

'No, it is only that . . .'

'You think all this merely exists in the feverish imagination of a silly old woman, a fantasy grown out of family feuds with no substance in fact.'

'No, it is not that,' Anna felt ashamed that her thoughts had been read so easily.

'Yes, it is and it is quite natural, but you need not worry. I am not crazy and I have papers made out with proof of the child's birth and you shall take them with you.' Suddenly she was clinging to Anna's hand, urgently whispering. 'You must go soon. Every day's delay adds to the danger now that Gregory is dead. If the boy dies or is kidnapped, then Kumaria and all our people who trust us will belong to Daniel Gadiani.'

'So it is he whom you fear.'

'I don't know, I tell you, all I know for certain is that envy and greed have been like a poison corroding our lives, a poison that will destroy Vanya as it has destroyed Gregory and his father and I want this done before Daniel can prevent it.'

'Wouldn't it be better if I sent Yakov to the Viceroy and asked for a military escort to Tiflis?'

'I thought that at first but Prince Vorontsov will have to

know the reason and Daniel holds a high position on his Council. They may not leave the child with you.' The Princess sat back, her voice suddenly cold. 'Is it too much to ask? If so, tell me now at once and I will find other means.'

For a moment Anna still hesitated, then she raised her head proudly. 'I will do as you ask. I will take the boy.'

'I knew I was not mistaken. That is what Gregory said of you, "If she makes a promise, she will keep it." Tomorrow we will arrange everything. You will go quietly, unobtrusively, with your servants and two of my men. We can tell everyone that you are taking the child to Tiflis for medical treatment and then no one will guess. It will be hard to part with him. He has been my joy, something to live for . . .'

Anna bent forward to take the Princess's hand. 'Is it really necessary to send him away? Surely here with so many people to guard and care for him, he will be safe.'

'No. I am being weak when I must be strong. It is Kumari that matters, not an old woman who has outlived her time.' She sighed, looking very old and frail. 'I am weary now. Come back to me in the morning, Anna. There will be much to do.'

On impulse she kissed the withered cheek and then she went out of the room. As she moved up the stairs, she saw the figure of a man cross in front of the single lamp burning in the shadowy hall. He turned and the light fell on his face. For an instant she thought it was the young man she had seen coming out of Bela'a room that night in Paul's house and she remembered the girl's distress and her fear of what her brother might do. Then he had gone towards the kitchen quarters and she went on to her own room thinking that she must have imagined it. There were so many servants at Kumari it was impossible to know them all.

The candles had already been lit, her nightgown laid out on the bed, the ewer filled with fresh water, everything quiet and as usual. Away from the Princess, away from the strange spell woven in that lavish room, the whole story seemed fantastic, more like something out of a melodrama than real life in the middle of the nineteenth century. She thought of how her father would smile at such a bizarre plot, violence and murder, a family twisted by old jealousies, old hatreds . . . and yet there had been a compelling power as the Princess had related it.

She stood for a moment, facing up squarely to what she had taken on herself. Then she dipped her face in the cool water and began to undress. After all what was there to fear? There was only the short journey to Tiflis and from then on, with Marya to help her, it should be easy. Something resolute and strong within her rose to meet the challenge. She would take Vanya to Moscow where she would have the advice and guidance of her father. She would fulfil her promise to Gregory and perhaps in the child who was his half brother, she would find something to satisfy the hunger for the baby she had lost.

——10——

It was Yakov who suggested that they should take two days over the journey.

'The child is young, Barina. It is a long ride for a little one and we will need to rest in the heat of midday.'

To Anna's surprise he had already become something of a hero to the fatherless little boy. It was a great relief for, having no brothers or sisters, she had never had very much to do with young children and now she had accepted the responsibility, she was feeling woefully inadequate.

Tears were not far away when Vanya said goodbye to his grandmother and his nurse. All his short life had been spent at Kumari and suddenly he was being taken away by a stranger, leaving his toys, his dog, the kittens in the kitchens, the ponies in the stables, everything that was dear and familiar. But he was a Gadiani and Gadianis never cry and are afraid of nothing, said the Princess sternly, so he tried hard to be brave when she hugged him to her.

'You must be good and obedient and do just as Anna tells you, Vanya, promise me. It won't be for long. I shall see you soon.' Her hand caressed the boy's dark hair and then abruptly she pushed him away from her and turned her back. 'Go,' she whispered in a muffled voice, 'go now quickly.'

Anna hesitated and then took the child's hand and led him from the room. Outside in the courtyard Yakov took one look at the small woebegone face.

'Come along, little master,' he said cheerfully, 'you're a man now and you're going to show us how splendidly you can ride, isn't that so?' He lifted him into the saddle of the pony, winking at Anna behind Vanya's back. 'When he tires, I'll take him up with me.'

They set off, two sturdy peasants from Kumari riding with them. The documents with the casket which the Princess had insisted on Anna taking with her were strapped with her valise to the back of the baggage mule.

Again it was Yakov who suggested that they should camp for the night in a quiet valley among the hills that lay between them and Tiflis.

'We shall be safer there, Barina, away from people who show too much interest and ask too many questions.'

Anna had told him nothing beyond the bare fact that she had been asked by the Princess to take the child to Tiflis for a consultation with the Viceroy's own physician since last winter he had developed a weakness in the chest. But Yakov was no fool and she was sure he had guessed something of the truth though he said nothing. It was not his fault that he had miscalculated. The dark young man in the kitchens at Kumari had been remarkably well informed about the most suitable camping sites on the road to Tiflis.

They stopped in the early evening on the banks of a little stream. Vanya who had slept most of the afternoon in the crook of Yakov's arm was lively as a grasshopper, running here, there and everywhere, fascinated by the unusual thrill of eating a picnic supper and sleeping in a little tent instead of his big painted bed at Kumari. He helped Marik gather wood for the fire, learned how to make a spark by rubbing two sticks together and was entranced to sit down to meat and tomatoes instead of his customary bread and milk.

'He'll never sleep,' said Anna ruefully as she wiped the child's mouth and hands with a damp towel.

'Let him run about a little. The air will soon make him drowsy and then he'll be crying for his bed,' answered Yakov easily. She only hoped that he was right.

The men sat down to their own supper at a little distance and Vanya tugged at her hand.

'I want to see where the river goes.'

'We'll walk a little way along the bank. Would you like that?'

He gave a whoop and ran ahead at once, now and again pausing on the brink to stir up the mud with a stick and then racing on again, kicking up stones to throw into the water.

The river ran through a copse of low scrubby trees and Anna hurried after him. 'Vanya,' she called, trying to keep him in sight, 'Vanya, take care. Don't go too far.'

There was no reply and suddenly she was afraid and began to run, stumbling over the broken ground. She came through the trees as she heard him call excitedly.

'Anna, Anna, come quickly. Look!'

Then she saw him. He was standing in the middle of a narrow bridge made of a split log and beside him was the slim dark young man whom she believed she had seen the night before at Kumari.

'Look, Anna,' exclaimed the boy again. 'Look what the man has given me,' and he held up a little dagger. 'It is a *kinjal* and it is for me, for my very own.'

'Vanya, come back here at once. It is dangerous. You might fall in.'

She took a step on the creaking log and instantly the young man picked up the child and leaped for the opposite bank. The boy cried out in fright and she stumbled after them, the log shaking and turning under her feet. She screamed as loudly as she could for Yakov. Vanya was kicking frantically in his captor's arms. She tried desperately to reach him and slipped in the mud falling to her knees. Then suddenly there were men all around her, black figures that seemed to emerge like magic from out of the trees.

She screamed again and immediately something was thrown over her head. She struggled wildly in the heavy stifling folds of a *bourka* but strong hands pinioned her arms to her sides and a rope was tied around her so that she could see nothing.

Through the muffling folds she could hear shouting, the sound of running footsteps, a heavy thud and a splash. Yakov and the other men must have reached them by now, but they were only four and there had seemed a dozen at least surrounding her. She was being dragged along the ground. She fell and was jerked to her feet stumbling against something that snorted and pawed the ground. Then she felt herself lifted and flung across a saddle, a man mounted behind her and held her firmly while the horse moved swiftly into a gallop.

It was the most terrifying experience of her life. She could not move or cry out. She had no idea of what had happened to Vanya or Yakov and the others. The only thing that she was sure of was that these were Shamyl's horsemen and they must be somehow linked with Daniel Gadiani. How could she and the Princess have been so naïve as to imagine they could outwit such a subtle and clever enemy? Why had she not believed in the danger and taken greater precautions against it? She had a sickening certainty that she had fallen headlong into a trap. Her guess at the dark young man's identity had been right and if she had only trusted her instinct and warned the Princess that he was in all probability a spy in

Daniel Gadiani's pay, she could have saved Vanya and herself.

The ride went on and on. She was nauseated by the musty smell of the enveloping cloak, bruised and battered as the rough ground threw her from side to side, so that it was impossible to think clearly and it took all her courage not to fall into a hopeless despair. Sometimes they seemed to be climbing, sometimes she felt the horse slither and slide as they descended some stony slope. Once they splashed through a stream and she felt the water soak her feet and skirts.

She had no idea of how long they had been travelling but it seemed hours before she felt the pace slacken to a trot. They were no longer climbing and after another interminable time there was a shout, the horse pulled up, her captor dismounted and lifted her to the ground, her feet and legs so numbed she could scarcely stand. The rope was undone, the heavy folds of the *bourka* pulled away and for a few seconds it was such a relief just to breathe clean air that she stood swaying giddily, close to collapse. Then she took hold of herself and looked around her. It was already quite dark and at first she could see little. Then gradually she realized they were on a kind of plateau completely surrounded by mountains. It was a bleak bare place with nothing but a partly ruined stone hut. About nine or ten men were standing by their horses and seemed to be waiting for something. Then everything came back to her with a rush.

'Where is the child?' she demanded furiously. 'What have you done with the boy?'

No one spoke. Then one of the men came forward and she saw that he was carrying Vanya. He put the child down and gave him a push. The little boy stumbled towards her, burying a dirty tearstained face against her. She knelt down, putting her arms around him, soothing and comforting him before she spoke.

'Where are you taking us?'

One of the men laughed. He swaggered up to her, pulling her to her feet, chucking her under the chin, saying something so that the others burst into loud guffaws, hushed instantly as a man appeared in the doorway of the hut.

He silenced them with a gesture, then came across to Anna. 'Come,' he said.

'I'm not going anywhere unless you tell me why we have been kidnapped and where you are taking us.'

He stared at her. He was tall and well made. In his way he

was good-looking despite the scar of a sabre cut across one cheek, but she was in no mood to appreciate it.

He said in slow Russian, 'You will find out in good time. Now it is best that you sleep, you and the child. We have a long way to go.'

She realized the uselessness of argument. She was completely in their hands, many miles from any kind of help. So far as she could see there were no other prisoners and there was no sign of the dark young man. What had happened to Yakov and Marik? Were they dead? Her whole body ached with fatigue. She was tormented by anxiety for the child and terror of what might happen to them, but he was right in one thing, they must rest if they were to go on living.

'Come, Vanya,' she said and walked towards the hut.

The man picked up the *bourka* and followed after her. At the door he threw it to her. 'Cover the boy. The night will be cold,' he said and shut the door.

There was nothing in the hut but a bundle of straw in one corner that she soon found to be verminous. She covered it with the cloak. Vanya was whimpering. She pulled him close to her, cradling him in her arms, talking to him, any words of comfort she could think of until presently, worn out by fatigue and fright, he fell asleep. But she lay long awake, hearing the jingle of harness, men laughing and talking as they moved around until at last there was silence and she slept fitfully until they were wakened at dawn. This time the man who had spoken to her the night before and who was apparently their leader, put her on a horse tying her to the saddle. Then he took Vanya up in front of him. They set out again, one of the other men seizing her bridle and pulling her horse after him.

There were times during the weeks that followed when she was astonished at the resilience of the human body. If anyone had told her that she and a five-year-old child reared in every kind of luxury could survive on a handful of rough millet meal moistened with water into a tasteless dough and a few strips of almost uneatable dried meat, she would never have believed it possible and yet they did. At first Vanya refused pointblank to touch any of the unpalatable food and one of the tribesmen brought them some goat's milk, but at last, driven by hunger, he ate it just as she did. In most of the villages they passed through, they were stared at with dislike but once or twice a woman would take pity on the child. Anna found herself desperately grateful for a withered apple, a crust of dry mouldy bread, for a mutton bone with a little meat on it that they gnawed for two days trying to soothe the pangs of starvation.

The journey was fearful, a dreary repetition of the first few hours only far worse. They climbed precipices so steep that they had to dismount and crawl up, dragging the horses behind them until her hands and knees were raw and bleeding. They descended into ravines of thick scrub where the men had to hack their way through with their swords and they were tormented by flies and mosquitoes. They crossed an icy torrent so deep that the horses floundered and, clinging to the bridle, she was soaked to the skin. They slept where they could, in one of the mountain huts, in a disused granary, in an old stone tower, or more often than not on the ground, huddled together and shivering with cold. She tried to preserve certain decencies but alone with a company of men it was a continuous misery.

The child recovered his spirits first. Rough and brutal as the men often were, they had a kindness for the sturdy little boy. They taught him how to use the dagger in his belt, they vied with each other to take him up on his horses; once she found him sitting with them as they lounged around their camp fire, singing their strange melancholy songs. He watched them at their Moslem ritual, twice a day prostrating themselves, facing the East, chanting and calling on Allah. Once she caught him imitating them, kneeling as they did, muttering and bowing to the ground, and snatched him away. She realized how easy it would be for so young a child to be trained in their ways, to forget his early life, to lose his Christian heritage for ever.

Again and again she questioned their leader whose name she discovered to be Kezia Mahommed, but he always returned the same answer. She would know when they reached their journey's end. In the meantime he drove them on relentlessly. One day they must have skirted a Russian outpost because unexpectedly they met up with a small band of soldiers. She saw the familiar uniform and for an instant her hopes ran high, but Kezia was not fighting. He relied on the magnificent horsemanship of his men and he drove straight through the little troop scattering them to right and left. Her despairing cries were lost in the blood-curdling shouts of the tribesmen waving their curved swords above their heads. She looked back with the worst feeling of despair she had known since she and the child had been captured.

That night they descended into a valley where the grass was green, where flowers still bloomed and the air was warm. By now she had grown accustomed to the violent contrasts in the Caucasian mountains. For the first time in many days she pulled off Vanya's little shirt and washed his face and neck in the river. Her riding skirt was torn and filthy, her blouse stained with sweat. She told him to sit quietly and walked further up the stream as far out of sight of the men as she could and then took off her blouse. The water was ice-cold but wonderfully refreshing. She had no soap or any washing material but greatly daring, she dipped her head in the rush of the river, letting it soak away the dust and stickiness. She was drying it as best she could with her petticoat when a sound made her look up. One of the men was standing only a few feet away, his eyes devouring her.

She huddled the rag of linen around her. 'Go away,' she said fiercely, 'Go away!'

He grunted but did not move. Then one of the others shouted something and reluctantly he dragged his eyes from her and walked quickly back along the bank.

Shivering with shock she pulled on her blouse again. Up till then, though the men sometimes eyed her curiously, none of them had touched her. That night it was stiflingly hot in the little windowless shack where they were to sleep and she would have liked to leave the door ajar but did not dare. There was no lock or catch so she wedged it with a piece of wood. She made up a bed for Vanya on one side of the hut and lay down half covered by the *bourka*, her damp hair spread around her.

She was awakened by the door being forced back, but before she could move a man was kneeling beside her, pinning her down. She smelled the rank odour of sweat, heard his heavy breathing. He tore open her blouse and she felt the rough touch of the bearded face pressed against her breast. She screamed, struggling violently before the greedy mouth clamped down on hers. His hands were already fumbling at her skirts when he was seized, lifted off her and booted through the door. Sick and terrified she saw Kezia staring down at her, his eyes glittering in the faint light, panting as if he had been running a race.

She tried to cover her breasts, so frozen with horror that she could not speak. So it had come. What she had feared from the beginning. The nightmare had become reality. First one, then the other. Would they all take their turn? He stood there for what seemed an eternity but was no more than a few seconds, then he turned and strode out of the hut. In a moment he was back with a loose white garment in his hand. He threw it to her.

'Cover yourself with that,' he said hoarsely and went out again, shutting the door behind him.

Vanya was calling out to her. 'It's all right,' she said, 'I am coming.'

It must have been one of his own shirts, she thought, as she pulled it over her head. It was coarse unbleached linen, far too big, but it covered her nakedness and she was grateful for it.

'What did the man want?' asked the boy as she knelt beside him.

'It was nothing. It was just that he heard a noise and came to see if we were all right.'

'When are we going home to Kumari, Anna?'

'Soon, darling soon. Go back to sleep now.'

After that night Kezia made sure that she was never left unguarded and at least she was sure of one thing. Whatever happened to her in the future, for the time being at least she was not to be given over to the mercies of his men.

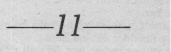

11

Anna first saw the mountain outpost of Karimat through sheets of icy blinding rain. They had been climbing for most of the day, all of them shrouded in their *bourkas* so that they looked like so many grey ghosts. At first sight it seemed impossible to imagine that anything human could live in such a desolate cluster of black huts clinging to the side of a precipice.

Dusk was falling when they rode in and she saw that it was built on a shelf of rock and was larger than she had thought; a great number of huts of all shapes and sizes surrounded a small square.

It had stopped raining but there was a bitter wind. Men, women and children came out to stare at them curiously when they dismounted but Kezia was brusque. Anna and the child were hustled through them into a small bare room. Tired and shivering she felt that she had reached the limit of her endurance and she rounded on him fiercely.

'The boy and I are soaked to the skin. Does the Imam Shamyl intend to murder us? If so, let him end our lives at once and not torture us needlessly. We cannot go on like this. We must have dry clothes, blankets, warm food . . .'

He looked considerably taken aback at her vehemence. When she paused for breath, he stared at her for an instant without speaking and then went out.

Wearily she looked around her. The room was comfortless but at least there were mattresses on the floor, a wooden table and two stools. According to their harsh standards, she thought hopelessly, she had little to complain about. There was one window that looked across the mountains. Up there amongst the high cloudy peaks, they had told her, was the fortress where Shamyl lived with his wives and children when he was not on campaign. She wondered whether they would be taken to him there and how long they were to stay in this wretched place. The room was very cold and Vanya's teeth were chattering. She must do something quickly. She was about to start hammering on the door when unexpectedly it opened and an old woman came in, dumped a great bundle of clothing on the floor, stared at her curiously and then went out again.

It was an extraordinary collection, worn and not very clean, but among them there were two rough blankets and a variety of garments which were better than nothing now that her skirt and blouse were almost in rags and her riding boots worn through to the uppers. She tried to make a game out of it, picking them over with Vanya, trying this one and that on him until he was dressed in dry shirt and breeches and a little jacket and boots somewhat too big for him. She had to stuff the toes with bits of rag.

He stuck his little *kinjal* in the belt and strutted up and down. 'Look at me, Anna. I look like Kezia now. I'm a Tartar.'

'No, you're not,' she said quickly and caught hold of him. 'You're a Gadiani, Vanya, never forget that.'

The child looked at her, bewildered. 'Why are you so cross?'

'I'm not cross.' She was annoyed with herself for spoiling the boy's innocent pleasure. She turned back to the pile of clothes. 'Now you come and help me choose.'

Vanya giggled as she picked out a pair of pink pantaloons, a long loose overdress and a shawl. The shoes were either too big or too small or all left feet so she had to shuffle about in a worn pair of embroidered slippers. The old woman came back with a copper bowl, a ewer of water and some clean pieces of linen to use as towels. Kezia must have taken note of what she had said because presently they were brought two bowls of onion soup, thin enough but at least it was hot, and with them a flat cake of unleavened bread with some goat's cheese, dry and hard but luxury after what they had been forced to swallow in the last few weeks.

That night when she tucked Vanya up on one of the mattresses, Anna thought that if ever she escaped from this terrible place, she would never lie in a comfortable bed or eat a decent meal without going down on her knees and thanking God for it.

For a day or so, worn out by the agonies of their journey, the bare miserable room seemed a kind of paradise, but it did not last long. Very soon time began to stretch interminably. To be shut up hour after hour with a five-year-old boy, with nothing to do, nothing to read, no one to talk to, became more and more unendurable. Without the stress of danger, the struggle simply to keep alive, there was time to brood. The unbearable tension of not knowing what was to happen to them nearly drove her crazy. Sometimes at night she would live through their ghastly journey, a nightmare of misery and hunger. Once or twice she dreamed of Paul, a fantasy when he seemed so near she would tremble with joy. Then when he took her in his arms, he would turn into the brute who had tried to rape her and she would wake with a start and lie sweating and shivering on the hard mattress.

It became desperately difficult to keep Vanya amused. She tried playing the simple games of childhood but even 'I spy' palled with nothing to look at but bare walls. She fell back on the stories her father had told her, inventing if she couldn't remember and when she ran out of them, she made them up.

Towards the end of the first week she discovered by accident that the old woman spoke a little Russian. Her name was Fatimah and she had been captured as a child so long ago that all memory of her native country had vanished, but she still had a few rusty words of Russian that came to life when Anna tried to speak to her. It was from her that she learned that everyone in the village was waiting for the arrival of the Imam Shamyl himself.

She found out other things too, that Kezia Mahommed was a cousin of the great man and therefore enjoyed special prestige and importance. One day when Fatimah brought their food, a woman came with her and stood in the doorway frowning at them. She was a tall handsome creature richly dressed in purple silk, her veil of golden gauze fastened with jewelled pins. She looked at Vanya as if she could eat him and then took a step into the room examining Anna from head to foot with undisguised curiosity and dislike. She said something in a sharp aggressive tone and went out.

The old woman chuckled to herself and Anna said, 'Who is she?'

'She is Ameera, Kezia's wife and she is jealous.'

'Jealous? Of what?'

'Of this,' and she touched the red-gold hair, 'and of the boy. She has no son.'

'But Vanya is not my child.'

The old woman grinned. 'Her husband talks of you too much. She does not like it.'

'Why should he? I haven't seen him since we came here.'

Fatimah glanced at her slyly. 'She fears he will ask the Imam for permission to take you as his second wife.'

'Oh no, that is too ridiculous!'

But was it? She suddenly remembered the way he had looked at her. The very thought of being condemned to live in this dreadful place made her sick with fear. They might hold her prisoner but she would not yield, she would die first, she would smash her way through the window and hurl herself down the precipice. It was a madness born of frustration and lasted only for a few hours. While she lived, there was always hope and she had to think of Vanya. She was worried about him. The enforced confinement had begun to tell on the boy accustomed to an open-air life. He grew pale and listless, refused to eat their scanty and monotonous food and seemed to want only to lie on the mattress or stand at the window where nothing was to be seen but mountains, sky and an occasional bird circling the peaks. It helped her to make up her mind. If Kezia looked on her with favour, then perhaps she could exploit it. Next time the old woman came, she demanded to see him.

'The child is sick. I must speak with him.'

Fatimah looked doubtful, but Anna was insistent and at last she promised to carry the message. He came the following morning, standing in the doorway, a fine figure of a man she had to admit. He had discarded his rough mountain garments and was dressed splendidly as befitted one of Shamyl's most important Naibs.

'What is wrong with the boy?' he said curtly.

'He is pining for lack of exercise. He is shut up in one stifling room without fresh air, with nothing to play with, nothing to do. If I had books, I could at least give him lessons.'

'Books?' he looked baffled. 'What does a man child want with books?' Then he strode across to the window. 'There is a path outside here. I will give orders that you may walk there each afternoon if you will also give me your word that you will not speak with anyone or try to escape.'

She had come to stand beside him. 'Am I a bird,' she said ironically, 'to fly over the mountains and no one here speaks my language except yourself.'

'Very well. See that you keep your promise.' She felt his dark eyes on her. He put out a hand and touched her hair as if it fascinated him and she stood quite still though inwardly she trembled. Then abruptly he turned on his heel and went out.

The next afternoon they were escorted out of the room and round to the back of the hut. It was a long narrow path with a sheer drop into a ravine at the further side, but after the confinement it seemed like heaven. At this altitude the air was cool but the sun could sometimes be hot still. Vanya raced up and down with the exuberance of a puppy let out for the first time and when they came back, there was a ball and some broken toys on the table with a tattered book that turned out to be an illustrated trade journal for ladies' underwear. How it had found its way up to this remote place, she couldn't imagine, but it became an invaluable lesson book. They ploughed their way through chemises, drawers, stockings, nightgowns, petticoats, examining the pictures and she began to teach Vanya French and English words while the hours passed less slowly.

It was a few days later when they saw the prisoners brought in. They had to stop in the square pressed back against the walls of the hut while they were marched through. There were about twenty of them, Russian soldiers, their uniforms so dilapidated as to be almost unrecognizable. Filthy and emaciated, they stumbled by chained together. One of them was limping so badly that he would have fallen if his comrade had not supported him.

Where they had come from and how far she did not know, but these were men who could never hope for ransom, never hope for freedom, and she was filled with pity.

The following afternoon she discovered why they had been brought here. A wall was to be built along the path where she walked with Vanya, obviously to provide protection in case of siege. Some of the prisoners were already at work digging foundations. She longed to speak to them but, mindful of Kezia's warning, she was afraid it might do more harm than good though it was difficult to keep Vanya away from them.

The child ran from one to the other, asking questions, delighted when they paused for a moment to answer. She saw some of the men smile, surprised at what looked like a Tartar boy speaking to them so boldly in their own language.

At the end of the row was the man who had limped so painfully the day before. He had stopped working and was leaning against the wall of the hut shading his face against the glare of the sun as if wearied beyond endurance. Vanya ran up to him and said something. He straightened himself. Then suddenly he clamped both hands on the boy's shoulders bending down to look into his face. A little scared Vanya cried out and Anna ran towards them.

'What is it? What is wrong? Please don't frighten the boy.'

The man dropped his hands and turned to her. He was dreadfully thin. His face, bearded, worn to the bone, pale as death, was still unmistakably Gregory's face. The shock was so tremendous that neither of them could speak and in that second the overseer had come striding up.

'Back to work,' he growled, 'back to work,' and cracked his whip.

Anna would have protested but Gregory shook his head imperceptibly, mouthing the one word tomorrow, then submissively he picked up his spade and returned to the digging.

'Who was that man?' demanded Vanya clinging to her hand.

She dare not tell him. 'Oh no one special, just a Russian soldier.'

'Why did he look at me in such a funny way? He asked what my name was.'

'Perhaps you reminded him of someone, his son perhaps or a little brother.'

Thank goodness the child accepted it without question but what was she going to do in the future? She had to speak with Gregory but how without attracting attention? Until she knew why he was here, she dare no reveal his identity in case it should be worse for him.

She lay awake all that night, her mind seething with unanswerable questions. At some time in the night she heard singing, faint and infinitely mournful. It must have been the prisoners and it was the song she had once heard with Paul in the mountains . . .

> The haunting sound of evening bells
> That bring me back my dreams . . .

Oh God, how strange it was that she should meet Gregory here like this . . . so Paul had not killed him after all . . . and it had not been his head that he had seen swinging from some Tartar's saddle bow. A great surge of thankfulness swept through her until she realized what it meant. Gregory, her husband, was alive and she was bound to him, now more than ever because of his weakness, his sickness . . . the new sweet thing that she had found with Paul, the dream that she had lived in all that summer, was over. She must not even think of him any longer. She buried her face in the coarse blanket and wept helplessly for what had vanished, forgetting that she was as much a prisoner as Gregory and that for both of them there might well be no future.

It took several days before she was able to piece the story together because they could not talk longer than a few minutes at a time and then only with extreme caution. She would walk along the path with Vanya running ahead and then pause as if by chance to look across the ravine. She did not look at Gregory and he did not stop working and they spoke in French, a language no one who overheard them was likely to understand. It was disjointed, fragmentary, but gradually the pieces formed a whole.

On the first afternoon, staring up at the cloudy peaks, she said under her breath, 'They told me that you were dead.'

'So I am . . . dead to all that matters.' There was so much despair in his voice that she wanted to turn to him, to give comfort, but did not dare.

'What happened? Daniel said you fought a duel with Paul Kuragin.'

A curious smile flitted across his gaunt face. 'So you have met Paul. He is a magnificent shot. I've wondered sometimes if he knew that was the one time he missed his aim.'

'You mean . . .?' Then the guard came, looking at her suspiciously so that maddeningly she had to walk on. It was so tantalizing, she could have wept with vexation.

At the next opportunity she said, 'Why did you fight?'

He shot her a quick glance. 'Didn't he tell you?' She shook her head. 'It was nothing, a triviality,' and she was certain that he lied.

'What happened?'

'What do you think?' he said dryly. 'We took our shots at one another and I was hit. I must have fainted. When I came round and realized I was not dead, I was alone.'

'He left you there . . . to die? How could he be so callous?'

Gregory shrugged his shoulders. 'He could have been intending to send someone back.'

'What did you do?'

'I managed to get on my feet. My horse was still where I had tethered him. I don't remember much only that I had not gone far when I was surrounded.'

'By Shamyl's horsemen?'

'Afterwards I guessed they must have been lying in wait for me. I was sick from loss of blood. I tried to get away from them but there were too many. I must have fainted again because the next thing I knew I was in the mountains.'

'A prisoner?'

'What else?'

'But why?'

'Haven't you grasped it yet? My dear beloved cousin Daniel, who had welcomed me back to the Caucasus with open arms, had found a splendid opportunity to get rid of me without any blame attaching to himself.'

'So your grandmother was right after all . . .'

'It's not easy to pull the wool over grandmamma's eyes! Didn't you believe her?'

'It seemed so . . . so impossible.'

He stopped working, staring down at his hands, so fine and slender and now grimed and calloused from the hard manual labour. 'Oh God, what have I done to you, Anna? I never thought, I never dreamed that he would harm you as well as the child . . .'

'It was not your fault.' Forgetting caution she put a hand on his and their eyes met. He bent his head and touched her fingers lightly with his lips. Then Vanya came running back to her and she moved away to see Kezia's wife standing at the end of the path watching her.

That night the rain came down heavily and continued without ceasing for two days so that they could not go out and she would watch the prisoners from the window working on in the bitter wind, soaked to the skin. It must be September, she thought, and already turning to winter in these high altitudes. In this extraordinary existence she seemed to have lost all count of time. She tried to sort out her few scraps of information. A pattern was beginning to emerge. She realized how Daniel Gadiani had contrived to put all blame on Paul's shoulders and take advantage of what had happened to further his own scheme, but there was still so much that she did not understand.

When they were allowed out again, she saw with painful pity how sick Gregory looked. Under the tan his skin had a greyish tinge and fresh blood was oozing from the rags that covered his thigh.

'What is wrong with your leg?' she whispered.

'I fell,' he said dully, 'when I tried to escape. The rocks lacerated it and it will not heal.'

'Has it been treated?'

He laughed and she realized the absurdity of her question. Why should they trouble themselves to cure a prisoner whose life or death mattered nothing to them?

She said, 'If I could find some clean rags, I could bandage it for you.'

'Better not. If they see you do so much for me, they might suspect something and punish you for it.'

They had momentarily forgotten their usual caution so that neither of them noticed that the overseer had come quietly up behind them until his whip curled across Gregory's back.

Anna turned on him in a fury of indignation. 'How dare you do that? Can't you see he is sick?'

The Tartar stared at her, slit eyes narrowed, then he raised the whip again. He might have slashed it across her face if Gregory had not seized his wrist.

'Let her be, you damned brute!'

The man flung him off so that he fell against the partly built wall and Anna found herself facing Kezia who had come to inspect the work with two of his men behind him.

'What is going on?' he demanded.

The overseer burst into angry explanation, but he silenced him with an impatient hand. 'What are you doing here?' he said to Anna.

Carried away by pity and anger she said defiantly, 'I tried to prevent him flogging a man who is already bleeding to death.'

'What!' Kezia was frowning at her.

'I did not think you so lacking in humanity,' she stormed at him. 'Even an animal shows more feeling!'

The men with him were looking at her with amazement. A grin spread across the brutal face of the overseer. With a furious exclamation Kezia seized her by the wrist and strode away pulling her after him. He thrust her inside the hut and slammed the door.

'Don't you know better than to speak to me like that where everyone can hear you? No other woman would dare raise her voice in such a way.'

'Then more fool they,' she retorted and then stopped appalled by the rage on his face.

He took hold of her, his hands hard on her shoulders.

'What is this man to you? My wife told me that she saw you speaking with him. Why? For what reason?'

Obviously he did not know who Gregory was so she temporized by defying him. 'I thought you did not listen to women's gossip. I have my eyes, haven't I? I could see how he was suffering and it sickened me.'

He dropped his hands. 'Are you so feeble that you cannot stand the sight of a little blood?' he said with contempt. 'You have your remedy. You can turn your back on it.'

She tried to calm herself. She must not show too much personal interest. 'Is that all you can say? At least let Fatimah tend him. She has skill with wounds, she told me so. Even you must realize that he will work better if he is cured and you want the wall built quickly, isn't that so? Before the winter is here.'

He did not answer at once, then he shrugged his shoulders. 'It is true that the work goes on slower than I could wish. I am a fool to listen to you . . . let the old woman look at this man, but that is all. Do you understand?'

'Yes . . . and thank you.'

'I want no thanks. I shall be glad when the Imam comes and I am rid of my responsibility,' and with that he swung out of the room.

No one stopped her when she insisted on going with Fatimah the next day. Escape from this remote place was unthinkable and the guards were becoming accustomed to the freedom allowed to her. There was something else too. Very early that morning she had been roused by the jingle of harness and the tramp of horses. She struggled up to see Kezia ride out at the head of his men. An air of relaxation seemed to pervade Karimat at his going.

Gregory was in his usual place, but he was not working. He was sitting propped up against the back wall of the hut. One of his comrades gave a quick look around and then put a hand tentatively on Anna's arm.

'He couldn't walk at all this morning,' he whispered, 'but he begged us to bring him here. He said if he was to die, then he'd rather it was in the open air.'

'He is not going to die. We've come to help him.'

Fatimah had brought a bowl of warm water and some clean cloths. Anna knelt beside her as she cut away the blood-caked rags. The sight of the festering wound turned her sick but she would not give way to it and resolutely held the bowl while the old woman swabbed and cleansed the raw flesh as well as she could. Gregory clenched his teeth against the pain and Anna protested when Fatimah covered the place with a mass of some kind of green moss before she began to wind the linen round it.

'It is good,' she said pushing Anna's hands away. 'We use it always when the men come back wounded. It cleans and it heals. He should lie down, not stand or walk for a time,' she went on, 'that is if they will let him.' She took the basin and soiled bandages and hobbled away while Anna stayed beside him.

After a moment Gregory stirred a little. 'I couldn't stay in that filthy hole where we sleep.' His clouded eyes were on Anna. 'This is your doing, isn't it? How did you manage it?'

'I told Kezia Mahommed that he was behaving worse than an animal.'

Gregory smiled faintly. 'He won't have liked that . . . from a woman too. I saw the way he looked at you. He wants you for himself, my dear.'

She contrived a little laugh. 'What an idea! He has a wife already.'

'But not one like you.'

'In these clothes . . . and looking like I do?'

'It's not the clothes that make the woman.' He shifted his position, stifling a groan, and moved with pity she put up a hand to touch his face. He caught at her fingers. 'Why are you doing this for me? You could have left me to die.'

'I could but I'm not going to,' she said lightly.

He still held her hand. 'Anna, is it too late to say I'm sorry?'

How many times he had said that before with the same boyish look of appeal and the words had meant nothing.

'Never mind about that now. There are other things more important.' She leaned towards him whispering. 'Gregory, what are we going to do?'

'What can we do?' He lay back, looking so deadly exhausted that she was frightened for him. She said quickly, 'It doesn't matter. We'll talk of it tomorrow.'

But after a moment he roused himself with an effort. 'No, you're right, and we don't know how much time we may have to speak like this. It is you I've been thinking of, Anna, over and over again ever since I knew you were here. Now listen to me. Your father is English. That is what you must play on. Shamyl would dearly love to have England on his side in his struggle with Russia and would not willingly offend them. When he comes here, demand to see him. Make your father sound far more influential than he is. If ransom is asked, then my grandmother will find the money somehow.'

'Even if he will listen to me, I could not go and leave Vanya behind . . . or you.'

'You may be forced to. But if he releases you, you could carry information back to Prince Vorontsov. He would know Daniel for what he is. He would have evidence of his treachery. If I had not played the fool, he would have known long since and all this might have been avoided.'

'How do you mean?'

'I had guessed that Daniel was playing a double game but I said nothing . . . because of Natalie . . .'

'Natalie?'

Gregory avoided looking at her 'I was sorry for her. She is his sister after all.' He went on quickly. 'It's useless thinking of that now. How many weeks is it since they kidnapped you, Anna?'

She thought back. It seemed endless but was not really so long. 'It's more than a month. Six weeks by now.'

'In that case Vorontsov will already have sent spies to find out where you have been taken.'

They were not able to talk together much longer that day. She dare not stay with him for more than a few minutes, particularly as she had left Vanya shut up in their prison room. But Kezia did not return and in the meantime Gregory recovered a little strength and each time she saw him, she learned more. Once he told her something of what had happened in the weeks after his capture.

'I soon realized one thing. Shamyl has no trust in Daniel's promises. I am sure he hoped for my death but Shamyl refused. He offered me a choice. If I would throw in my lot with him, if I would take Kumaria and all that that implies to him, he would set me free"

'And you refused?'

'I may not have amounted to much, but I have my pride. I would not betray my people, nor Russia.'

'Did it anger him?'

'I don't know. He is a man who gives nothing away and you cannot guess at his thoughts. He stood me up before a firing squad and then at the last possible moment when the guns were already levelled at me, I was granted a reprieve. "I will give you time to think it over," he said to me.'

Gregory shut his eyes for a moment before he went on dryly,

'I did not know how often I was to wish the reprieve had come too late.'

'Oh Gregory . . .' she thought of what he must have gone through, her young husband who had never known a day's discomfort, 'all those months. It must have been terrible.'

'Don't pity me. That's something I have never wanted.'

She said slowly, 'That must have been when Paul believed you to have been already murdered.'

'Paul?'

'Part of his mission had been to find out where you might have been imprisoned. He thought he had come too late.'

'Do you believe that?'

'Yes, now I think I do.'

'Why do you say that? How well did you know him, Anna?'

'I travelled with him and his Cossacks from Pyatigorsk.'

'I see.' He looked at her curiously. 'Did you know that he was Natalie's lover?'

'Yes, I knew.' She met his eyes and looked away. She did not want to talk about Paul and she evaded his questions. They turned again to the all-absorbing topic of how they could contrive to escape from the impossible position in which they had been trapped.

By the end of the week though he was still sick and fevered, they set him to work again. The building of the wall had proceeded very slowly. The prisoners, weak and badly fed, made poor progress. Kezia had been gone about ten days when she was aware of a ripple of excitement running all through the village. The guards were more alert, they harried the prisoners, shouting at them if they paused even for a few minutes, and one evening just as dusk was falling, she understood why.

Up the steep road from the ravine came a detachment of splendid horsemen, their black banners streaming in the wind, with Kezia at their head. As they entered the village they parted, drawing to each side, and through them came a tall man on a magnificent horse caparisoned in scarlet leather with fine silver tassels. In the centre of the square he pulled up and in the flare of the torches held by two of his men she saw the austere figure with the long white cloak falling behind him and the silver-hilted daggers in his belt. He was just as Paul had once described, the pale face, the dark smouldering eyes, the reddish beard and behind him was the executioner, the man with the uplifted silver axe, symbol of his authority and power. No one moved or spoke. He raised his hand, giving one sweeping glance around him, taking in the whole square.

'Allah is great,' he said in his deep voice.

'Allah is all-merciful,' they answered him in one long chant.

It was the Imam Shamyl, the Lion of Daghestan, who held their fate, hers and Vanya's and Gregory's in the hollow of his hand. Then he turned and rode on with his Naibs following after him.

—12—

Three days of nerve-racking tension went by when every hour Anna expected to be taken before Shamyl and did not know whether she felt relieved or sorry when no summons came. She was kept locked into her prison room since it was not decent for an unveiled woman to be seen by the returned warriors who now stalked about Karimat showing off their weapons and their battle trophies. Vanya had developed a cold and was fretful and listless by turns so that she was at her wits' end trying to keep him amused.

Then on the fourth morning Fatimah appeared with their breakfast, bubbling over with news. There had been a great victory, hundreds of Russians killed, she told Anna, and the following day they would be celebrating, a whole sheep roasted, a goat too, meat for everyone with new bread and cakes, the bakers were hard at work already. There would be dancing and singing. The Imam had decreed it and would grace it with his presence before he left to ride up to Dargo-Vedin with a few chosen followers.

'But today you are to see him, you and the child,' babbled the old woman breathlessly. 'It is a great honour and you must prepare yourself.'

The moment had come and although she had thought about it over and over again, she still felt unprepared. She did not know what bargain Daniel Gadiani had struck with the Moslem leader. She understood why he had taken the child, but what did he mean to do with her or was he merely indifferent to her fate? She tried to remember everything Gregory had said, but what would a professor of literature at Moscow University, even if he was English, mean to a man like Shamyl? If she was allowed to write to him or to the Viceroy or to the Princess Gadiani, it would be weeks, perhaps months, before any reply could reach this remote place. Then there was the question of ransom. Her father was not a rich man. The Tartars had no idea of the value of money.

They believed all Russians to be fabulously wealthy and demanded huge sums. Fatimah had told her once that if the price was slow in coming, the men fought over who should take the captive women, particularly if they were young and still attractive.

All these thoughts jumbled together in her mind as she tried to make some preparation, combing Vanya's hair and her own, tidying their clothes as best she could. Another fretting hour passed before Kezia came himself to fetch her. He brought a piece of black cloth with him and handed it to her.

'Cover your face,' he said. 'It is not fitting that you should come into the presence of the Imam unveiled.'

'But I am a Christian,' she protested, 'I do not follow the law of Islam.'

'Do not argue,' he said curtly. 'Do you wish to anger him?'

She tied the veil as the other women did and he took Vanya by the hand leading them through the village to the far end where there was a house better built than the others with a balcony running along one side. The two guards saluted and they went up the stairs and into a large room that must have covered the whole of the upper storey.

There were several men grouped together at one end but she had eyes only for Shamyl seated in the one chair and by his immense dignity and presence converting it into a throne. Behind him as always stood his executioner, still holding aloft the great axe, and with him an impressive array of his dark-skinned, hawk-faced Naibs.

A man was lying prostrate before the leader, his arms stretched out, and Kezia put a hand on Anna's shoulder and drew her to one side. There was no sound except the babble of the high-pitched voice, pleading and pleading, but Shamyl's stony face showed no pity. He raised his hand and two guards jerked the man to his feet and marched him through the door followed by the executioner. Anna saw the prisoner's face, white and distraught as he passed them.

'What has he done?' she whispered.

'He robbed his comrade so his right hand will be struck off,' said Kezia indifferently.

'Oh no!' She was appalled at the barbarity.

'He is no longer fit to ride with warriors. It is the Imam's justice. Come.'

Kezia led her to the centre of the room and then stepped to one side. For a whole minute Shamyl sat motionless fixing her with his strange slit-like eyes. When he spoke in his deep voice, though it was through an interpreter, she felt as if he addressed her direct.

'Kezia Mahommed tells me that you have found favour in his sight. He has asked that I should give you to him as his wife.'

She was so taken by surprise that her thoughts scattered all over the place and unwisely she let her indignation and fear carry her away.

'You cannot do this, you cannot. You insult me even to suggest it. I will never submit to such a thing, never, never, never!'

His reply was chilling though he did not raise his voice. 'Kezia is my cousin, a fine warrior, victor in many battles. It is an honour that he should regard you as worthy of his choice. Would you prefer that we sell you in the market as a slave?'

'You don't understand.' In her vehemence she tore off the veil and a stir ran all around the room at her daring insolence. 'I am Princess Gadiani. My husband is Gregory Gadiani, Prince of Kumaria. How can I be wife to any other man?'

Shamyl stopped her with uplifted hand. 'I am aware of your identity, but your husband is dead.'

'He is not dead. He is here among your prisoners . . .'

'Silence,' thundered Shamyl suddenly and turned to Kezia. 'If this is so why have I been misinformed?'

'There are a number of prisoners here. I do not know all their cursed names,' he replied sullenly.

'Ascertain them and bring them to me.'

He clicked his fingers imperiously. To her horror Daniel Gadiani stepped forward from those around him and too late she realized her mistake. They must have believed Gregory to be already dead and by reminding them that he still lived, she could have condemned him once again.

Daniel leaned towards Shamyl whispering and the Imam nodded. Belatedly she remembered what Gregory had said and boldly she took a step forward.

'My father is English and I have been kidnapped unjustly and for no reason. You cannot keep me here as your prisoner. You must permit me to write to him.'

'English? Is that so?' She had caught his attention. He stroked his beard thoughtfully, his eyes narrowed, watching her.

Again Daniel intervened. 'He is a man of no account, Highness,' but this time Shamyl put him aside.

'We will consider further of this matter. What of the child? Is he your son?'

'He is my husband's half-brother.'

'A bastard child of no importance,' said Daniel Gadiani quickly.

'Is that so? He is a fine upstanding boy for all that.' The stern unrelenting face broke into a smile and Shamyl held out his hand. 'Come. Are you afraid of me?'

Vanya hesitated, looking up at Anna. But a Gadiani never cries and does not show fear. Slowly he went forward and Shamyl lifted him on to his knee. He drew the silver-hilted dagger from his belt and held it up to the child.

'What is this?'

'It is a *kinjal*, like mine.' The boy laughed and gripped it as the men had taught him, lunging forward. Shamyl caught his wrist. 'So . . . you would threaten me.' He smiled grimly. 'See . . . he holds it already like a man. We will make a fine warrior out of him.'

He ruffled the boy's hair and set him down again. 'Take them away. Before I leave for Dargo-Vedin, I will decide what is to be done with them.' He lifted his hand as a sign that the audience was ended. Then he rose and stalked from the room followed by his lieutenant.

Kezia took her back through the village with Vanya chattering excitedly beside them. Inside their prison he paused for a moment.

'You acted foolishly.'

'I know. You don't need to tell me.'

'Am I so hateful to you?'

'It is not that,' and because in his own way he had been kind to her, she said, 'Can't you understand? It is my husband who is out there, one of your prisoners.'

'So that is why you pleaded for him. He is not worthy of you. Any man who allows himself to be taken prisoner is a coward.'

'That is not true. He has already faced death with courage and he was reprieved. Should he then hurl himself down a precipice?'

'That is what I would have done. I would fall on my sword rather than be made prisoner by the Russians. In any case he will die soon.'

'Why do you say that?'

'He is sick. We cannot feed those who cannot work.'

Revolted she said, 'Are you all so ruthless?'

He shrugged his shoulders. 'It is how we must live.'

'What will the Imam decide?'

'It is for him to judge and for us to obey.' Then his calm broke. He took a step towards her and caught her to him. His kiss was hard and compelling. She fought against it fiercely and after a moment he drew back, the dark face very close to hers.

'I would make you happy. You could have everything you desire . . . I would give you clothes, jewels . . .'

'As you give them to Ameera.'

'She is nothing beside you. You have courage. All these weeks I have seen it. You would give me fine brave sons. Why do you deny me?'

'Because it is impossible,' she said desperately. 'To me it would be like a prison. I would die rather than submit.'

He stared at her for an instant, his eyes alight with anger and then he went out quickly, slamming the door.

All that afternoon she could hear the preparations going forward for the celebration on the next day. When Fatimah brought their supper, she asked her what was happening outside.

'The packmen have come. It is a whole year since they were last here. Such things as they have brought, silks and satins, all kinds of finery, the women are going crazy to get at them.'

'Do you think I might go out and see them too? I have been shut in for so long.' Once outside, she thought, it might be possible to find Gregory and warn him about what had happened.

She had to plead for a long time before Fatimah would consent to leave the door unlocked.

'Maybe there's no harm,' she said at last grudgingly. 'But not for long, mind you. If they were to find out, they would kill me.'

'They won't find out, I promise. I will only stay for a few minutes. I will come back almost at once.'

She tucked Vanya up on his mattress and made him promise to remain very quiet. 'I will not be long.' She kissed him before she slipped out of the door.

She could see the women at one end of the square gathered in a gabbling excited group. There were horses tethered and a pack mule with two men in soiled finery, turbans pulled down to their brows, one of them tall and the other, older and broader, with a fine black moustache. They were holding up lengths of cloth, cheap trinkets, beads, mirrors, pocket combs . . . treasures to these women who had lived all their lives so far from the luxuries of cities. She drew the veil across her face and went to join them, hoping to move away unnoticed after a few minutes and look for Gregory.

The women were too intent on the bargaining to take much notice of her. She began to turn over some of the articles laid out. The tall peddler held up a length of silk, spreading it out, smoothing its folds, and with a start she saw the large onyx ring on the long brown hand. He turned towards her, swinging the silk around to show it off, and she met his eyes, the luminous brown eyes in the lean face, stained and darkened. Her heart gave a great leap. It couldn't be and yet it was . . . it had to be Paul. But how could he possibly be here unless he knew about her capture and he had gone from Tiflis long before it happened? Veiled and in these outlandish clothes he had not recognized her. She wondered if Varga was the other man, who was now throwing the material round his shoulders, taking a few dancing steps, acting the fool and sending the women into gales of laughter. Under cover of his antics, she plucked at Paul's sleeve. He looked towards her and she dropped the veil. She saw his eyes widen in recognition but he said nothing. Instead he picked up one of the saddle bags.

'There's more here,' he said with a flourish, 'everything for a lady's pleasure!' He put it on the ground kneeling beside it. She sank down beside him as he brought out the trinkets.

'What in God's name are you doing here?' he murmured in English as they both bent over the bag.

'I was kidnapped by Daniel Gadiani when I was taking Vanya to Tiflis.'

'Didn't the Prince give you a military escort?'

'I didn't ask him for one. Why have you come to Karimat?'

'Never mind that now. Do they keep you shut up? Is there anywhere we can talk?'

'I'm in one of the huts with a window on the ravine.'

'I'll try to come there tonight.'

For an instant his hand was on hers and the very touch seemed to give her fresh courage. Then he raised his voice.

'Do you see, lady? Combs of every colour!' He pushed

them towards her as if completing a bargain and rose to his
feet, lifting up the saddle bag and turning back to the other
women.

She drew the veil across her face again, looking quickly
around her, wondering in what part of the village the prisoners were housed, and then she saw Ameera. She was standing
a little apart from the others, the black eyes above the gauze
veil watching her curiously. To arouse suspicion now by trying to find Gregory would be sheer madness. She got up,
pulling her shawl around her and walking unconcernedly
back to the hut.

Presently when Fatimah returned to lock the door, she
gave her one of the coloured combs and the old woman
grunted with pleasure.

'I saw Ameera there. Did she buy anything?' asked Anna
casually.

'Bless you, no. Nothing but the best is good enough for
that one. The Imam reproaches Kezia for his wife's extrava-
gance. Once he was so angry, he had her baggage seized and
burned, but she did not care a rap. She knows her husband
will buy her more for the asking.' She grinned at Anna,
chuckling. 'It's lucky for you that you please him. A fine man
to take you to his bed . . .'

'And share it with Ameera,' said Anna dryly.

'What's in that? Bear him a son and he'll pluck the stars
out of the sky for you. Better that than the slave market and
a master who would beat you black and blue.'

The old woman was garrulous and Anna was thankful
when she talked herself out of the room. Thank goodness,
Vanya was sleeping quietly. She walked up and down, her
mind in a turmoil of excitement and hope. She was not sure
why Paul was there or what he could do to help her, but just
to know he was near was so wonderful that she could not
keep still. That he would find some means of coming to her,
she never doubted for an instant, but it could not be yet and
she did not know how she was to endure the endless hours
until darkness fell.

It was still only early evening and though it was light outside, the shadows were already gathering in the little room.
She stood at the window for a long time watching the mountains turn from pink and gold to a deep grape purple. Then
she lit the one candle allowed to her and tried to settle herself
to wait with patience.

The sound of someone at the door sent her heart leaping

up into her throat. Fatimah never came as late as this. Had Ameera guessed after all that Paul was not what he pretended to be and told Kezia? She was on her feet, breathlessly trying to still her wildly thudding heart, when the door opened and Daniel Gadiani slipped in, closing it behind him. The very sight of him angered her so much that it helped to steady her.

She said coldly, 'Why have you come here? I do not wish to speak to you.'

'I think you will when you hear what I have to say,' he replied smoothly.

'I doubt it and please keep your voice down. Vanya is asleep.'

He crossed to the mattress and looked down at the boy's flushed face. 'The little warrior, eh? Shamyl has a fondness for children, a curious weakness in a tyrant and a murderer, is it not?'

'A weakness which you obviously don't share,' she said tartly. 'Would you please say what you have come to say and leave me alone?'

'You have a quite extraordinary spirit, my dear. I have never met it in a woman before and I must confess I never expected it. Where does it spring from, I wonder? Is it the English blood of which you're so proud? I fear it will do you very little good.' He came and perched himself on the table, the flaring candle flame illuminating the dark face into strange planes of light and shadow.

She sat on the stool, clasping her hands tightly together, trying to still her fear and her overwrought nerves.

He watched her for an instant before he said, 'How much has Gregory told you?'

'Enough. I know that you hoped Shamyl would have him murdered so that you could take his place at Kumari.'

'My rightful place,' he said with a sudden frightening ferocity, 'a place that has been owed to us for three generations. While Gregory rioted in a life of luxury in Petersburg, I lived a hole-in-corner existence in a country that should have been mine if there was any justice in this world. The Russians never granted me any favours.'

'Have you deserved any?'

For a moment she thought he would strike her, but he didn't. He smiled grimly. 'I've already said that I admire your spirit, but don't tempt me too far.' He leaned forward suddenly, his face so close to hers that she drew back. 'Now listen to me. What was it that the old woman at Kumari gave you to take to the Viceroy?'

She looked at him startled. So he didn't know for certain about the child. Somehow she must play for time.

'Didn't Kezia's men bring everything to you when they kidnapped us?'

'No, damn them! The fools let it go.'

So Yakov and Marik must have got away after all. She tried to think quickly. Once he knew Vanya was the rightful heir if Gregory died, then he would destroy him. A child is so easily disposed of . . . an accident . . . a sickness . . . She spoke slowly, feeling her way. 'There was a casket of jewels, old-fashioned pieces, family heirlooms. The Princess wished me to sell them for her in Tiflis.'

He frowned. 'And that was all?'

She forced herself to meet his eyes. 'What else should there be?'

'And the child?'

'He had been sick during the winter. The Princess was worried about him. She wanted the Prince's physician to examine him.'

He stared down at her, then got up and took a turn across the room, swinging round to face her. 'I don't believe you.'

'It is the truth.'

'Kamil told me differently.'

'Kamil?' She remembered the slim young man whom she had seen at Kumari, who had been the first to entice Vanya away from her. 'So he was your spy.'

'He has a grudge against all Russians and against Paul Kuragin in particular because of his sister.'

'Is he here?'

'He is of no importance.' He moved towards her, his hands gripping her shoulders, pulling her roughly to her feet. 'Do you realize the position you are in? Have no illusions about these people. To Shamyl you are no more than a counter to bargain with and once I have persuaded him that you are of little value to his purpose, he will give you to Kezia without a second thought. Would you like that? To be his woman, his plaything, shut up in his harem with his other women, to serve his pleasure whenever it suits him.' He put a hand under her chin and jerked it up so that she was staring into his face. 'I have a better suggestion. Forget Vanya, marry me and we will rule Kumaria together.'

She was shaking but tried to keep her voice steady. 'I would rather be Kezia's slave.'

'You talk like a fool.' He released her so that she fell against the table. 'Do you imagine that I intend to drag out a life in these mountains? Shamyl would doublecross me tomorrow if it suited him. I owe him no more loyalty than I do the Russians. I do as I please.'

'And serve both parties for your own advantage.'

'If necessary. It's the only way to live and succeed.'

She took a deep breath. 'You seem to forget that Gregory is still alive.'

He shrugged his shoulders. 'For how long? A prisoner is got rid of very easily. He is sick already. He will not survive a week in one of the prison pits.'

The callous cruelty revolted her so much that she longed to spit her disgust into his face, but some instinct kept her silent while her brain worked feverishly. She did not think he was as secure as he sounded. Shamyl was no fool. If he had guessed about the child, he could hold him as a threat if Daniel should try treachery. In this devious world there seemed to be no trust anywhere.

Daniel Gadiani was watching her with an unpleasant smile. 'Don't think that Paul Kuragin will come riding to your rescue. He is a romantic. He is pursuing a madcap scheme to capture Shamyl himself and he will be damned lucky if he ends up without having his throat cut, he and the Cossacks with him.'

So that was the reason why Paul was here. The audacity of it appalled her. She said, 'How do you know?'

'I have always had my informants.'

'Where is he now?'

'God knows. At this moment he doesn't matter.' Then he looked at her with suddden suspicion. 'Have you heard something? Has there been some message?'

'How could there be when I have been shut up here day after day for weeks?'

She knew now what she must do. Though every instinct urged her to fling defiance at him, she must temporize, show weakness, gain time until she could speak with Paul. She let herself drop on the stool again.

'I'm so afraid . . . I can't think any longer . . .' she said despairingly burying her face in her hands.

He bent down to her whispering. She felt his breath on her cheek, smelled the strange subtle perfume he used. 'Gregory never appreciated you, did he? He threw away his chances. Believe me, Anna, I shall not do that. I know many ways of pleasing a woman.' He drew her hands away from her face forcing her to look up at him before he kissed her. His lips were cold and a shudder ran through her. It took all her strength of will not to flinch away from him. Then he straightened himself. 'Shamyl will not leave here until after the victory feast. I will come to you again.'

She held herself quite still until he had gone and then fell across the table trembling so much that it was some time before she could pull herself together and try to marshal her thoughts so that when Paul came, she could tell him everything calmly without breaking down.

The hours crept by with a torturing slowness so that hope died and despair took its place. It was quite dark now. Outside everything was silent and still he did not come. Something must have happened. All kinds of fears darted through her mind. Paul had been discovered . . . he had thought better of it . . . he had decided to pursue his own mission leaving her and Vanya to their fate. Daniel Gadiani would return and she would have no answer for him. She shivered as she blew out the candle and lay down on the mattress.

It must have been long after midnight when she heard the faint tapping at the window. She was up in an instant. It was a black night, no moon or stars, and she could see nothing. She fumbled with the latch. Then strong hands took hold of it and moved it silently back. The space was so small that she did not know how he got through but somehow he slithered into the room. She went to relight the candle and he stopped her.

'If it is seen at this hour, it will arouse suspicion.'

He groped for her hand gripping it strongly and drawing her to the window. She could scarcely see him through the thick darkness, but it was immensely comforting to feel him so close.

'Now tell me what has happened, quickly,' he said.

So she told him about Kumari, about the child, the family feud, the Pricesss's fears and about Daniel Gadiani, but something prevented her from mentioning Gregory.

'I believe Prince Vorontsov guessed part of it,' he said thoughtfully. 'But he could not step in unless he was asked. These native rulers can be confoundedly touchy and the old

Princess has always had the reputation of a martinet. That is why you should have sent to him. He was prepared to help.'

'I realize that now. But it seemed so fantastic at the time and she was so against it. I thought she exaggerated . . . I didn't believe in the threat of danger.'

'Well, it's done now and it's no use crying over it. What is important is to get you away from here.'

'Oh Paul, is it possible?' she breathed.

'It's got to be possible. If they take you to Dargo-Vedin as they may very well do until Shamyl makes up his mind, escape would be out of the question. It is guarded at every point.'

'Paul, I know what your mission is . . .'

'Who told you of it?'

'Daniel Gadiani when he came here today. He does not think you can succeed.'

'What he thinks is of no importance,' he said curtly. 'What else did he say?'

She looked away from him trying to speak lightly. 'It seems that I am to be faced with a choice. To marry him or be given to Kezia.'

'Damned scoundrel! He has been playing a double game for too long.' He drew her closer to him whispering. 'Now listen carefully. Varga and I are camped in the valley. The rest of the Cossacks are hidden about a mile away. The ravine is steep but it is not sheer. I have come up that way tonight so as to avoid the road, and we have ropes to help you and the child. Tomorrow there is going to be this celebration. The whole village will be involved, guards as well, and we can only hope that security for that one night at any rate will be slackened. I don't know at what time we will come. We will have to seize our opportunity, so be ready. Stay in here. If they offer to let you out to see the fun, pretend sickness, you or the boy, any excuse you can think of. Somehow we will get you over the wall and down into the valley. With reasonable luck they won't discover you've gone till morning and by then we will have joined up with the rest of my men and must take our chance if we are pursued. Have you got that clear?'

'Yes, I think so, but there is something else . . .'

'What is it?'

'Gregory is here.'

'What!' She felt him stiffen, saw the glitter of his eyes as he turned to her. 'But that is not possible. Gregory is dead. Who told you? Was it Daniel?'

'No, I have seen him and spoken with him. He is among the prisoners who are building the wall.'

'Oh Christ! It is no use, Anna, I can't take him . . . you and the child, but not Gregory.'

'Paul, you must. He is sick and he has gone through so much . . . I cannot leave him here to die.'

'Now that we know where he is, we can carry the information back to the Viceroy. He will arrange ransom.'

'They will never agree to it, never. Long before then, Daniel Gadiani will make sure that he dies. We must do something to help him, we must, Paul.'

'No, it is impossible,' he said violently, and then controlled himself quickly. 'Anna, you must understand. Prisoners will be housed together and strongly guarded. How can I take one man out from among them? It is crazy even to think of such a thing.'

'You could try . . .'

'And ruin everything? Will it help if we are all taken prisoner? I won't do it.'

'It's because you hate him, isn't it? It is your fault that he is here. You tried to kill him once, you left him to die and now you would do it again. If he stays, then I must stay too.'

He suddenly seized hold of her, pulling her close to him 'You love him still, don't you, in spite of everything? He means more to you than I do, or the child, or the lives of my men.'

'No, it isn't that.' She was weeping as she pleaded with him. 'If you'd seen him as I have . . . he is my husband . . .'

'He forfeited all right to that name long ago,' he said savagely. 'He was Natalie's lover, didn't you realize that? In Petersburg first, all the time you were bearing your child, and then here in Tiflis. He took her from me, laughed about it, exulted in it, holding me up to ridicule . . . that was why we fought and I wish to God that I had killed him then!'

She slipped through his hands, falling to her knees, weeping helplessly, the long strain taking its toll at last, and after a moment he bent down, raising her up, holding her against him, speaking soothingly.

'Oh God, I'm sorry . . . I had never meant to tell you . . . don't cry like that, Anna. It's long past, finished and done with. Hush now, you will wake the boy.'

'Yes, yes, I know.' With an heroic effort she tried to control her sobs.

'Listen,' he whispered. 'I can't promise but I'll do what I can. Perhaps Varga will think of something. You say he is sick. How bad is he? Can he walk?'

'His leg is injured, but it has improved a little.'

'Well, he can ride, I suppose, if we do succeed in getting him out.' He turned to the window. 'I shouldn't stay any longer. We mustn't stretch our luck too far.'

She clung to him then, hating to let him leave her. She saw him smile, then he bent his head and kissed her lightly on the lips.

'Pray to everyone you can think of,' he said, 'including Allah the Great, the All-Merciful, because, by heaven, we're going to need it!'

He hoisted himself up, slid through the window and she saw him vanish into the night with an agonizing feeling of loss before she refastened the latch.

Halfway down the slope of the ravine, Varga materialized out of the darkness and joined him.

'Everything arranged, Colonel?'

'I think so. It may not be so difficult as I imagined at first. We can pass the Princess and the child through the window and get them down with the ropes.'

'Good.'

They plodded on, edging their way down step by step before he said, 'There is one hitch that I had not expected. Gregory Gadiani is among the prisoners.'

'He can't be. We saw him dead,' exclaimed the Cossack. 'You remember, sir, months ago, in the spring.'

'That's what we were told, Varga. We must have been mistaken. She has seen him. He is undoubtedly here and wounded.'

'What the devil can we do? We cannot work miracles.'

'We will have to try,' said Paul grimly. 'Find out what you can during the day, where they are imprisoned, whether they are guarded and how. It shouldn't be too difficult with the whole village in a turmoil.'

Varga gave his master a quick look. 'Must we do this, sir? Can't it wait until afterwards? We'll never get such an opportunity again. Shamyl will go up to Dargo-Vedin with no more than half a dozen of his men. With him safely in our hands, we can come back here and rescue the Princess . . . the whole damned lot if necessary.'

'We've already been through all this, Varga. You know as well as I do that there is only a slim chance of us taking Shamyl alive, or dead for that matter, a chance I was prepared to take when it involved only us. But if we fail, or even if we succeed, you know what will happen. They will cut the throats of their prisoners before they cut their own rather than surrender and we can't risk that.'

'The men won't like it, sir. They have waited a long time for this.'

'The men will obey their orders,' said Paul coldly. 'Once we have taken the Princess to safety, we can return.'

'And a lot of good that will be,' muttered Varga under his breath, but he knew that when the Colonel spoke like that, there was no point in arguing with him. Damn all women! he thought to himself. In his opinion they were good for two things only, to give pleasure and to bear strong sons. Yet here was his cool and level-headed master so blinded by love for one of them that he was willing to sacrifice a plan carefully nursed for many months and, even worse, was prepared to jeopardize all their lives by trying to rescue her husband at the same time instead of leaving him to rot as any other sensible person would have done. He would never understand the Russians, never!

———13———

After Paul had gone, Anna sat for a long time, a prey to conflicting feelings that threatened to tear her apart. It surprised
her that Gregory's infidelity still had so much power to hurt.
All those wretched weeks when his son was born and died, he
had been with Natalie. How could he have been so heartless?
What a fool she had been to be so easily deceived. She felt
again the numbing sense of humiliation and rejection. Why
then had she pleaded so strongly for him? Anger struggled
with pity. She knew how much she had asked from Paul. It
was not simply the danger, she was demanding that he risk
his life to rescue a man for whom he felt nothing but contempt and dislike, a man who was her husband. She buried
her face in her hands unable to come to terms with her own
heart. Just to see and speak with Paul, even for those few
minutes, had brought her overwhelming joy and yet she was
preparing to stifle that joy for ever. But how could she leave
Gregory to die in such misery and degradation while the faint-
est chance remained of resucing him? To abandon him deliberately, however they might excuse it to themselves, would
inevitably destroy the love that had sprung between her and
Paul. She could see no way out of the dilemma and as soon
as it was light, she tried to distract her thoughts by going
through their scanty garments and making as much preparation as she could for when the time came, if indeed it ever
did come. At one moment she was dizzy with hope and at the
next plunged into despair thinking of a hundred unforeseen
accidents that could so easily make it impossible.

The day dragged on. Fatimah brought them food, full of
excited talk about the festivities in the village. Vanya was
restless. She tried to interest him in a word and picture game
she had devised but he suddenly flew into a temper, throwing
the worn book to the floor and stamping on it.

'I hate it here. I hate it, I hate it! I want to go home to
Grandmamma,' he screamed.

Exasperated by his tantrum she slapped him hard and he burst into noisy sobs, collapsing into a forlorn heartbroken little heap on the floor. She was repentant at once. The child's nerves were as ragged as her own. She put her arms round him, hugging him to her, whispering comforting words. She would have liked to tell him that soon they might be leaving their hateful prison behind them for ever, but did not dare in case he should blurt it out to Fatimah the next time she came.

Late in the afternoon Kezia Mahommed came, standing cold and aloof in the doorway. 'The Imam wishes me to take the child to him.'

'It's impossible,' she said quickly. 'He is not well.'

'What is wrong with him?'

'He has a cold and a fever. You have only to look at him.'

'Sick or not, the Imam has to be obeyed.'

'Then I must go with him.'

He frowned and then shrugged his shoulders. 'Come then.'

She threw the veil over her face and followed him. The men and women of the village were all crowded together each side of the track with Shamyl seated in a position of honour in the front. He beckoned to her and took Vanya on his knee. Uneasily she saw that Ameera stood close behind him and leaned over, offering the child sweetmeats. Vanya looked at her before he took one and she nodded. Better not to offend anyone with escape so near.

The mountain road out of Karimat was surmounted by a stone arch so low that it was almost impossible for a rider to pass beneath it even if crouched over his horse's neck. The warriors were showing off their skill, galloping up the slope one after the other at breakneck speed. As they approached the arch, they swung themselves sideways in the saddle without slackening speed, seeming to cling by no more than their fingertips. Then as they went under the arch, they rose up in the stirrups with a wild whoop only to wheel their horses and return, repeating the performance. It was the most dazzling piece of horsemanship she had ever seen and at any other time she would have been utterly fascinated. As it was, she could not prevent a lurking anxiety. Supposing Shamyl took the child away from her now? Her mind scurried about distractedly trying to think what she could do.

Then it was all over. Shamyl rose, putting the boy down but still keeping a hand on his shoulder. She moved to go to him but Kezia stopped her.

'The Imam has decided that my wife shall have the care of the boy. You need have no fear, he will be well looked after.'

She stared at him with horror. 'But you can't do that.'

'It is done already.'

'No, no!' She burst through the people around Shamyl, falling on her knees before him, stretching out her hands, imploring him.

'You cannot take him away from me, you cannot. It is too sudden. He is only a little child and he has no father or mother. I am all he has. Please, please, let him stay with me.'

There was dead silence while Shamyl looked at her, his face grave, immovable, with no touch of pity. She had thought all along that he understood more Russian than he pretended and this proved it. For an agonizing moment it seemed their fate hung in the balance. Then Vanya broke away from the restraining hand and ran to her, burrowing his head into her like a little animal seeking refuge. She held him close, waiting breathlessly.

Shamyl said slowly, 'You may keep him for one more day, but in that time you must prepare him for his new life.'

She stumbled to her feet, faint with relief at the narrowness of their escape, but before she could move away Ameera had come swiftly across to her, seizing hold of Vanya and trying to drag him away.

'You promised . . . you promised that he should be mine,' she screamed at her husband.

In an instant they were fighting like madwomen over the helpless child while Kezia did nothing, simply stood by laughing.

Desperately Anna tried to thrust Ameera away, but she was tall and strong. In jealousy and spite she clawed at her rival's hated face and made a vicious grab at the red-gold hair. It was Shamyl who drove them apart.

'Stop!' he thundered. 'Stop! Have you no shame?' Even Ameera did not dare to disobey when the Imam spoke in such a tone. She drew back, panting and dishevelled, her veil torn from her face. 'Kezia, take your wife,' he went on sternly, 'it is not decent to behave thus before me. Do you hear what I say?'

Kezia still grinning gripped Ameera round the waist and lifted her bodily away though she kicked and screeched at him. Anna picked up Vanya and fled down the street. For the first time she was glad to be locked into the comparative safety of their prison room.

All that evening there was noise and laughter as the feast went on outside. She could hear the haunting wail of the pipes and then the stamping of feet as they began to dance. Her face felt sore from Ameera's scratching fingers. She peered through the window but the prisoners were not working on the wall. Perhaps they had been securely locked away or even put in chains. Neither Paul nor Varga would be able to do anything about that. Oh God, would the day never end?

Fatimah brought their supper, a better one than usual, including some scraps from the food they had all been enjoying, but she could not swallow more than a mouthful. Vanya sensed her nervousness. He kept sitting up and refusing to go to sleep when she made him lie down on the mattress.

It was already pitch dark when suddenly there was a fusillade of shots outside. Her heart nearly stopped beating. It went on and on and she was so paralysed with fear and anxiety that she nearly missed the quiet opening of the window she had left unlatched.

'Put out the light,' whispered Paul.

She felt giddy with relief as she hurried to obey him. 'What is that shooting?'

'They are amusing themselves trying their skill by torchlight. With any luck they will end up shooting each other. It's a good moment. They're making enough noise to wake the dead. Quickly now, give me the child.'

When she roused him, Vanya said sleepily, 'Where are we going?'

'Home, we're going home. Come now.' She lifted the boy up and Paul took him through the window passing him to someone else outside.

'Now you,' he said.

She climbed on to the stool and felt him take a firm hold of her. The leg of her pantaloons caught as he eased her through and there was a rending tear. Then he was lifting her down. He closed the window quietly and took her arm. Gradually as her eyes grew accustomed to the darkness she could see over the partly built wall down to the shadowy depths below.

'Don't be afraid,' he said reassuringly. 'It is not as bad as it looks.'

'Where is Gregory?'

'Varga is looking after him, I hope. Now I will go first so that if you slip, I will be there to hold you.' He climbed over, showing her where to place her feet. 'Take hold of the rope. It is quite strong and come down slowly, step by step.'

She did not think she would ever have been able to do it if it had not been for Paul's voice, quietly confident, constantly reassuring her, his hands holding her when she slipped on the rocks and her fingers loosened on the rope. Slowly, bit by bit, they edged their way down until at last they reached the valley. She was standing on grass, there was the sound of water somewhere nearby, and through the darkness she could make out horses, one of the Cossacks standing beside them with Vanya. The boy came running to her, half scared, half excited.

'Are we really going home, Anna?'

'Yes, darling, we are . . . very soon.'

He did a little dance. 'Goody, goody, goody!'

The Cossack said, 'Shall we go on now, Colonel?'

Paul was looking up the ravine. 'If Varga does not come in a few minutes, Grishka, you will take the Princess and the boy. I will wait for him.'

'I would rather stay,' she said quickly. She went to stand beside him. 'Do you think Varga will find Gregory?'

'How can I tell?'

The minutes passed and the tension grew. Everything in the valley was quiet though faintly they could still hear the sound of shooting from Karimat.

Paul said quietly, 'I think you should go on, Anna, the sooner we get you away from here and join the rest of my men the better.'

'No, I will wait.'

They stood close together. She could feel his anger. There was a gulf between them that she did not know how to cross. Then Grishka pointed.

'Isn't that Varga now, your honour?'

They strained their eyes. A shape, darker than the surrounding scrub, was moving slowly down but whether it was one man or two it was impossible to make out.

The Tartars were using the prisoners as target practice, not shooting them down, but what was more nerve-racking, standing them up against the wall and firing all around them by the light of the torches.

Varga pushed his way through the cheering shouting spectators. 'These devils certainly think up some pretty nasty games!' he muttered to himself.

The Russians were standing in a dejected line, each one wondering when his turn would come, hoping he would have the courage to stand and be fired at without crumpling into a faint as one had done already to hoots of derision. Varga slowly moved towards them. There was so much enthusiasm and noise, so much jostling to get a better view, that no one was taking any notice of the peddler marvelling at the fine show and now and again exchanging a coarse jest at the expense of the victims. Gregory was at the end of the line, a little apart from the others, one hand supporting himself against the wall to take the weight off his injured leg. Varga waited until the fun was at its height and then sidled up to him and touched his arm.

'Come,' he whispered.

Gregory opened his mouth to speak and the Cossack immediately clapped his hand over it. 'Don't argue. If you want to get out of this hell hole, keep your trap shut and follow me.'

Taken by surprise, the young man still had the sense to make no outcry but seized his chance to slide away into the shadows. Varga quickened his pace.

'Hurry.'

'I'm doing my best.'

Varga hooked Gregory's arm round his shoulders, taking half his weight. 'There's no time to lose.'

'Who the devil are you?'

'Never mind about that.'

They slid along the back of the huts and Gregory pulled back a little. 'I can't go alone . . .'

'Your wife and the boy are already gone. This way . . . over you go.'

Gregory looked down the steep slope despairingly. 'I'll never do it.'

'You must. Come on, sir.'

Varga had released the rope and let it fall. No point in telling the pursuers which way they had gone.

'Now I will go first. This way . . . give me your hand.'

It was fortunate that Gregory had lost so much weight during his imprisonment or it might have been too much even for Varga's great strength. As it was, he was half carrying him most of the way.

Down in the valley Anna was watching intently. At every moment she expected them to fall, but slowly and surely the dark shape crawled crabwise down the mountain slope until the last dozen feet when Varga suddenly missed his footing and they rolled down together. The Cossack was up in an instant but Gregory lay in a crumpled heap.

Anna started forward but Paul drew her back. 'Let me.' He bent down. 'Are you hurt?'

'Winded, that's all.'

'Good. Come now, on your feet.' Paul took hold of his hands and pulled him up. They were standing face to face.

'My God! Kuragin! It can't be!' exclaimed Gregory breathlessly and then began to laugh. 'You . . . of all people! How damned funny. What the devil are you doing here?'

'Never mind that now,' said Paul curtly. 'What's more to the point, can you ride?'

'I can try.'

'Come on then. Varga, give him a hand. Now you, Anna. We've no saddle for ladies, I'm afraid.'

'It doesn't matter. I can manage.'

He lifted her to the back of the horse, then swung himself into his own saddle. Grishka lifted the boy and Paul took him up before him. He turned round to face them.

'After about a mile we shall meet up with the rest of my party. We need to put as much distance as we can between us and this place before morning. Follow me and for God's sake, take care. It's a devilishly rough road.'

It might have been only a mile, but it took them the best part of an hour. Paul had hidden his men in an inaccessible cleft of the mountain to which there was no regular path. They rode in single file picking their way carefully through the darkness lit only by a few stars.

'Does he think we are mountain goats?' grumbled Gregory as his horse stumbled for the third time jerking an exclamation of pain out of him.

'Better a mountain goat than being riddled like a colander by Tartar bullets,' grunted Varga behind him.

It must have been close on three o'clock when at last they reached the rest of the Cossacks. They came swarming around them, staring at Anna in her torn pantaloons and dirty shawl and plying Varga and Grishka with questions until Paul silenced them. 'Keep your voices down. We're not out of the wood yet by a long chalk.'

They dismounted wearily. Vanya was half asleep and Paul handed him over to Varga.

'Now listen,' he said as they gathered round him. 'I've

been thinking. To push on now through the night is too dangerous. We dare not take the obvious route and it's a stony difficult track we must follow quite apart from the risk of losing our way. In two hours it will be dawn. I'd advise you to get some rest, particularly you Anna . . . and Gregory too. Grishka and I will go back and see if by any unlucky chance your escape has yet been discovered. If, for one reason or another, we don't return, Varga knows what to do.'

'Is that wise?' interrupted Gregory. 'Wouldn't it be best for all of us to keep together?'

'I know what I'm doing,' said Paul abruptly. 'When they take the prisoners back to their quarters, you may be missed.'

'The others are good fellows. They will cover up for me.'

'We can't count on that.'

'If they are already in pursuit,' argued Gregory, 'they could follow you back here.'

'Afraid for your skin, Gadiani?' said Paul witheringly. 'Don't worry. After having taken the trouble to get you out, I'll not give you up so easily.'

The young man flushed. 'God damn it! I'll not take that lying down . . .'

'Gregory, please . . .' Anna put a restraining hand on his arm.

Paul had already swung himself into the saddle and turned his horse's head along the way they had come with Grishka hurrying to keep up with him.

Gregory stared after him. 'Who the hell does he think he is?'

'He has already risked a great deal. Can't you understand? We are all on edge. Paul as much as any of us.'

The night had turned cold and Anna shivered in her flimsy rags. The Cossacks had built a small fire and Varga busied himself with spreading thick felt *bourkas* on the ground.

'Warm yourselves,' he said to them, 'and take some rest as the Colonel says. We could have a very long day tomorrow.'

He wrapped Vanya in a rug and put him close to Anna. The little boy went on mumbling for a while and then suddenly fell asleep in the way children do. Anna pulled the cloak round her gratefully. Gregory had dropped down beside her, holding his hands out to the comforting heat.

'By heaven, this feels good. I still can't believe I'm free, Anna. How did it happen? How in God's name did Paul come to be here? Did Vorontsov send him on a rescue mission?'

'No. It was the purest chance. He came to Karimat for quite another purpose.'

'And threw it up for your sake?'

'Not just for me. There was Vanya.'

'It's not like Paul. He can be ruthless when it suits him. I ought to know.'

'I have not found him so.'

'How did he know about me?'

'I told him.'

Gregory leaned back, his hands behind his head. 'You know it's damned amusing. Last time we met he was doing his level best to kill me, now he is playing the hero and risking his life to get me to safety. I wonder why.'

'Does it matter why?' she said wearily. 'And I don't find it at all amusing. Don't you think you had better do as he says and try to sleep?'

He raised himself on his elbow, looking at her. 'How did you persuade him? He detests me, he always did. You know that, don't you?'

'He had good reason.'

'What did he tell you?'

'A great many things which I don't want to talk about now.'

Deliberately she turned away from him, huddling herself into the thick cloak and pulling Vanya into the circle of her arm.

'Is he in love with you?'

'Oh for heaven's sake, must you go on about things like that now? Why on earth should he be?'

'Because you have grown quite astonishingly beautiful, Anna. I saw that up in that vile hole . . . that very first day.'

'No, Gregory please. . . don't talk such nonsense.'

'It is not nonsense.'

He lay watching her through half-closed eyes. It was true, he thought, even in those dirty rags with her hair wild and uncombed. The firelight lit her face, thinner than he remembered it but that only accentuated the fine bones. No wonder that fellow Kezia had wanted her and now Paul . . . She was no longer the lovely child he had married, but a mature woman who had suffered and learned to overcome it, and he felt a sharp pang of jealousy that other men should desire what he had wantonly thrown away.

They were roused at dawn. It was very cold and everything was shrouded in a thick white mist so that men and horses seemed to move about in it like ghosts. Varga brought them mugs of boiling tea. There was no lemon or sugar but it was the first she had tasted for so long that Anna sipped the pale amber liquid gratefully. With it there was hard-baked biscuit, some of which she dipped into the tea and fed to Vanya.

Then Paul, mug in hand, came striding up to them through the mist. He had discarded his peddler's disguise and washed some of the stain from his face. He wore the tight-fitting coat and breeches of the mountaineers, indistinguishable from his men. Apart from their weapons there was nothing about any of them to suggest that they were soldiers engaged in a military mission.

'This fog will clear as soon as the sun comes up,' he said cheerfully. 'I hope you got some sleep.'

Gregor had struggled to his feet. His face looked grey and exhausted in the pallid morning light. He said, 'What happened when you went back to Karimat last night?'

'Very little. It was quiet enough until just before we decided to turn back. Then we saw a small party, not more than six or so, ride out, but there was no alarm so that I'm not sure whether it was a routine patrol or whether they were in search of you and Anna. At any rate they took a completely different route and we are well hidden here. By now they will believe us to be much further away. With reasonable luck we should be able to avoid them.' He looked them over keenly. 'The thing that has been troubling me is how to provide you both with more adequate clothing. At this time of the year we could get any kind of weather, even snow. Varga has been searching through our saddle bags. We can't provide Parisian fashions, but I think we can do a little better than what you are wearing.'

Anna took the bundle the Cossack handed over to her and retreated into the shelter of the rocks. A tiny spring trickled from above her head into a little stone basin before disappearing into the ferns and undergrowth. She stripped off the motley garments she had worn for so long and bathed her face and neck in the ice-cold water. Then she pulled on a pair of voluminous black breeches, a calico shirt and a thick embroidered jacket, bizarre certainly but far warmer and more practical than the soiled rags they had given her at Karimat.

Her spirits rose. She felt gay and cheerful. She came back, swaggering a little, hands on hips.

'What do you think? Will I do?'

'Excellently,' said Paul smiling, 'except for the feet and I think we can even do something about that. Varga, where are those boots you took in exchange for a roll of silk?'

Varga dived into the bag again and came up like a jack-in-the-box with a pair of red leather boots adorned with large gold tassels.

'Great Heaven, they're whore's boots!' exclaimed Gregory.

'Actually she was a gypsy dancer,' mumbled the Cossack repressively.

'I don't know what else Varga had to give for them,' said Paul grinning, 'but they were a bargain.'

'I don't care where they came from so long as they fit,' and Anna sat down, kicking off her worn slippers and pulling on the boots. She stretched out her feet. 'I shall have to stuff the toes but that's better than being too small. Shall I cut off my hair then I shall really look like a boy?

'No,' said Paul quickly, 'don't do that. There's no need. I daresay we can find you a cap somewhere.'

Gregory's Persian coat and breeches would have fitted a man twice his size. He tied the sash around his waist looking down at himself ruefully. 'Not exactly Petersburg style but what the hell! Anna looks good though, doesn't she, Paul? Pretty enough to eat. Our little camp follower . . . Vive la Vivandière!' and he seized Anna's hands, twirling her round and round before pulling her into his arms and kissing her violently. Then he staggered and might have fallen but for her arm holding him up.

Paul's amusement abruptly vanished. 'I think you had better reserve your high spirits until we reach the end of our journey.'

'Damn it, I know you're right, but after the last hellish months it feels marvellous just to be free.'

'I've no doubt it does. Let's hope we can keep it that way. Now here's what I intend to do. We are making for a Russian garrison in South Caucasia. We should reach it in four or five days.'

'Five days!' exclaimed Anna. 'It took far longer than that when they brought me here.'

'Very likely they would have taken devious routes so as to avoid Russian patrols. It is quite possible that we may have to do the same if Shamyl's horsemen are on the war path. Once we reach the garrison, a military escort will take you and Gregory to Tiflis.'

'What about you?'

'I have other plans.'

'What plans?'

'I don't think they need concern us at the moment. Today I hope to reach a mountain settlement I know of. They are neutral, neither for Shamyl nor against him and I am afraid they are not entirely trustworthy but we must risk it. I badly need extra food for all of us and milk for the boy. Provided we look like any ordinary folk travelling with our merchandise and you leave the bargaining to Varga and me, I think we may do well enough and avoid suspicion. Now if you're ready, we should be on our way.'

It was a long and arduous day. There was little sun and the wind blew cold at times. On the high peaks snow had already fallen and lay in long white streaks, but they made good progress. Despite the confinement and poor food of the last weeks, Anna kept up remarkably well, the sense of freedom after the apathy and despair helping to counter fatigue. It was in the late afternoon when, nose to tail, they were following down a long defile that Gregory suddenly collapsed. He would have fallen from his horse if Grishka had not ridden up and supported him. Anna moved quickly to his other side. The Cossacks halted and Paul who had been riding ahead, came trotting back.

'What's the trouble?'

Gregory had recovered a little. He tried to hold himself upright. 'I'm all right now. Let us go on.'

Paul looked at him keenly. 'We have about another two hours' riding by my reckoning. Do you think you can do it?'

Gregory managed a weak smile. 'I will have to, won't I?'

'It will help if you can.' Paul pulled a flask from his pocket, unscrewed the silver top and handed it over. 'Take a pull of this.' Gregory swallowed a mouthful and a faint tinge of colour came back into his face. 'Do you want to keep it with you?'

'No.'

'Right.' Paul put the flask back in his pocket. 'It will serve for another emergency. Two of you men had better ride close beside him. Let me know how he goes on.'

He turned his horse and rode forward again. Anna took one look at Gregory's drawn face and cantered after him.

'He is very sick, Paul. Can't we make camp here?'

'It would be most unwise. There is no cover and we wouldn't be able to light a fire. Besides it is better for him that he should pull himself together. Once he gives up, it will be all over with him . . . and maybe with us too.'

'You are being very hard.'

'Not hard, practical.'

'Are you angry with me?'

'Why should I be angry? Go back to your husband, Anna, keep his spirits up. He needs you.'

It was going to be an impossible situation, Anna had already realized that, but it had happened and there was nothing she could do about it. She thought that Paul was being unreasonable, but he was also doing everything within his power to help them so how could she blame him? She longed to tell him she loved him, that Gregory meant nothing to her any longer, but how could she when he held her at a distance and she could not get close to him?

Somehow Gregory kept up until the end of their day's journey. It was dark when they reached the village, a poor place of some dozen black huts clinging to the hillside, a few scrawny sheep on the thin pasture and one or two hens scratching in the dirt road. They halted outside while Paul went forward to talk to the headman. Presently he came back.

'There is an empty granary we can use. It will provide some kind of shelter.' They followed him through the village and further up the mountainside. Then he drew rein. 'Carry Prince Gadiani in,' he commanded.

'I can walk,' said Gregory unsteadily.

'This is no time for heroics. Take care of him now.'

He helped Anna to dismount and she followed the men into the bare barn-like place. They laid Gregory down on a bed of straw. He was obviously in great pain. He groaned, moving restlessly. She was kneeling beside him when Paul came in.

He looked down at him for a moment. 'Better let me see that leg of yours.'

'What can you do? It's only the riding. I shall be better tomorrow.'

'Don't talk like a damned fool.' He knelt down beside Anna. Gregory glared at him.

'Leave me alone. I want nothing from you.'

But Paul ignored him. 'Help me,' he said to Anna.

Together they eased off the breeches and Paul unwound the bandages round his thigh. The wound had festered and there was a sickening smell. All around the thigh and stretching down to his knee, the flesh was hideously swollen and streaked with red. Gregory winced as Paul prodded it gently.

'God knows I'm no doctor but there is infection there. It will have to be opened up before it spreads any further.'

'Can you do it?'

'There is no one else,' he said grimly. 'Can you assist me or shall I call one of the men?'

'No, I'll do it.'

They made what preparations they could. Varga brought a lantern and some clean cloths with a bowl of heated water. Paul drew his dagger.

'You had better hold him down,' he said to the Cossack.

'Keep your damned hands off me,' said Gregory fiercely through clenched teeth.

'Very well. Please yourself.'

Paul held the blade in the candle flame for a moment, then cut across the swollen purple flesh. Anna held the bowl as he pressed on the wound, wiping away the pus and blood and then cleansing it as well as he could before pouring into it a little of the brandy from the flask. He began to wind the clean bandages around it. Gregory was shivering with cold and shock. Paul covered him with the blanket that Varga had brought and poured a little more of the brandy into the silver top of the flask. He held it to Gregory's lips.

'Drink it. It will warm you. It's the best I can do. It should at least do something to relieve the pain.'

He got to his feet. 'They will be bringing some soup soon,' he said to Anna. 'Give him a little, not too much. It will help him to sleep.'

Varga had taken away the bowl and the soiled bandages. Anna followed Paul to the door. It was good to breathe the clean cold air after the nauseating stench of infection and blood.

'How bad is he?'

'Bad enough, but he should improve a little now and if we can get him to the garrison in a few days, there may well be a regimental surgeon. What worries me is that we may have to stay here for a day or so if he cannot ride.'

'Will that matter?'

'Any delay is dangerous. Still, the folk here have promised us eggs and milk tomorrow. Some decent food may help him.'

'Paul, I am sorry to have caused you all this trouble.'

In the faint light she saw him smile. 'It's not exactly your fault, is it? It is what novelists would call the workings of fate. I ought to be used to them by now. Don't worry. I'll get you both to safety if it is humanly possible. And now go and lie down yourself. You must be worn out.'

'Oh heaven, I forgot all about Vanya. Where is he?'

'He is with the men and enjoying himself hugely. Don't fret. I'll make sure he is looked after and comes to no harm. Good-night, Anna.'

He walked away from her into the night and she went back to Gregory. Varga had left the lantern and she carried it nearer to the bed.

He said, 'What were you talking about out there?'

'You.' She helped him to sit up a little, putting a rolled cloak behind him and trying to make him comfortable. 'Paul thinks we may have to stay here for a day or two to give you time to recover.'

'He must have been wishing he had left me to rot in Karimat.'

'Don't talk so foolishly.'

'Do you wish that, Anna, do you?' Feverishly he sought for her hand. She let it lie in his and was saved from answering by Grishka coming in with bowls of hot soup, some bread and half a cup of vodka. She knew they had spared it out of their own ration and was deeply grateful.

She persuaded Gregory to take the soup and a little of the spirit and after a while, worn out with pain and fatigue, he fell asleep. Every bone in her body ached from the unaccustomed riding, but she sat on beside him, trying not to think of what would happen when finally they got back to Tiflis. At the moment in his pain it was easy to tend him as she would a sick child, but when he recovered, then it would be different. Then he would make demands on her and how could she refuse him? She was his wife after all. It was a long time before she spread the blanket on the bundle of straw and lay down on the other side of the barn, and longer still before she slept.

——14——

It was early when Anna woke up. Light was filtering through the wooden slats at the top of the door. The barn was cold and smelled mustily of the grass and straw and animal fodder which had been stored there and still lay heaped untidily in the corners where rats and mice had scuffled and squeaked all through the night.

After a moment she pushed back the blanket and went across to look at Gregory. He was still asleep, one arm flung out, the black hair matted with sweat. He looked young and vulnerable and so like the handsome boy she had married that she felt a pang of pity because so much had happened to them since then and it was impossible to go back. You cannot revive the dead ashes of love. She had been aware of that during the night when he had woken asking for water and after she had brought it to him, had tried to pull her down to lie beside him. She had hidden her instinctive revulsion, drawing herself away from him gently, but she knew then with an absolute certainty that she would never willingly sleep with him again.

She groped for her boots and her thick jacket, pulled them on, tucked her hair under the red cap Paul had found for her, opened the door and crept out.

Outside the wind was sharp and keen, the mountain peaks flushed a rosy pink in the first light. The Cossacks were already up, brewing tea over a little fire. There was an appetizing smell of frying that made her realize how hungry she was. She hesitated and then went to join them. They rose respectfully, but she waved them down again, preferring the easy comradeship that her boy's dress made possible. One of them brought her a mug of tea. Vanya was sitting on Grishka's knee munching a crust of bread, his face covered with egg. He looked healthy, dirty and very happy. He had been shy with Gregory the previous day, staring at him, not recognizing his elegant half brother in the gaunt bearded stranger. She thought that in the circumstances he was better with the Cossacks than shut up with her and a sick man.

Then Paul came walking up the track from the village. Somehow he had contrived to shave and clean himself up. He looked strong and attractive and she had to school herself not to run to meet him. He was carrying a crock in his hand and set it down before the fire.

'It's goat's milk. Give some to the boy. Good morning, Anna. You're awake early. How is Gregory?'

'He is still sleeping.'

'I'd better see if there is anything I can do for him.'

She did not go with him. There were things a man could do to help his weakness that Gregory would resent from her. She knelt down by the fire, glad of the warmth in the chill morning air and one of the soldiers shyly offered her a slice of bread with a fried egg on it. She accepted it with pleasure and ate it hungrily. Presently she went back to the barn and paused in the doorway for a moment.

Gregory was saying irritably, 'I can manage alone. There is no need for you to play sick nurse.'

'Better me than one of my men.'

'Where the devil is Anna?'

'Eating her breakfast if she has any sense. They will bring you food in a few minutes. I wouldn't stand on that leg too much today if I were you. We still have a long way to go.'

'I am aware of that. What do you take me for?'

Paul did not answer and a few minutes later when he came through the door, Anna stopped him.

'Have you made up your mind what you are going to do?'

'Remain here for a few hours at any rate. We have kept guard during the night and so far there are no signs of pursuit but we can never be sure. In these mountains an ambush can be lurking anywhere. I'm going to take a short ride above the village. I've been talking to some of the peasants and I'm wondering if I can find a route that will provide easier riding for Gregory.'

'Can I come with you?'

'Shouldn't you stay with your husband?'

'There's nothing I can do for him just now and after so much confinement, it feels good to be free and able to breathe fresh air. Please, Paul.'

He hesitated and then said abruptly, 'Very well. In about ten minutes then.'

When she went into the barn she saw that Paul had banked up the bales of straw to make a sort of chair bed so that Gregory could lean back against it with his bad leg stretched out in front of him.

'Where the hell have you been?' he said.

'Nowhere in particular. I wanted to make sure that Vanya was all right.'

'Oh God, yes, the boy. I had forgotten him. Where is he?'

'He is with the Cossacks, having a wonderful time.'

'He should be here with us.'

She paused in folding up the blanket she had used during the night. 'Oh I don't know, Gregory, why? They spoil him outrageously, but it is only for a few days. He is happier with them than being cooped up in here.'

'Why do you say that? God knows what he will pick up from them. He is not a brat out of the gutter. He is my brother, isn't he, a Gadiani?'

'Of course he is but we're not as Kumari now. Does it matter what he picks up? He'll forget it again in a week and you are sick. You need to rest and be quiet. A small boy playing around you would drive you out of your mind.'

'You will be here, won't you?'

'No. I'm going out for a little while.' She moved over, tidying his makeshift bed as best she could.

He looked up at her quickly. 'Where?'

'I'm going with Paul. He wants to try and find an easier track for you to travel by,' she said calmly, shaking out the blanket, then putting it over him again and tucking it in.

His fingers closed on her wrist in a bruising grip. 'You're not going.'

She did not struggle. She stood quite still. 'Oh yes I am. Gregory, let me go.'

'You are my wife,' he said stubbornly. 'I forbid you to go with him.'

'You cannot forbid me to do anything, not now,' she said quietly. 'You have no right. You had better realize that once and for all.'

'What exactly do you mean by that?'

'What I say. I'm not a child any longer, Gregory. I've grown up. I make my own decisions.'

He stared into her face for a moment and then let his hand fall to his side.

'I thought you would be glad to stay with me,' he said pathetically.

He could turn so quickly from arrogance to pleading and once it had possessed power to charm her, but not any more. She was armoured against it.

'I shall not be long,' she said, 'not more than hour.'

The hard pressure of his fingers had bruised her wrist. She was rubbing it when Paul came in, but if he noticed anything, he made no comment.

'The men will be keeping watch,' he said, 'and Varga is in command. I don't anticipate any danger, but one can never tell and I don't care to think of you unarmed. You had better have this.' He put one of his silver-mounted pistols on the blanket. 'It is loaded, so take care. I don't want to come back and find one of my Cossacks with his head blown off.'

With a curious half smile Gregory's hand closed round the butt. 'You're very trusting. I owe you a shot, you know. Hasn't it occurred to you that I might blow your head off?'

'Reserve it until we reach somewhere safe,' said Paul lightly. 'You may need me till then.'

They were joking of course and yet beneath the banter Anna detected a latent hostility that at the slightest thing could flare into an explosion.

Gregory said suddenly, angrily, 'Go if you're going and send someone back with some food. Have I to wait all day?'

Paul smiled. 'Hunger is a good sign. You must be feeling better, and we've got eggs and milk. I'll see that they bring it to you and afterwards I'll tell Grishka to fetch my razors and shave you. It's a great thing for keeping up one's morale. Believe me, I speak from experience.'

Riding beside Paul up the mountain road and then down into the valley, Anna was reminded of the many days they had spent together on the way from Pyatigorsk. It was only just over six months ago and yet so much had changed. Then she had lived from day to day, uncertain of the future, but imperceptibly something had sparked between them, a feeling that at any other time might have taken time to grow, but that danger and circumstances had brought to sudden flowering. She felt uneasily that it would have been wiser not to have come with him this morning, that she was perhaps playing with fire, and yet she had been unable to resist the temptation. She stole a glance at the lean face beside her and wondered if he felt the same. Ever since she had pleaded with him to rescue Gregory, he had deliberately kept himself aloof, kind and considerate, but with no hint of the intimacy they had known in Tiflis. She knew it was for the best and yet she rebelled against it.

For a while he said very little. Every now and again he halted, looking keenly around him, observing the countryside, referring to the position of the sun and making comments which she did not fully understand and answered at random. He did not touch on anything personal until they were walking their horses along a stretch of green turf.

'I'm not sure that you should have done this,' he said.

'Done what?'

'Come with me this morning. Gregory is bound to resent it.'

The fact that he echoed her own uneasiness put her on the defensive. 'Why should he?'

'He is sick and in pain and it enrages him that you should apparently find pleasure in the company of another man. I understand. In similar circumstances I might feel much the same.'

'You're quite wrong. Gregory has not been in love with me for a very long time. I knew that nearly a year before he left me to come to the Caucasus.'

'I don't think that matters. He has had many months to brood on it and you are still his wife. He resents losing you.'

'He does not own me and I do everything I can for him.'

'I am not blind, Anna. You care for him as you would care for Vanya or for one of my men if it were necessary.'

'Is that my fault?' He did not answer and she glanced at him curiously. 'Would you really feel like that if you were he?'

He was staring straight before him. 'Every time I see you with him, I have an entirely primitive desire to seize him by the throat and strangle him,' he said savagely. 'Does that please you?'

She gave a little gasp. That must have been how he looked when he faced Gregory, pistol in hand. She said shakily, 'You are making fun of me.'

'Perhaps,' he smiled grimly. 'It is true all the same.'

'Then it does please me. Is that very wicked of me? Should I be going down on my knees and thanking God that Gregory has been given back to me? I wish I could, Paul, I do really wish I could!' And in a sudden rage at the trick life had played on her, she kicked her horse and it sprang forward.

He followed her at once, putting a hand on her bridle to slow her up. 'Take care. This is not a time to act rashly.'

'I know. I'm sorry.'

They rode side by side in silence for a little while and then Paul said, 'Do you remember that night at Daniel Gadiani's party?'

'Of course I do.'

'Do you still believe that I callously left him to die?'

'How can I after what you have done for him?'

'I don't know what Gregory has told you, but it is true enough that when I went out to meet him that morning, I had murder in my heart. I suppose it can happen to all men at some time or another. The Prince had issued an edict against duelling which is why we had no seconds. If it had leaked out, he would have had us both put under arrest. It was not until I faced him that I realized what a damned fool I was making of myself. It was Natalie who should have been standing there. She had played us off one against the other and Gregory was as much her victim as I had been. I was bitter and resentful, loathing myself and him, so I shot at random and rode away. But I did go back. God knows why. I had no reason to believe him seriously hurt, but when I got there, he had gone, and it was not until much later that I guessed at what had happened. You know the rest.'

'I wish you had told me when we first spoke of Gregory.'

'How could I? How can you say to a young woman you scarcely know that you had every intention of killing her husband?'

'But afterwards when we knew one another better . . .'

'Afterwards,' he said wryly, 'I cared too much. I thought you would hate me for it and I was right, wasn't I?'

'Not for long.'

'Is that really true?' He had turned to her when she saw his face change. His hand clamped down on her bridle. 'Quickly,' he whispered, 'this way . . .'

'What is it?'

'Into the trees.' He was pulling her horse after him into the shelter of the copse beside the track. He slid from the saddle and bewildered she did the same.

'What is wrong?'

'Ssh, keep very quiet and still.' Cautiously he parted the branches a little and pointed. 'Look—up there on the ridge.'

She could see them clearly, the line of black horsemen, banners fluttering from their long lances. She felt her heart thud unpleasantly and drew nearer to him.

'Are they hunting for us?'

'I doubt it. They are a war party, I should say, and they are moving in the opposite direction, but if they have scouts scouring the countryside who knows what they might find out and in this wilderness we would be horribly conspicuous.'

They watched them until they had disappeared and all was silent again except for the sound of birds and the whistle of wind in the high rocks. Then he said, 'We ought to go back.'

They were very close under the trees. In her fright she had taken his arm. Strands of red-gold hair had escaped from under the absurd little hat and blew across her face. She put up a hand to push them out of her eyes, those velvet eyes with the long curling lashes that had first attracted his attention, and he knew that he wanted her passionately. He had been deliberately holding himself in check, determined to say nothing, reveal nothing, until the question of Gregory was settled once and for all, but now without warning, his self control slipped. His kisses took her by surprise; she stumbled back against the tree and then hopelessly, ravenously, gave herself up to them. He kissed her eyes, her throat, the first swell of her breast through the open neck of the shirt and then came back to her mouth until he felt her body tremble and relax against him. He knew that he could have taken her there and then on the short green turf, that she wanted him as much as he wanted her and it would have been joy and release. But this had never been an idle affair. This was like nothing else, it was the best thing that had happened to him and he would not cheapen it. Still holding her, he drew away a little.

'Anna, when this is all over, will you come to me? Will you leave Gregory and come away with me?'

She had been bowled over by a storm of feeling that had nearly engulfed her and she was shaking as she looked up at him, scarcely taking in what he asked of her.

'Leave Gregory? How can I?'

'Have you the courage to let him divorce you?'

'Divorce?' she repeated faintly. 'But the scandal, the shame ... you would have to give up your army career ...'

'To hell with that!'

'Then there is your home, your uncle . . .'

'There is no one close to me who matters. We could live abroad if necessary . . . in Europe . . .'

'You wouldn't like that.' She was slowly pulling herself together. She said more firmly, 'I cannot abandon Gregory, not until he has recovered, and then there is Vanya. I promised the Princess that I would look after him.'

He brushed it aside. 'I will make sure that the child is properly brought up and educated.'

'Gregory would never give him up to you and he is not fit to have the care of a child. Vanya is my responsibility now.'

He released her suddenly. 'You think of too many excuses. Is it so important to you to remain the Princess Gadiani?'

'You know it is not.'

'Because if it is,' he went on, 'I do not intend to be your lap-dog lover. I've finished with all that. I want a wife, Anna. I want your children.'

'So do I, more than anything in the world, but this is not the way.'

'Then what is the way?' he said brutally. 'Do we wait for him to die or do I push him down a precipice?'

'Don't say such things.'

'I'm sorry but what else is there to say?' Abruptly he turned away. 'We must go back. We've wasted too much time already.'

He began to disentangle the horses' bridles and then helped her into the saddle, but she could not bear to let him go with this sudden coldness that had sprung between them. She grasped his hand.

'Paul, I love you. You must believe that.'

He looked long into her eyes. 'I wish I could,' and then because he could not trust himself, he leaped into the saddle and set a fast pace to take them back to the village.

The moment Anna went into the barn she knew that Gregory was in one of the difficult maddening moods she had known so well in the past, a mood when he was at odds with the whole world and when nothing she or anyone else did would be right.

'I didn't expect you to be gone the whole morning,' he burst out almost at once. 'I wonder you took the trouble to come back at all.'

She was still emotionally shaken by the scene with Paul. It

was hard to be patient with him. She said quietly, 'It took time and we had to be very careful.'

'I might have been dead lying here for all the notice anyone took of me.' It was so like a fractious child that she could not help smiling and that made it worse.

'It is nothing to laugh about.'

'I'm not laughing, but Gregory, you only had to call. Paul left one of his men on guard outside. He would have come at once.'

'I don't care to be dependent on serfs,' he said angrily.

'Oh Gregory, don't be childish. At the moment we all depend on one another. We were longer than we intended because we saw a party of Shamyl's horsemen and we had to take cover for a while.'

He pushed himself up against the straw. 'Are they coming here?'

'Paul doesn't think so, but he has gone to talk to his men now. We may have to move on sooner than he intended.'

'God, if only I weren't so damned crippled! I seem to have escaped out of one hell-hole only to find myself in another.'

'How can you say that?' she exclaimed indignantly. 'At least you are here with us, with your friends. You ought to be grateful to Paul for bringing you out of Karimat.'

'Paul, Paul, Paul! Can't you ever talk about anyone else?'

'We'd be in a poor way without him,' she said dryly.

She had not fully realized the depth of his frustration. He had been lying there all the morning, still very feverish, anger boiling up in him against Daniel Gadiani for his treachery, against Paul and the crazy quarrel over Natalie that had put him where he was, above all against pain and the tormenting fear that the poison in his leg, despite Paul's rough surgery, would creep up and up until it killed him. Rather die now, fighting his enemies, gun in hand, than be dragged mile after mile, helpless as a log.

He watched Anna as she picked up a cloth, dipping it in a bowl of water and wringing it out. It maddened him that imprisonment and privation had only made her stronger and more beautiful, even in those ridiculous clothes. He had not had a woman for so long and she was his wife. Last night she had refused to come to him when he wanted to feel her close to him and he had thought it due to his sickness but now he was not so sure. His inflamed imagination saw her going out among the men, flaunting her body in front of the Cossacks, laughing and joking with Paul, when she should have been with him, caring for him, loving him.

Anna brought the cool damp cloth and wiped the sweat from his face. She too was on edge, but trying hard to be calm and reasonable. She put the cloth aside and sat down beside him.

'Have you thought what you will do when we get back to Tiflis?' she said.

'I shall make damned sure that Daniel gets what is coming to him.'

'But after that. Will you go to Kumari?'

'For a while, I suppose,' he said indifferently. 'I shall have to see Grandmother, but not for long.' He hoisted himself up suddenly, his eyes lighting up. 'We'll go back to Petersburg, Anna, back to the old life. I was a fool ever to come to the Caucasus.'

'But surely you ought to stay here now. It is your home and your people expect it of you. There is so much that you can do. Your grandmother told me about it. Kumaria is beautiful, far more so than I ever expected. Why didn't you tell me more about it, Gregory?'

'It was a hell of a place when I was a child. Half the time we were being driven out of it. Besides Grandmother can take care of it.' He laughed. 'She could run the whole Caucasus singlehanded if given the chance.'

'But she is old now. You ought to shoulder some of the responsibility.'

'Oh be damned to that! That's your father in you, Anna, always worrying about his duty to his fellow men. Grandmother has still got a good few years yet. No, it's Petersburg for me. I want to enjoy myself, make up for all the time I've lost.'

She sat back on her heels. 'I don't want to go back to that old life, Gregory. Have you forgotten what it was like?'

'What was wrong with it?'

'Everything . . . wrong for me and for you. I realize that now. It was empty and futile and I hated it.' And quite suddenly all the things she had meant never to mention swept over her, the pain and humiliation she had suffered at his hands, the months of wretchedness, Natalie's openly shown contempt, and she could not stop herself, the words poured out. 'Have you forgotten that you left me to go to Natalie? All those weeks when the baby was coming and afterwards, you were with her, laughing at me, making fun of me when I needed you so badly . . .'

'How do you know that?'

'Does it matter how I know?'

He was staring at her as if she were mad. 'But that's all over and done with. What's the use of bringing it up now? It's forgotten.'

'Finished with perhaps but not forgotten,' she said passionately. 'How could I forget? Natalie is there in Tiflis waiting for you, and if not her, then some other woman. I'm not going back to that life, Gregory, nothing will make me.'

'You have no choice. You are my wife.'

'You cannot force it on me,' and in her vehemence the words came out which she had never really intended to say. 'I want a separation.'

'A separation? What the devil do you mean by that? Are you talking of divorce?'

'Yes,' she said recklessly. 'Yes, a divorce, if there is no other way.'

'No,' he said violently. 'Never. It is unthinkable. A Gadiani could never stoop to such dishonour.'

'Maybe not, but he can take a mistress, he can treat his wife like a slave, walk out on her and leave her to face humiliation alone,' she retorted bitterly. 'That is not dishonourable I suppose.'

'This is Paul's doing, isn't it? I might have known. It's been staring me in the face all the time. I took Natalie from him and now out of revenge, he would take you from me. It's as simple as that.'

'No,' she said wildly, 'no, it is not like that at all.'

'Isn't it?' He smiled derisively. 'What do you really know about him, Anna? What were you doing during the morning? Did he make love to you in the mountains?'

'You shame me and yourself by saying such things,' but the memory of Paul's kisses sent the colour flying up into her face and Gregory saw it.

He was sitting upright, all the frustration, all the pain and jealousy of the morning surging together into a furious rage. 'You were lovers on that trip from Pyatigorsk, weren't you? You couldn't even wait to be sure that I was dead.'

'No, it's a lie. We were not even alone. I had my cousin with me . . .'

'What difference does that make? I've never known Paul to

be at a loss when he wants anything. How many nights did he creep into your bed, coupling with you . . . ?'

'You are vile, vile . . .'

He reached out and seized hold of her, pulling her down to him. 'Now listen to me. If you leave me for Paul, I'll make sure that he is hounded through Russia . . . I will break him . . .'

She looked into his face and what she saw there frightened her. 'You're mad,' she whispered. She struggled wildly to free herself but his grip tightened until she cried out with the pain. It was Paul's voice, hard, incisive, that drove them apart.

'Don't you think you had better let her go?'

Gregory released her and she stood up, sick and ashamed that he should see her brawling so vulgarly with her husband. Paul came further into the barn letting the door swing to behind him.

He said levelly, 'Do that to Anna again and I swear to God it is I who will break you.'

But Gregory was lost to all reason. The sight of his rival, strong and healthy, was more than he could endure. He had gone very pale, the sweat running freely down his face.

He said slowly, 'Anna has just told me that she is going to leave me. She wants a divorce and I know why. It's because of you, isn't it, you damned philanderer, you cursed murderer!' His fingers closed around the pistol and he raised it. Anna heard the click as he cocked it. She cried out in fear.

Paul had not moved. He said quietly, 'You had better put that gun down, Gadiani, before you do something silly.'

But Gregory was beyond listening to anyone. 'I owe you a shot,' he said in fury, 'and now, by God, you're going to have it!'

He fired, the sound echoed around the rafters and through the smoke, Anna saw Paul stagger and fall to his knees. Gregory looked dazed, the pistol still in his hand.

Blood was streaming down Paul's face. He pulled out a handkerchief as he got shakily to his feet. If the bullet had been a hairsbreadth nearer the right he would have been dead. As it was, it had scored along the side of his forehead leaving a raw red furrow before it buried itself in a wooden post.

There was the sound of running feet, the door burst open and Varga came in with Grishka close behind him.

'We heard a shot . . .'

'It's all right. It was an accident. Prince Gadiani was trying out my pistol.'

Varga gave a quick glance round and turned back to Paul. 'Better let me take a look at that, Colonel.'

'In a moment.'

'It seems we may have more useful work for our weapons soon, sir. One of the scouts has come in with something to report to you.'

'Very well. I'll come in a few minutes.'

'You'll not be long?'

'No.'

The two Cossacks withdrew reluctantly and Paul went on speaking quietly as though nothing at all had happened, as though Gregory had not just tried to murder him.

'I had intended to tell you to be prepared. We may have to leave here in the next hour or so.'

Anna longed to go to him, but didn't dare. She bitterly regretted her folly. Why hadn't she kept her mouth shut? She said in a stifled voice, 'You should have that wound bandaged.'

'Varga will see to it.' He walked across to Gregory and took the pistol out of his hand. 'I think this would be safer with me for the time being.'

When he had gone, Anna felt her legs give way and sank down on the straw bed too unnerved even to speak. Gregory's voice, strained but normal, roused her.

'Help me to get up. If we have to fight out way out, I'd rather be on my feet.'

She turned on him, angry that he should sound so calm, so ordinary after what he had done, and then realized the futility of it. It was so typical of Gregory. Now the madness had passed, it was better to say nothing, to let it rest as Paul had done. She helped him up. He limped slowly to the door, holding on to it, while she silently folded up the blankets and put together their few possessions.

Within an hour they had taken to the road. One of the Cossacks who had been on watch had seen a small party of horsemen too close for comfort. There were not more than four or five, he reported, but from his description Paul had little doubt that two of them at least were Daniel Gadiani and Kezia Mahommed. They were not yet on their track, but it could only be a matter of time before they came to the village and Paul could place no reliance on the silence of the peasants. They must go on as far as they could into the mountains, find somewhere to lie up and hope they could elude the pursuit.

——15——

For days it seemed they played a desperate game of hide and seek, with Paul trying hard to keep his main objective always in view and travel towards the Russian garrison and safety, but he was hopelessly hampered by a sick man, a woman and a child. There was no time or opportunity to think of anything but keeping themselves alive and eluding the hunters who appeared and then vanished again, stalking them as though they were wild animals so that their nerves were always at the stretch.

On the second night after leaving the village, they were forced to take refuge in a cave under the lee of the mountain. It was dry enough but bitterly cold and Paul would not permit them to light a fire because of the tell-tale smoke. They were all huddled together except for the two always on guard. They ate a little cheese with dry bread and no more than a mouthful of water and lay shivering under their blankets.

Gregory had ridden doggedly during the day and was utterly spent. At some time in the night hours he shivered so much that Anna drew near to him putting her arms around him and trying to give him something of her own warmth. He clung to her convulsively. She felt the sweat on his face though he shook with chill and she soothed him with the words she might have used to Vanya. Waking early from an uncomfortable doze she found that another blanket had been wrapped closely around them and guessed that Paul must have put it there before he went out to take his turn on watch.

They started off again at first light and when the men came to help Gregory on to his horse, he stood swaying, hanging on to the bridle, turning to face Paul.

'Must we go on running like this? Can't we stand and fight it out? We are seven after all with the Cossacks. Surely it would be better than this endless game of cat and mouse?'

'I've thought of it,' said Paul steadily, 'more than once. I don't like it any more than you do, but I daren't risk it. I have Anna and the child to think of. We don't even know for certain how many of them there are or whether they can call upon others. We must go on. Once we are free of the mountains and into the foothills, the going will be easier and we shall be within a day of the garrison. I doubt if they will follow us there.'

He spoke with more confidence than he felt. With every hour that passed, he saw Gregory weakening and they were only able to travel slowly with frequent rests.

And so they went on. Days and nights seemed to blend into one long agony. Sometimes Anna wondered if it was deliberate, something born in Daniel Gadiani's tortuous mind. He was playing with them as a cat plays with mice; it amused him to watch their misery, to let them feel themselves safe and then when they least expected it, he would pounce.

One morning, climbing up and up a narrow ridge, they were caught in an early snowstorm. The wind blew the whirling stinging flakes into their faces, blinding them; the horses stumbled and slipped in the slush so that in the afternoon, Paul realized they could go no further and called a halt.

'We must wait until it goes over,' he said. 'It is too early in the year for it to last long.'

They found some sort of shelter among the towering rocks and in desperation the Cossacks lit a small fire. They crouched together over it, drinking the hot tea made with the melted snow, their fingers numbed and their faces whipped raw by the storm's buffeting. It was the worst moment they had encountered so far and Paul had a hard job to keep up their spirits.

He came to sit beside Anna and Gregory, a little apart from the men. He looked incredibly tired, the plaster on his forehead showed traces of fresh blood, and she wondered if he had managed to get any sleep at all. He leaned forward, his arms round his knees, and she slid out a hand and put it on his. He smiled faintly and bent his head to brush his lips against her fingers.

'Don't lose heart. This won't last for ever.'

Gregory was holding the cup between both trembling hands, his face pinched and drawn. He said in a hoarse whisper, 'If it wasn't for me, you could have outdistanced them

long ago. You would be safe by now, all of you. Go on without me. Leave me here.'

'No,' exclaimed Anna in horror. 'No! How can you say
such a thing!'

'Be quiet, Anna. It's Paul who makes the decisions and he
understands what I mean. We have to face it. I'm never going to reach Tiflis alive. This damned leg will see to that.
What is the use of keeping up this ridiculous pretence? You
know it as well as I do. Leave me a pistol. I'll not let them
take me easily.'

'Don't listen to him. He is feverish. He doesn't realize what
he is saying.'

Paul did not answer at once. He knew perfectly well that
Gregory was probably right. It was more than likely that if
they did not reach skilled medical help very soon, then the
poison from the damaged leg would kill him if fever and exposure didn't and yet he could not accept such a solution. The
very fact that he was the husband of the woman he loved and
passionately wanted made it imperative that he should save
him if he could at whatever sacrifice. It was perverse and
paradoxical, he thought grimly, but there it was.

He said hearteningly, 'Nonsense, man. You're depressed at
what we've been through today and I don't wonder at it, but
we're not giving up. We're in this together, sink or swim, and
I'd not leave a dog behind for those devils to amuse themselves with.'

Gregory's eyes narrowed. 'Don't play the hero too long,' he
murmured ironically, 'you may regret it.'

Paul said nothing, only shifted a little away from Anna
and nearer the fire as if he were cold.

Gregory lay back and watched them broodingly. They
rarely made any move towards each other and yet he knew
what was between them, he knew that he had lost Anna to
Paul though his pride would not let him accept it. It was one
more torment to add to his physical wretchedness.

By the morning of the fifth day since they had first realized
that they were being followed, they had come down from the
high peaks and the snow had gone. It was warmer and the
sun was shining again. For a day and a night there had been
no sign of their pursuers. The snow followed by sleet and a
thick mist in which they had lost their way for some hours
seemed to have done the trick. The hunters had either lost

heart or else they had really been given the slip, and a certain cautious optimism pervaded everyone. Grishka had found some hen's eggs hidden under a hedge and he had boiled them over a tiny fire. They were deep yellow and tasted strange, but they were all glad of a mouthful of hot food with the dry biscuit.

Vanya was sitting close beside Gregory, his face shining with the grease Anna had rubbed on it to soothe the soreness caused by the altitude and the biting winds. He had survived better than any of them, she thought. Children are so resilient. One of the men had carved a wooden figure for him from an old tree root and he was pretending it was a soldier and fighting a battle all over his half brother's blanket. Gregory had eaten some of the food and was lying back letting the boy prattle on, only putting in a word now and again.

The strain had lifted a little and Anna felt rested and more at peace with herself. They had taken shelter in a stone hut that must at some time have been a shrine, but the statue of the saint was broken from its pedestal and nothing remained but the little spring flowing in and out of the cracked basin.

There was no door and she stood outside for a moment looking around her. On the other side of the track a steep cliff went down to the river valley. She knew she must not go too far from the camp, but the Cossacks were within call and she could see Paul talking to Varga close to where the horses had been tethered. Ever since the day when Gregory had shot at him, they had not spoken privately, partly deliberate, partly because there had been so much else to occupy him. And so it must continue, she told herself. She could not forsake Gregory, nor must she do anything to provoke him again. When he had made his absurd suggestion that Paul should abandon him and go on, there had been a sudden leap of her heart and immediately she had felt deeply, horribly ashamed.

In remorse she had tried to do more and more for him until one night when she had begged him to let her rebandage his bad leg, he had turned on her furiously.

'For God's sake, leave me alone. I don't need you. I don't need anyone. I know what you want. I can read it in your face every time you look at him. Go to him then, go. Don't make me your conscience.'

He had thrust her away so roughly that she stumbled bruising her face badly against the rocks at their back. She had tried to hide it but she knew that Paul had noticed it.

He found a moment to say quietly, 'Did Gregory do that?'

'No,' she said quickly. 'No, of course not. I fell.' But the anger in his eyes told her that he didn't believe her.

She had fought a hard battle with herself. Gregory was right. Divorce was unthinkable, something so shocking, so remote from all she had been brought up to believe, that she must not, dare not contemplate it; and though he never asked for it, she knew that she still had power to comfort and strengthen Gregory.

She woke up from her thoughts and looked around her, aware suddenly that she had let her feet carry her further than she had intended. The air that morning was soft and sweet, the grass green, and she glimpsed a clump of flowers, pink rock roses, still blooming in a sheltered spot. It was like a good omen, a sign that they had at last left the black horsemen behind them and she started forward to pick the flowers, thinking how the sight of them would hearten everyone, making the end of their journey seem all the closer.

As she knelt down, the shadow that had been lurking in the rocks and watching her every movement, leaped forward and seized hold of her.

'Captured you at last, my beauty! Why did you run from me?'

She twisted in his arms and saw the dark face of Kezia Mahommed, the flash of white teeth as he smiled. He must have been lying in wait for her and she had given him the opportunity he wanted. The flowers dropped from her hand. Panic-stricken she screamed for help but he only laughed. He whistled and his horse came obediently to his call. In an instant he was on its back and had lifted her in front of him. They were already galloping along the narrow track when Anna heard the sound of hooves thundering behind them. Kezia was urging his horse on, but for once he was being pursued by a rider as skilled and determined as himself.

Paul had heard the scream but it took him a couple of minutes to locate it and then capture one of the horses which they kept always saddled. He shouted a warning to his men as he galloped after Kezia. He gained on him very slowly, waited till the path widened a trifle, slithered dangerously past, wheeled his horse and swung round to face them.

Kezia taken by surprise made a desperate attempt to turn around and go up the side of the mountain, but his mare, straining under the double weight, balked at the steep incline and fell backwards. Anna wriggled out of Kezia's grasp and fell to the ground. To save her from being trampled, he flung himself out of the saddle, dragging his horse away, and found himself confronted by Paul, pistol in hand.

Anna was scrambling to her feet. 'Get behind me,' shouted Paul at her.

Kezia had whipped the dagger from his belt, paused an instant and then lunged at the same moment as Paul fired. The Tartar's arm fell to his side, blood streaming from his hand and the dagger dropped to the ground.

Kezia's horse had moved away, his gun was out of reach, he pressed himself against the rock at the side of the track. 'Kill me,' he said defiantly. 'I do not submit. I will never be made prisoner.'

'We don't want any damned prisoners,' said Paul. 'Where are the others in your party?'

'They will be in your camp by now,' he flung back at him. 'I am not one of them. I come only for the woman.'

'She is not for you.'

They were glaring at one another and Anna, bruised and shaken, could not bear that Paul should kill in cold blood the only man among Shamyl's horsemen who had shown her some kindness.

'Let him go, Paul, please, please let him go . . .'

For a moment she thought he did not even hear her, then he said curtly, 'You heard what she said. Get to hell out of here.'

Kezia looked baffled. 'You do not kill me?'

'It is not my custom to murder an unarmed man. Go and don't come back.'

He stared at them both and then turned his back, stalking towards his horse with an air of bravado. Then he made a flying leap into the saddle, gave a wild whoop and careered up the road in a crazy gallop.

'He would not beg for his life,' said Anna, 'but he will not come back, I'm sure he won't.'

'I hope to God you're right. I don't know which of us is the greater fool. What the devil were you doing up here anyway? Come on now, hurry. The Lord knows what is happening back at the camp.'

Somehow she clambered up behind him, clinging to his belt as he galloped back.

He slowed up as they came in sight of the stone shrine,

stunned by what they saw. It seemed impossible that so much could have happened in the short time since she had walked out so peacefully that morning. The camp looked as if a tornado had hit it, blankets, cooking pots, all their few possessions were scattered everywhere. The Tartar horsemen must have gone through it at a gallop. There was no sign of the Cossacks, but on the beaten track immediately below them was Daniel Gadiani, still in the saddle, with the child held in front of him and in his other hand a long rope, a rope that tautened behind him and had been bound round his cousin's wrists. Gregory was covered with dirt, his clothes ripped, as if there had been a hard struggle.

Paul swore under his breath. He backed his horse a little, slid from the saddle and drew the second pistol from its holster.

'Get back, Anna, and keep quiet,' he whispered.

Daniel Gadiani twitched the rope viciously so that Gregory stumbled forward falling to his knees. 'Now, my dear cousin,' he jeered, 'we're going to amuse ourselves. Let us see how fast you can run.'

He raised his whip to bring it down on his horse's flank and Paul fired. Daniel slumped forward in the saddle. Vanya slid out of his hands and tumbled to the ground, screaming in terror. The frightened horse bolted forward as Paul dropped the pistol and ran like an madman to take hold of Gregory. He flung his arms around him, the rope jerked violently. He was caught off balance but did not let go his grip. The horse with its dead rider went crashing over the edge of the ravine taking Paul and Gregory with it.

It had happened so swiftly that Anna could not move, paralysed with shock. At one moment they were there and at the next there was nothing, only the child running to her, flinging himself against her, sobbing out something that she was too dazed to take in.

Automatically her arms went round him. Then still holding his hand, she ran to the edge of the track. At first she could see nothing, but it was not so sheer as she had feared. There were crags and ledges thick with scrubby undergrowth. She thought she could see something move but wasn't sure. She looked frantically for a way to climb down, but could not find any foothold. She must reach them, she must, but how? She could not think what to do. She was trembling and near desperation when she heard a shout. A man was running

towards her and at first she thought it was one of the tribesmen coming back and then, sobbing with relief, she saw it
was Varga.

'They had us cornered,' he said breathlessly as he ran, 'but
we fought our way out. The damned rascals have taken to
their heels. Where is the Colonel?'

'They went over the cliff, both of them,' she clung to him,
incoherently stammering out what had happened.

'God Almighty,' he breathed, 'what a devilish thing!' He
put her aside and lay down on the edge peering over. 'I can
see something,' he said after a moment. 'We'll get ropes and
go down.'

By that time Grishka and two more of the men had joined
them. Anna sank down on the edge with Vanya clutched
against her, feeling utterly helpless and tormented with anxiety while they fetched the rope. They fastened it securely
and then climbed down, hand over hand, down and down,
until she could not bear to look any longer. Surely no one
could have fallen so far and still be alive.

Vanya was going on and on in his shrill childish voice.
'That man came into the hut and he was horrible. He got
hold of me. He hurt me, Anna. Gregory tried to stop him but
he knocked him down and then tied him up. Oh Anna, where
have they gone? Are they dead?'

'Ssh, darling, don't cry. It will be all right.'

Something inside her was praying over and over again. 'Oh
God, don't let Paul die! Please don't let him die!'

She could see the Cossacks on a kind of ledge so they must
have found them. Varga shouted. The sound came up faintly
and another man went edging down to join them.

They began the slow climb up and she waited, not daring
to look, her heart thudding so thickly that it made her feel
sick. Then Paul's dark head came over the ridge; his clothes
were torn, his face smudged with dirt, one arm hanging useless at his side, but he was alive. She could not stop herself.
She ran to him throwing her arms around him.

'I thought you were dead ... Oh Paul, Paul, darling ...'

He held her with one arm. 'All right, my love, it's all
right.'

It was the first thing that Gregory saw as they hoisted him
up. They were clasped in one another's arms, the passion between them naked and unashamed, and he closed his eyes
against it. Then Paul put her from him and knelt beside him.

'Are you hurt? Is anything broken?'

Gregory's eyes stared up at him. 'I'm sorry I'm so hard to kill.'

Anna was kneeling at his other side. 'How can you say that? Paul saved your life.'

'Did he? I thought he pushed me over.'

'Oh Gregory please . . .'

'Sorry,' he muttered weakly. 'Not a very good joke really.' He lay back, his eyes closed.

She looked at Paul fearfully. 'He's not . . . he can't be . . .'

'No, I think he will be all right.' He summoned two of the men. 'Carry him inside. Careful now in case there is any fracture.'

'What happened?' she breathed as they followed Gregory into the stone hut.

'I hardly know. We went down at such a rate, but somehow or other I kept my hold on Gregory. We landed on a kind of ledge and the shrubs growing out of the scree saved us from falling any further. The jerk must have snapped the rope. The horse and Daniel Gadiani are somewhere down there at the bottom of the ravine.'

Anna caught her breath. 'Do you think that he was dead before he went over?'

'I hope so.'

It was a savage end, but he would have murdered Gregory in the cruellest possible manner and no doubt the child also without a second thought so she could feel nothing but an enormous relief as if a weight had been lifted off her shoulders.

The men had put Gregory down on the straw mattress and looked at Paul enquiringly.

'That will do,' he said. 'Varga, you had better stay, the rest of you set about clearing up the camp and keep watch in case any of those devils come back. Two of you climb down if you can and find out what has happened to Daniel Gadiani, but I don't want any risk to anyone's life, d'you hear? It is not worth it. If it is possible we will move on even if it is only a few miles into some more secure shelter.'

The fall had ripped Gregory's breeches exposing the injured leg that for days he had refused to let Anna touch. The flesh had swollen horribly around the bandage and was a dull purple. There was a faint sweet nauseating stench.

'We'll have to do what we can for him, Varga. Fetch some

water and clean bandages. Some fresh clothes too. There must be something in our baggage. There is a coat of mine. Bring that with you.' Paul straightened himself painfully.

Anna said quickly, 'You're hurt.'

'Bruised, that's all, we both are. It's just my wrist. I've fractured it, I think.'

'Let me see.' He winced as she felt it with gentle fingers. 'It ought to be tightly bound.' She looked around her. 'I don't know what I can use. Have you a handkerchief?'

He groped awkwardly in his pocket with his other hand and pulled out something which she recognized instantly as the silk scarf she had once loaned him as a sling and which he had never returned.

He smiled wryly, 'Romantic fool, aren't I?'

'Oh Paul . . .' she leaned against him for a moment, moved almost to tears that he who was so strong and self reliant should have kept it with him for so long. Then briskly she ripped it in half and carefully bound it round his wrist, knotting it firmly. 'It's not too good, but it should help a little.'

'It will do very well.' Paul glanced at Gregory and then put his hand on her arm drawing her towards the door. 'I know we're all exhausted but we must go on at whatever cost. I am very much afraid Gregory may lose his leg if we don't get him to a surgeon quickly.'

'Oh no, no, not that. He would hate that above everything.'

'I could be wrong. I hope to God I am.'

'It's my fault,' said Anna wretchedly. 'I should not have gone so far from the camp. Then Kezia would not have found me and you would not have had to come after me.'

'It's easy to be wise afterwards,' he said wearily. 'I am just as much to blame. I should have realized that Daniel Gadiani wouldn't give up so easily, but we were so damned tired.'

Gregory was lying with closed eyes. He drifted in and out of consciousness hearing what was said dreamily as if it were a long way off. He could move his arms and legs but his whole body ached unbearably. He had faced a hideous death at his cousin's hands and in that frantic moment when he and Paul had hurtled over the cliff, he had been sure they would die together and in a curious way had been glad of it. But it had not happened. With all the breath knocked out of him, he had opened his eyes to see Paul bending over him. He heard him say, 'We're safe, I think. We're on a ledge. In a moment I'll try to find a way to climb up and get help.'

He had felt his hands moving over him drawing him back from the edge. It seemed a miracle that except for horrible bruising they were both without serious injury. Paul had saved him, he thought bitterly, only to condemn him to a living death. Oh God, to be a cripple, an object of pity, despised by other men. Never to walk freely again, never to dance, never to love or be loved. He would far rather be dead.

His mind drifted away and some time later he was aware that they were kneeling beside him again. Anna was bathing his face while Paul with Varga's help was rebandaging his leg.

'They caught us napping, didn't they?' he muttered. 'When they rode through the camp, I kept tight hold of Vanya and thought we were safe but Daniel came back. Where is he by the way?'

'At the bottom of the ravine.'

'Dead as mutton,' said Varga grimly. 'He'll not trouble us again. Sit up, sir, let me help you into the Colonel's coat.'

Gregory was silent for a moment, the fever clearing from his mind and leaving it sharp as a diamond.

'What a pity you and Anna didn't come back five minutes later, Paul, you would have been rid of me with no trouble to yourself.'

Anna drew away from him, close to tears. 'Gregory, please don't . . .'

'Don't what, my dear? It's the truth, isn't it?'

Paul stood up. 'She had been captured by Kezia Mahommed,' he said curtly. 'I thank God I reached them in time. Do you think you can sit a horse? I want to get away from this place.'

'I can do it if I must.'

'Good. We'll get packed up now.'

He went out with Varga and Anna wearily got to her feet and moved across to her own bed. She began folding up the blankets once again.

'Three men, and all of them hot as mustard for you, my dear. Does it please you?' The hoarse whisper followed her, ironic, mocking. 'It's amusing really. In the old days back in Petersburg I would never have believed it possible.'

No, she thought bitterly, and so you left me for Natalie

who was beautiful and clever and unscrupulous. You cared nothing about me then. I was the wife you never really wanted, the wife who couldn't even give you a living son . . . the biting words hovered on her lips but she didn't say any of them. He was sick and miserable and if it helped him to needle her, then she must bear it as part of her punishment for not being able to love him as she should.

——16——

So much had happened in a few hours that it seemed almost impossible to believe that it was still not long past midday. Without Daniel Gadiani to spur them on, Paul doubted if the Tartars would pursue them any further, but he could not be sure and the nearer they were to the garrison, the greater the chance of falling in with a Russian patrol. So weary as they were, he urged haste.

They could not travel as far or as fast as he would have wished, but at least now they were leaving the mountains behind them. After the intense cold, the snow and bitter winds of the high peaks, it was strange to remember that it was still only early autumn. There was a mildness in the air and a mellow warmth in the brief glimpses of sun.

For most of the time Anna was riding close beside Gregory. They did not speak much. He needed all his strength to keep upright in the saddle. Once he swayed forward and she gripped his arm. He pulled away at once.

'I'm all right. Don't fuss.'

'I think we ought to stop. You've had enough. I'm going to speak to Paul.'

'No, Anna, it is not necessary,' but she had already cantered forward to the head of the party.

Paul had tucked his injured wrist into his jacket to ease the pain and held the reins in his left hand.

'What is wrong?' he asked as she came up beside him. 'Is it Gregory?'

'He is very exhausted, Paul. Are we stopping soon?'

'In about another hour. If our maps are correct, we shall have left these woods behind by then and be in more open country with a stream. Can he hold up that long?'

'He will go on until he collapses.'

'He has great courage.'

'Yes, he has.' She knew what she must say. They were so

rarely alone that now was the time, but it was not easy to begin. She glanced at him. 'Is your wrist painful?'

'On and off. Luckily I once practised shooting with my left hand.'

'Are we still in danger?'

'I hope not, but it is as well to be prepared. I dare not take any chances.'

She looked about her fearfully, the shock of the morning still with her. The trees were dense on each side of the track. Anyone could be following them and yet be completely hidden from view. Her nerves were on edge. A bird flying out of the bush, the rustle of a small animal in the undergrowth alarmed her though she tried to hide it.

They were quiet for a few minutes, then she said, 'I've been thinking, Paul. If the worst should happen, if Gregory does lose his leg, then I couldn't leave him. I know so well how he will feel. He has always had such a dread of sickness. He will take it very badly. He will need me.'

'I guessed you would say that. If you want to make a martyr of yourself, then go ahead and do so. He won't thank you for it. No man would.'

'Oh Paul, please understand. Don't make it harder for me.'

'Oh I understand perfectly,' he said wearily. 'I was a fool ever to believe that you would do anything else. You wouldn't be you if you did. It's absurd, isn't it? More than anything in the world I want you to leave him and come to me and at the same time I want you to remain the person you are, the woman I have fallen in love with, and it is not possible. I can't have it both ways.'

She could find no ready answer. She said slowly, 'It's just that . . . I did once love him and now I find I can't leave him to face this alone.'

'I know. He has the advantage of both of us. If he had not been sick, we might have fought it out between us,' he said grimly, 'as it is, my hands are tied.'

'What will you do?'

He shrugged his shoulders. 'Is that important?'

'It is to me.'

'Very well. I've been doing some thinking too. Once I know you and Gregory are safe, I shall come back.'

'Come back? Why?'

'Have you forgotten? I did have a purpose, a plan which might have succeeded . . .'

'If it had not been for me and Gregory.'

'Don't think I regret it. I don't, not for a single second, but I detest leaving things unfinished. I'd like to make another attempt at it.'

'But you cannot, not now. They know too much about you. You could never get so far a second time.'

'There are other ways,' he said obstinately. 'I have no intention of sitting down, twiddling my thumbs, while the Tsar makes up his mind how he can use me. I prefer to be master of my own life.'

'Free as an eagle,' she said dryly. 'You told me that once.'

'Did I?'

She turned to him pleadingly. 'Paul, don't do it, please don't. I don't think I could bear it.'

He gave her his ironic smile. 'You could stop me very easily, but you won't, will you?'

'Why do you make it so difficult for me?'

'I don't mean to, believe me, but it is not easy for me either.' He was staring straight ahead of him. 'I'm not a patient man, Anna. There are times when I don't know how to keep my hands off him. Can't you understand that?'

She saw the look on his face and was frightened at the passion she had aroused, the violence that he usually kept well in check. Then he relaxed, became again the man she thought she knew. 'You had better go back to Gregory,' he went on quietly. 'Tell him we will be making camp very soon now.'

When she had gone, he rode on, angry and frustrated, aware of a sickening sense of failure. Why in the name of God should this have happened to him? He had loved her for her simplicity, her spontaneity, her joy in living. She awoke in him a tenderness, a protectiveness he did not know he possessed. He had wanted to bring back the laughter into her eyes, make her feel her value to him after the humiliation she had suffered at Gregory's hands, and now he would have to watch her devoting herself to a man who would turn her life into hell all over again. For a few seconds when they had fallen together on to the craggy ledge, he had fought an appalling temptation to give Gregory the final push that would have taken him to death with his cousin in the ravine. No one would have known except himself and that was what had made it utterly impossible. I was a fool, he thought savagely. Why wasn't I ruthless enough to kill him and make Anna happy for the rest of her life?

That evening, sitting under the shelter the Cossacks had rigged up between two trees at the edge of the clearing, Paul pored over the crude and unreliable maps by the light of a lantern.

He looked up to say, 'I think after we reach the garrison, we will cross the river and make for Kumari. It is some fifty miles nearer than Tiflis. Will it be too much for your grandmother, Gregory?'

'On the contrary she will be delighted to be the first to hear the news.' Gregory who had been lying with his eyes closed gave a little laugh. 'You don't know her. She adores surprises. They must have given us up for lost long ago. We shall come out of the mountains like ghosts.'

'Scarecrows rather than ghosts,' said Paul wryly, folding up the maps, 'and we still have to get there.'

They were all utterly exhausted. Vanya fell asleep in the midst of his supper and Anna rolled him in a blanket and put him close to her own bed. Gregory ate scarcely anything but drank thirstily cup after cup of the thin tea made with boiled river water.

All that day the fever had come in sickly waves so that he sometimes felt as though he were floating disembodied, detached from all those around him. He had watched Anna riding beside Paul, saw how earnestly they spoke together, and one part of him no longer cared and another was hot with jealousy and resentment.

The Cossacks had done what they could to make them comfortable under the rough shelter. His eyes followed her as she pulled off her boots and jacket and tried to comb the tangles out of her hair. None of them undressed. The nights had been far too cold.

He held out his hand. 'Anna.'

'What is it?'

'Come here to me.'

The light from the lantern was very feeble, but he felt a flush of desire surge through him as she came across to him, her hair loose on her shoulders, the swell of her breasts easily visible through the thin shirt.

He seized her hand. 'Kiss me.'

She touched her lips to his cheek and impatiently he pulled her closer. She felt his mouth burning on hers. His other hand was on her breast and she had to steel herself not to repulse him. For an instant they stayed locked together and then, sensing her lack of response, he thrust her away.

'Are they the kisses you give to Paul?'

To answer would only provoke another quarrel so she said nothing, but busied herself with putting a cup of water within reach of his hand before she blew out the lantern and went silently back to her own bed.

She lay awake hour after hour in a torment of misery and indecision until she could bear it no longer. She owed a duty to Gregory and yet because of her, Paul intended to throw away his life in a crazy reckless venture. Her thoughts tossed this way and that, strain and exhaustion adding to the tension until she could not lie still for another moment. She forced herself to listen for Gregory's quiet breathing and then noiselessly crept out of the shelter. Her longing for Paul was like a sharp pain. She wanted to feel his arms around her. She yearned for the comfort of his strength and his love. She would go to him, make him understand, persuade him to give up his plan. In the quiet of the night they could talk together as they never could during the day.

Gregory did not know what time it was when he woke up. His mouth was dry and parched. He groped for the mug of water and knocked it over.

'Anna,' he called softly, and then again louder, 'Anna!'

There was no answer and yet always before she had come at once. He sat up listening and after an instant realized that, except for the child, he was alone in the shelter. Anna was not there. He lay quietly for a little but when she did not come back, it was as if everything crystallized in his feverish mind. A black wave of anger shook him. She had gone to Paul. He was sure of it. Something snapped inside him. A crazy desire to make them suffer for all he had been through had floated in and out of his consciousness for days and now suddenly it was real. He knew exactly what he was going to do.

It took him some time to get on his feet and then, swaying dangerously, he had to grope about for the pistol that Paul had given back to him in case of any further attack on the journey. Panting he held on to one of the trees until he could steady himself and get his breath. The moon had risen and hung golden and full in the dark sky. The fire had died down to a tiny glow but he could see the humped figures of the sol-

diers grouped around it and some distance away Grishka
stood on watch, a rifle in his hands.

Anna and Paul would be somewhere not far away, lying
close in each other's arms. His head swam and he was glad to
feel the pistol heavy in his hand. He took a deep breath. His
eyes grown accustomed to the night, he could distinguish the
dark shape lying on the other side of the clearing. He braced
himself, gritting his teeth against the pain, and crept slowly
and silently across the soft turf, moving from tree to tree to
help himself along. He was only a few feet away when he realized that Paul was alone, wrapped in a blanket, sleeping
profoundly.

The pressure on Gregory's brain lifted. He shivered, feeling
the sweat cold on his back. He had been in the clutch of a
nightmare and now it was over. The moon slid behind a
cloud. Gregory waited, gathering strength, the cocked pistol
in his hand. Through the thick darkness, he heard a sound
and thought he saw Paul stir and sit up, then everything
around him suddenly exploded into violence.

It was the sound of the shots that startled Anna to her feet.
She had gone out from the shelter with every intention of going to Paul but, once outside, she had known that it was impossible. Alone in the night she could trust him no more than
she could trust herself. She had sat under the trees, huddled
into herself, until slowly the torment in her mind had eased
and drowsiness overcame her. Now, fear gripping her, she
ran across the clearing. Gregory was lying face upwards, a
dark stain spreading on his jacket while Paul was standing
over him, the gun in his left hand.

'My God, you've killed him!' It was the first thought that
came into her head as she fell on her knees beside Gregory.

'No, no,' he shook his head, still dazed because everything
had happened so quickly, 'there was someone here . . .'

'Where? There is no one,' she cried out wildly.

Gregory stirred a little and Paul dropped the pistol and
knelt beside him.

'Damned stupid,' he was muttering, 'I thought . . . I
thought . . . you and Anna . . .' his voice died away and a
little bubble of blood formed on his lips.

Paul tore open the coat and thrust a hand under the
ragged shirt. Varga and some of the men had come running

towards them. They crowded around looking down at Gregory, appalled at what they saw.

'What happened, sir? We heard the shots.'

'I wish I knew.' Paul rubbed a hand over his face. 'There was a man here, a tribesman . . . didn't you see him?'

Varga looked at the Cossacks and then back at Paul. 'Are you sure, sir? We saw no one.'

'Of course I'm sure,' he said angrily. 'Grishka, were you asleep at your post or what? You had better make a search. He could still be hiding somewhere.'

'If you say so, Colonel.' Varga nodded to Grishka and gave a few brief orders while Paul slowly got to his feet. He stared down at the blood on his hands.

Varga gave him a sharp glance. 'Is he . . . dead, sir?'

'Yes.'

Anna sat very still. Her mouth was so dry, she could scarcely speak. 'It can't be true . . . not quickly like that . . . it can't be . . .'

Paul bent down to her, his voice gentle. 'I am afraid it is. There is nothing we can do for him now.' He put his hand on her shoulder and she shrank away from him with a violent shudder.

'Don't touch me.'

'I didn't kill him, Anna,' he said steadily. 'Don't you believe me? I did not kill him.'

'Then who did?' She looked up at him and he read the accusation in her eyes. 'Don't lie to me, Paul, please don't lie to me.' She dragged herself up. She felt as if her limbs were weighted with lead. 'I had better go to Vanya. He will be frightened if he heard the shots.' She walked stiffly away from him.

Varga said tentatively, 'Maybe it was for the best, seeing how sick he was, sir . . . I mean him going quickly like that.'

Paul turned on him. 'Don't say such a thing, d'you hear me? Don't dare to say it. I would have given anything, anything in the world for this not to have happened.' Then he pulled himself together. 'Fetch a blanket and wrap him in it. I'm going to look around outside the camp.'

'Very good, sir.'

Varga watched him stride away. What the devil! he thought to himself. Even if they had quarrelled over the woman and the Prince had got himself killed, neither he nor the men would ever breathe a word, and wasn't it an easy solution to their problem? Yet there was his Colonel with a grim look on his face biting his head off and the young woman he fancied looking at him as though she were ready to stick a dagger into his heart! He shrugged his shoulders at such folly and turned back to the job in hand. He had seen violent death often enough to find it not unduly disturbing. He called to one of the men to bring a blanket and be damned quick about it!

Vanya was sitting up dazed with sleep. He reached for Anna's hand fearfully. 'Have those men come back?'

'No, darling. There has been an accident and Gregory . . .' Then she choked over it. 'It's all right. Don't get upset. I'll tell you in the morning.'

She tucked him in warmly and sat beside him, trying to soothe him until at last he fell asleep again. Then she got up, walking restlessly up and down, shocked and sick at heart. The moment she had seen Gregory lying there, she knew what had happened. The anger, the jealousy, had always been there. She had seen it on Paul's face that very afternoon and she was to blame. It was her fault, all her fault. She let herself drop on the makeshift bed, hoping that he would come so that she could relieve her wretchedness and her guilt by flinging the bitter words into his face. Then, when she looked up and saw him standing there, only a few feet away from her, the words would not come. It was almost dawn already. There was a sound of waking birds and he was a dark shadow against the faint light of early morning.

He said tonelessly, 'I think it best that we move on as soon as possible. We can't be far from the garrison now.'

'Paul . . .'

He paused, not looking at her. 'What is it?'

She took a step nearer, whispering so as not to wake the boy. 'Paul, what happened out there?'

'How do I know?'

'But you must know. Paul, why did you do it? Why, why, after all this time? How could you do such a thing?'

He did not answer at once and then he turned to face her, speaking with a biting irony. 'He came looking for you, expecting to find you in my arms, shouting unspeakable insults and so I killed him for it. That is what you want to believe, isn't it?'

'No . . . I don't know . . . how can you say that? I want the truth.'

He stared at her fighting an insane desire to seize hold of her, kiss her, make love to her, force her to believe him, anything to bridge the gulf that had opened between them, not realizing how the intolerable strain of the last few days had brought them both close to breaking point.

'What is the truth?' he said wearily. 'We both wanted him dead and now he is. If that is the kind of man you think I am, then what the hell does it matter whether you believe it or not?' and he walked quickly away to where the Cossacks were beginning to roll up blankets and bedding.

He did not come back. It was Varga who presently brought her a mug of hot tea and told her they would be moving on in an hour. She roused Vanya and wiped his face and hands with a damp cloth. It was hard to tell him about Gregory and he was very silent while she tried to explain how he must have got up in the night and been accidentally shot.

'But you said those men didn't come back.'

'I didn't want to frighten you.'

'Have they gone now?'

'Yes.'

He looked at her with wide eyes. 'Did they kill Paul too?'

'No.'

'I'm glad. I like Paul.'

When she took him outside into the freshness of the morning, he ran to the men as he always did. She saw Paul stoop to pick him up saying something that made the boy laugh and she thought how sad it was that the death of the brother he had scarcely known should mean so little to him. But then Gregory had never tried to win the child's affection.

The horses were already saddled and she averted her eyes from the long, dark shape that had been roped to the back of one of them. They set out almost at once, Paul riding ahead with Varga, leaving Anna to follow with Vanya, the men closing in around them.

They spent only one day in the village where the garrison had its headquarters. It was a small place and though the Commander did his best, he could offer little in the way of comfort. Their appearance was greeted with amazement by soldiers and officers alike. They crowded around besieging Paul and the Cossacks with questions and the peasants, coming to the doors of their black huts, stared at Anna in her bedraggled boy's clothes. One of the women brought some sweet cakes out of her scanty store and put them into Vanya's hands and another shyly offered Anna a clean white blouse in place of the ragged garment stained with Gregory's blood. She accepted it gratefully. Now that the stress and danger were over, she felt utterly exhausted, scarcely able to speak, and was only thankful that because of Gregory nothing was expected from her. She was treated with respectful sympathy and left largely to herself.

Paul spent most of the day with the Commander who wanted to know every detail of their escape. It was evening before he came at last to the room where she had been trying to rest during the afternoon. He stood in the doorway as she struggled to sit up.

'Do you feel strong enough to ride on to Kumari tomorrow?'

'Yes. I shall be glad to go.'

'The Commander expects me to accompany you. If you would prefer it, I can ask him to send his lieutenant.'

'No, it is not necessary.'

'The soldiers will follow with your husband. The Princess will wish her grandson to be buried at Kumari.'

'Yes, of course.'

They might have been strangers, they were so formal with one another. But how could they be anything else with the garrison all eager curiosity and Gregory lying in the next room? No one had questioned how he died. The war in the Caucasus had been filled with such tragedies and she had said nothing. How could she condemn the man who had done so much for them? It was something that lay between her and Paul alone, a chasm that became more and more difficult to cross.

The following day they were riding through the handsome wrought-iron gates of Kumari. Vanya, perched in front of Paul and enchanted to be going home, had never ceased chattering about the dogs, the horses, the old donkey that pulled his little cart and the kittens in the kitchens. It had helped to cover the silence between them.

Autumn had touched everything with gold. Kumari was still beautiful, thought Anna, peacefully sleeping in the glow of early evening. The turmoil and distress of the last few days eased a little.

Grishka had been sent ahead to warn the Princess and she was there in the porch, tiny, bejewelled, indomitable, the long purple veils fluttering in the wind, the servants crowding at her back.

Paul dismounted and set Vanya on his feet. He raced up the steps crying out ecstatically, 'I'm home, Grandmamma, I've come home!'

She held him to her tightly, the black eyes suspiciously bright. 'There, there, my little one, you have come back safe and sound and after such an adventure.'

'I've lots and lots to tell you,' he announced and then was on his knees, hugging Suki and being hugged in turn by his old nurse and the maidservants.

The Princess turned to Anna, deeply moved. 'My dear child, it is a miracle. I never thought to see you. and the boy again.' The old voice broke for the first time and they clung together. Then Anna gently freed herself.

'This is Colonel Paul Kuragin. If it had not been for him, neither I nor Vanya would be here.'

'How can I ever thank you, Colonel?'

'There is no need.' Paul bent to kiss the Princess's hand. 'I happened to be there at the right time, that is all.'

'Come in, come in.' The old lady was quite taken out of herself, laughing and crying at the same time. 'Such a terrible time as you must have had, you must be worn out and such clothes . . . Anna, my dear, we must find you something to wear. The servants shall prepare baths and food.'

They supped together that evening, the Princess doing most of the talking, asking question after question. Paul's right wrist was still useless. After watching him struggle to eat with his left hand, Anna quietly took the plate from him and cut up the roasted kid and spicy salad.

Much later she sat with the old Princess in the room she remembered so well, the birds still in their silver cage, the lamps burning softly and the air fragrant with the delicate perfume the Princess favoured.

Anna had been telling her of Gregory, of their meeting at Karimat, their rescue, the agonizing days that had ended in his death and now they were silent.

The Princess said at last, 'I wept for him a year ago when I believed him gone from us and now I can weep no more.

I'm only thankful that he died honourably and his body will lie here with his father and grandfather and not be thrown into the lime pit of Shamyl's prisoners.'

Anna was astonished that she took it so calmly. She had the fatalism of the East that accepts death without question as part of life.

She turned away her head. 'I am ashamed, deeply ashamed that I cannot grieve more for him.'

'There are very few of us who go through our days without something we are ashamed of.'

'But it was my fault, all mine.'

'My dear, I think you ceased to love him a long time ago, isn't that so?'

'Not until he had rejected me.'

'Perhaps. Your marriage was a mistake but to go on regretting a mistake all one's life is nothing but folly.' She lay back among her piled cushions. 'Tell me about this Colonel Kuragin.'

'What is there to tell except what you know already?'

'My dear, I may be old but I am not in my dotage and I have my eyes. I watched him while we supped. He was so obviously cool towards you, he was at such pains to look everywhere but at you, that I knew immediately that he was afraid of giving himself away. He is in love with you, isn't that so?' And when Anna did not answer, she leaned forward, putting a finger under her chin and turning her face towards her. 'And you? Are you in love with him?'

'He is the man I told you of, the Russian officer who quarrelled with Gregory over Natalie. But for him, Gregory would never have been captured.'

The Princess made an impatient sound. 'Natalie is a whore and well aware of her brother's schemes. I am afraid that Gregory played into their hands,' she said crisply. 'That is not the reason for the coldness between you, is it?'

'No.' Anna looked down at the hands in her lap. 'I think he and Gregory quarrelled over me that night and he killed him.'

If the Princess was startled, she did not show it. 'Have you said this to anyone else?'

'No, only to you.'

'And he denies it?'

'Yes.' Anna looked away.

'Don't you believe him?'

'I want to, but I can't, I can't,' she said passionately. 'Don't you understand? More than anything he wanted to be rid of Gregory, he told me so that very afternoon, and then this happened . . .' she buried her face in her hands. She had accused him openly now and she was suddenly afraid of what Gregory's grandmother might do.

There was a long pause before the Princess said thoughtfully, 'He seems to me a man who hides his feelings, a proud man who would not stoop to a lie to save himself, and from what you have told me, he did a great deal for Gregory.' She leaned forward, 'Anna, my dear, look at me and answer truthfully. You had learned to love Paul Kuragin, isn't that right, and for that reason you wished Gregory had not come back into your life.'

'No, it was not like that.' Anna turned a tormented face towards her. 'It was a shock when I saw him at Karimat, but I was desperately sorry for him. I tried to help him. It was Paul who wanted me to leave him. He wanted a divorce but I wouldn't agree. I would not listen to him. I would have stayed with Gregory and cared for him. I did everything for him.'

'Except give him your love.'

'Was that my fault? I tried not to let him see it.'

'But he did see it. It is never possible to stifle the yearnings in one's heart and so now you are placing the burden of your guilt on Paul's shoulders.'

'I don't know what you mean.'

'I think you do. I don't know what happened that night but if he had killed Gregory, deliberately or in self defence, he would have told you at whatever cost to himself. You are letting yourself believe it because that is what you desired in your own heart.'

Anna was staring at her appalled. 'No,' she whispered. 'No, that is horrible.'

'Is it so strange?' went on the Princess calmly, relentlessly. ' "The sweet with the bitter . . . whom among us hath the furnace not consumed? Who has e'er yet plucked a thornless rose?" One of our wisest poets said that. We all have secret thoughts which we deeply regret. Face up to it and then go to him. Tell him so. Here in the Caucasus men like him are forced to live dangerously. I know that only too well. To waste even an hour of your life is like mocking the God who has given you a second chance.'

* * *

Paul was standing by the window in the long room that looked on to the garden. He turned as he heard the door open. Only one lamp was burning and he saw her coming towards him out of the darkness. The Princess had loaned her one of her own floating garments so that she reminded him of the moths that blew in and out on their wide grey wings. He moved to the table putting down the glass in his hand.

'I've been waiting to tell you. I shall be leaving early tomorrow morning. Is there any message you would like me to take to Marya Petrovna? I understand that she is still in the city.'

'Poor Marya, she must have been so anxious . . . give her my love and tell her I'll be with her soon,' said Anna unsteadily.

'The men are here already,' he went on, 'I've spoken with Varga. You will wish to stay of course until after the funeral.'

'Yes. It would please the Princess.'

She was very pale and there were dark smudges under the velvet eyes. He thought what a fool he had been to let this division come between them after they had gone through so much together.

He said, 'Do you still believe I killed him, Anna?'

She raised her eyes to his. 'I believe we killed him between us.'

'No, Anna, no. You mustn't blame yourself.' He looked away from her. 'The truth is that Gregory took what was meant for me.'

'How? I don't understand,' she breathed.

'It was Kamil, Bela's brother. When I woke that night, I saw his face just for an instant before he fired. It was very dark and Gregory was wearing my coat. He must have taken him for me.' He made a helpless gesture. 'It all happened so quickly. I tried to hold him, but he slipped through my hands. By the time I had picked up my gun, he was gone.'

'Why didn't you tell me?'

'I tried to, but you wouldn't listen,' he said wryly, 'and afterwards I was angry, with myself as much as with you. I had failed you. Somehow or other I should have prevented it. I find it hard to forgive myself for that.'

She thought how strange it was that Kamil would have re-paid his generosity to Bela with death if Gregory had not been there to die for him. She leaned one hand on the table, weak with relief and exhaustion.

Paul watched her for a moment before he said quietly, 'Anna, before I go from here, there is something I must know.'

'Not now, Paul, please,' she said uncertainly, 'it is too soon. I have to think of Vanya, I gave my promise. I owe it to Gregory.'

'I know that, but don't you owe a little to me?'

'Yes, yes, I do, but . . .' She moved away from him to the window. The sky was a deep plum colour and beyond lay the mountains, the Caucasus with its beauty, its mystery and its danger. She said suddenly, 'I wonder if the cock still crows and flaps his wings on Mount Elbruz.'

He smiled a little. How young she was still in spite of everything that had happened. He wanted to take her in his arms but knew he must be patient. Instead he said, 'Shall we climb it and find out?'

'I think I have had enough of mountains.'

'Anna,' he said gently, 'I want an answer.'

'The Princess says it is folly to waste even an hour of one's life.'

'How right she is. I will take a long leave and we'll go to Arachino. It's as flat as a billiard table there. Not a mountain in sight.'

'Oh Paul . . .' in spite of herself a tiny gurgle of laughter escaped her.

'That's better.' He came round the table to stand beside her. 'Will you come?'

It was like seeing the light at the end of a long dark tunnel. She stretched out her hand. 'Yes, I will come.'

ABOUT THE AUTHOR

Constance Heaven, a former actress and one of the leading mistresses of the historical romance, is the author of THE PLACE OF STONES, THE FIRES OF GLENLOCHY, THE QUEEN AND THE GYPSY, and LORD OF RAVENSLEY, also available in Signet editions. She lives in London, where she is currently at work on a new novel.

SIGNET Books You'll Enjoy

☐ **BEDFORD ROW** by Claire Rayner. (#E8819—$2.50)

☐ **SWEETWATER SAGA** by Roxanne Dent. (#E8850—$2.25)

☐ **FURY'S SUN, PASSION'S MOON** by Gimone Hall.
(#E8748—$2.50)

☐ **RAPTURE'S MISTRESS** by Gimone Hall. (#E8422—$2.25)

☐ **THE LONG WALK** by Richard Bachman. (#J8754—$1.95)

☐ **DAYLIGHT MOON** by Thomas Carney. (#J8755—$1.95)

☐ **MAKING IT** by Bryn Chandler. (#E8756—$2.25)

☐ **THE CORAL KILL** by Bryn Chandler. (#E8347—$1.75)

☐ **ON THE ROAD** by Jack Kerouac. (#E8973—$2.50)

☐ **THE DHARMA BUMS** by Jack Kerouac. (#J9138—$1.95)

☐ **FLICKERS** by Phillip Rock. (#E8839—$2.25)

☐ **FOOLS DIE** by Mario Puzo. (#E8881—$3.50)

☐ **THE GODFATHER** by Mario Puzo. (#E8970—$2.75)

☐ **THE MOSSAD** by Dennis Eisenberg, Uri Dan and Eli Landau.
(#E8883—$2.50)

☐ **PHOENIX** by Amos Aricha and Eli Landau. (#E8692—$2.50)

Buy them at your local
bookstore or use coupon
on next page for ordering.

More Bestsellers from SIGNET

- [ ] ASPEN INCIDENT by Tom Murphy. (#J8889—$1.95)
- [ ] BALLET! by Tom Murphy. (#E8112—$2.25)
- [ ] LILY CIGAR by Tom Murphy. (#E8810—$2.75)
- [ ] WINGS by Robert J. Serling. (#E8811—$2.75)
- [ ] CITY OF WHISPERING STONE by George Chesbro. (#J8812—$1.95)
- [ ] SHADOW OF A BROKEN MAN by George Chesbro. (#J8114—$1.95)
- [ ] TIMES OF TRIUMPH by Charlotte Vale Allen. (#E8955—$2.50)
- [ ] JUST LIKE HUMPHREY BOGART by Adam Kennedy. (#J8820—$1.95)
- [ ] THE DOMINO PRINCIPLE by Adam Kennedy. (#J7389—$1.95)
- [ ] THE FRENCH LIEUTENANT'S WOMAN by John Fowles. (#E9003—$2.95)
- [ ] FEAR OF FLYING by Erica Jong. (#E8677—$2.50)
- [ ] HOW TO SAVE YOUR OWN LIFE by Erica Jong. (#E7959—$2.50)
- [ ] FLICKERS by Phillip Rock. (#E8839—$2.25)
- [ ] LUCETTA by Elinor Jones. (#E8698—$2.25)